THE DISTRACTED

By M.C.ROONEY

The Van Diemen Chronicles

The Last Politician
The Lightning Lords
The Violent Society
The Arrogant Horseman
The King of Control
Tales from the Collapse
The Distracted
The Cykam War
The Lunatics of Sydney
The Two Realms
The Water Planet

Hobart, Tasmania, Year 2033

It was late at night at the Tasmanian Parliament, and work was still going on. The public may think that the politicians were bludgers who didn't work really hard for a living, but nothing could be farther from the truth. They worked very long hours, and if anybody could tell you how much time they spent away from home, it would be the politicians' families, especially one family member, the Opposition Leader Joseph Pratt's wife. Mara was her name, and she would berate her husband for hours on end as to how neglected she felt. And looking at the last remaining agenda tonight, it appeared this was one of the nights of neglect.

'You're never here!' she would shout at him.

'Mara, I have a job to do,' would be his exasperated reply.

'Cooper has a job to do; he is the Premier. All you have to do is complain about any plans he comes up with.'

'Yes, but I need to complain all around the whole State. Loudly and often. That's how the Opposition works.'

'Perhaps you could help the government instead of opposing everything they do?' she asked.

'Are you fucking serious?' he shouted back, astounded at this ignorant comment. 'I have to oppose them.'

'Even when they make good decisions?'

'Some-sometimes,' he stammered in a much softer voice than before. 'You know, it's . . . it's what we need to do—for the people. Yes . . . yes, the people.'

'Your party and the government are so similar,' she said, shaking her head in an almost sad gesture. 'The people don't know the difference between the two of you anymore.'

'We are different,' he replied, deeply offended. 'Why, just last week the Business Council of Tasmania said we had better policies than the government.'

'You didn't listen to what I just said, did you?' She frowned.

'What?' Joseph asked, confused.

Mara rolled her eyes and walked out of the room.

'What?' Joseph said again.

She had no idea how politics really worked, and he did feel bad for not being the best husband he could be, but he had warned Mara that being a politician's partner was a tough life before they were ever married.

Thank God we didn't have kids, Joseph thought. *The guilt would be overwhelming then. And what did she mean about differences?*

The Police Minister Bill Cooper was addressing the parliament about the increasingly high statistics of crime in this State.

Bill Cooper was the Premier Michael Cooper's younger brother and a seasoned politician. He wasn't as hard-faced as the Premier, but there were strong leadership qualities about Bill Cooper that worried Joseph. Rumours said Michael Cooper intended to retire in a few years, so Joseph and his political party members were looking at ways of undermining Bill's popularity with the voters. A smooth transition between the old party leader and the new party leader usually resulted in a longer time in government for that party. Arguments and clashes of egos between the leader and the want-to-be leader usually led to the Opposition party winning the next election.

People also voted for the strong political leaders such as Bill because they were as rare as hen's teeth. The politicians who displayed a smidgen of charisma, Joseph ruefully had to admit, had disappeared decades ago.

Speaking of having no charisma, Joseph glanced across the floor at the large figure that was Bruce Cunnington. He knew that Bruce was desperate to become the next Premier, everybody did, really. He was very glad of that because he believed Bruce made the voters feel the way they would if they discovered a cockroach in their sandwich . . . after they had taken a bite.

He also felt there was something quite odd about Bruce Cunnington—something was out of place. Maybe it was his eyes; whenever Joseph talked to Bruce, he felt like he was looking at a man who had hidden emotions just waiting to explode.

Mara would think I was nuts if I told her what I thought. She would think I had gone all new age all of a sudden.

"Why, just today, a security guard was badly beaten by a gang of thugs . . ."

Joseph hardly listened to what was being said by the Police

Minister as he prepared for his political attack; he looked across at the other ten members of his party and saw most of them were almost nodding off. It was a tiring business listening to the never-ending business of politics. And as much as Joseph loved his job, the speeches he gave *himself* almost put him to sleep. *Get ready, people,* he thought in growing anticipation. *This is going to be fun.*

The fourteen members of the governing party were also trying to stay awake, some succeeding, some failing, but Bill Cooper, the fifteenth member, looked the most tired out of the lot of them, and he was the one speaking.

It's a wonder he doesn't fall over, Joseph thought. It was the perfect time for the trap.

"Mr Speaker," Joseph said, standing up after Bill Cooper had finished his statistically sound, but meaningless and heartless, speech and sat down. "A matter has come to our attention, of a scurrilous bribe from the member of Denison, the Honourable Bill Cooper."

Cooper seemed to wake up a little at this accusation.

"And what is that . . . Pratt?" Cooper called out coldly from across the parliament floor.

People always think my name is funny and a way of being condescending, Pratt thought with a shake of his head.

But Joseph Pratt had reached that dreaded age of forty, and whilst it was sad to think he was no longer what everybody thought of as young, with that age came peace. For once you turn forty, something very good happens to you. You stop giving a shit about the trivial things in life.

I wish I had been this way when I was a teenager, Pratt thought. *It would have saved me a lot of unnecessary stress.*

"I will show you myself, Bill," he said as he brought out his Holophone. "This is the Honourable Bill Cooper discussing his plans for the next multi-complex business centre in his own electorate."

Bill Cooper frowned at this statement.

You'll love this, Bill, Pratt thought smugly. *You never knew you were being recorded, did you?*

The Holophone soon showed Bill Cooper in deep discussion

with a few business leaders.

'Surely an anonymous donation would help the matter, Mr Cooper?' a weasel of a man in a flashy suit said.

'We cannot accept anonymous donations,' Cooper replied in a firm voice.

'Well, an upfront donation then,' the man insisted.

'That will be fine; upfront donations are legal and honest,' Cooper replied.

'And we expect no special favours for our generous donation,' the man added with a grin.

'Of course not. That would be unethical,' Cooper replied with a small grin of his own.

Bill Cooper now went very pale in the face.

Joseph saw all of his party members suddenly come alive; half of them were even leaning forward in their seats now. A small murmur was now heard on his side of the chamber.

"Joe, please tell me I just saw that," Joe's Deputy Opposition Leader Craddock said beside him with a shocked look on his face. "He looked so guilty."

"He did say that, and he is guilty," Pratt replied firmly and with a great deal of satisfaction. "That man he was dealing with *did* receive preferential treatment for his new business last week."

"Unbelievable," Craddock replied. "And where did you get that footage?" he now whispered.

"I have my friends." And high-placed friends they were. The murmur was now getting louder.

Bill Cooper still looked shocked at what he had been caught saying, and his elder brother was glaring at him angrily. Bruce Cunnington, on the other hand, looked absolutely ecstatic.

"What I meant to say . . . is . . . w-was," Bill Cooper stammered. The Parliament went wild; the murmur was replaced by righteous anger with a touch of political opportunism.

You're finished, Bill, Joseph thought with an inward smile as he looked at Cooper's devastated face. *You know the rules and how it works, but you got caught.*

Pratt received 'incentives' from big businesses himself, they all did, but he was always careful to cover his tracks . . . unlike Bill Cooper.

The camera crews in the parliament were now in deep discussion—no doubt this would be all over the Holonews come tomorrow.

Sucked in, Bill, Pratt thought. *Suffer in your jocks, old mate.*

Joseph now had many calls to make. His wife, Mara, would just have to wait to see him for just a little bit longer.

The night was very cold, as it could get in Hobart during winter's heart, but a young girl must work in any conditions to pay her rent; a young girl must do what she has to, to buy what she needed the most in this world.

She had met some disgusting men during her work as a prostitute over the years, but apart from a few cuts and bruises, she had never really been seriously hurt . . . until now.

"The leader wants culling, the big man was mulling. They do, they do, it's true. The woman was yelling, the fat man was shelling. She did, he did, it's true."

"Please stop," the young girl moaned. "Please . . . please, I am begging you."

"What, stop my sing-singing or the blade cut-cutting?" The hugely obese man with lank, greasy brown hair and deep-set beady brown eyes smiled as he sat on top of the young woman and cut deep into her skin.

"The blade, please," she sobbed. "It hurts so much."

The pain as he flayed her skin was excruciating, and the mass of weight on her back pressed her hard against the bed and made it almost impossible for her to breathe. Sweat poured from her hair to her face, though whether it was only from her own body or from his she didn't know.

"Help me," she gasped.

She worked on her own, so she wouldn't be missed by anybody, except maybe Trevor, her drug dealer, and she had no doubt her client knew that as well, given who he was. She almost wished the man would just kill her and be done with it.

"Hmm, yeah . . . nah, no can do, I am afraid, young lady," the fat man replied as he kept stabbing her and blood splattered all over his face.

This is heaven, he thought. *This is truly heaven.*

"You are probably aware of who I am," he continued, "so we have gone past the point of no return, haven't we? And the

7

politicians of course, now *they* do wish to get under everybody's skin. Oh yes, they do." He giggled as he wiped the blood from his face.

"Please stop," she begged again. "I will . . . do anything."

"Ha-ha." The fat man chuckled. "As a prostitute, that could mean a wide number of things, as you are all so depraved and evil, and besides, you have already fucked me, so now you just have to sit there whilst I play with my knife, okay?"

"No . . . no, please, stop."

"Nope!" he replied and gave a demented smile and went back to doing what he most enjoyed.

"PLEASE!"

"Screaming won't help you none," the fat man replied as he adjusted his weight, making her gasp more desperately for air. "My 'scouts' chose this house because of its privacy." He grinned. "So we will continue, shall we? By the way, I do like your hair. What product do you use?"

"Stop, please, stop."

But he didn't stop. He wouldn't stop until his 'appetites' were sated and her heart finally stopped.

Taking a deep breath, covered in her blood, he sang once more. *"The fat man wants death, to come from your breath. He does, you do, it's true. The fat man kept singing and the young girl kept screaming. He did, she did, it's true."*

"He's doing it again." A young man in his twenties with short brown hair named Jerry McGuiness reported in disgust to his boss in Canberra.

"For fuck's sake," his boss snapped. "That's the third one this year."

When will he stop? Jerry wondered. *How many young girls is he going to kill?*

Jerry was in an empty house across the road from the fat man and the prostitute. The latest spying technologies allowed him to not only listen in on the conversation—which he didn't want to do—but also bring up a holographic scan for him to see the two people in the house, also something he didn't want to do.

"It's going to be reported on eventually," Jerry replied, then winced as he had to endure another gut-wrenching scream from the victim through his earpiece.

"He does well in disposing of the bodies. Those three 'associates' of his are very clever," his boss replied. "But yes, I agree, someone is bound to notice all these prostitutes disappearing."

"The clientele?"

"No, more likely the cops, don't you think?" the boss replied calmly.

Ah, yes, them too, Jerry thought ruefully, then winced again as another scream was heard.

"Yes, Boss. What should I do next?"

Jerry's boss was a man named Brook Raller, and Jerry was a nervous wreck around him. Some spymasters and their charges got along well, but Raller gave him nightmares. He would have liked to ask for a new spymaster, if not for the fact that Raller was one of the leading figures in the entire department of ASIO. Making this man angry would hinder his career greatly.

He heard a big sigh from Raller.

"Follow him. Make sure he and his 'friends' get rid of the body properly, and then we shall see."

Oh, the high and mighty gets away with so much, Jerry thought with a grimace. *And what do his three friends get out of this?*

"All right, then, Boss," Jerry replied and then winced again. "But if I may comment, this cannot go on forever."

"Leave that sort of decision to me, Jerry," Raller replied firmly.

"Yes, Boss."

He did his job well, as a good spy was supposed to do, but he just wished this murdering bastard would not take so long in satisfying his perversions.

Yet another scream could be heard through his earpiece. This scream sounded fainter than the last, and he hoped he wouldn't have to listen for much longer, but he knew it was going to be a long night.

The Assassin known only to a select few as 'Flowers' listened to the two spies—one very well known to Flowers and the other an unknown rookie—as they, in turn, listened to another sick murder.

Sick murder, you might say, was a strange and hypocritical label from someone who chose to kill people for a living, but Flowers always made sure the assassinations were quick and relatively painless, with none of the disgusting perversion like the fat man was displaying right now.

But I'm not making a living and have to work part time in a normal job to make ends meet, Flowers thought, frowning. *I need some more money urgently. There are four men involved in this serial killing; surely they must want at least one of them killed.*

That was the reason Flowers had told Raller about the killings to begin with. The assassin was hired solely by a group known as The Cabal to 'take out' anybody they felt was hindering their objectives. Unfortunately, due to the oppressive movement that dominated today's political and social landscape, not many people *were* hindering The Cabal's agenda, so Flowers was not needed very often at all. So, in desperation, Flowers took to spying on a few of the local politicians in an attempt to find work, and had somehow come across the fat psycho who was now murdering yet another victim.

I have to do something; this can't go on forever. An assassin who works part time in a bakery is embarrassing, Flowers thought jokingly. *I need to talk about my worker's rights with the Assassins Union.*

The Assassin then frowned once more and sat in a rusty old car, deep in thought, as the screaming continued. The Assassin's contemplative thoughts were only occasionally interrupted by the strange sight of a young man running around naked in the park across the road.

Paulo Smythen was a young man who had an obsessive passion for swords. Not the 'sword' dangling between his legs as he moved gracefully, naked, through the poorly lit park, but an actual sword obtained from an antique shop, that he had lovingly restored to all of its former glory. Paulo was only seventeen years of age, but as he was a cousin of the fat man, who was now most likely brutally murdering another prostitute, he had obtained a temporary government job in the same building where the fat man worked and could now afford to buy all sorts of interesting items over the Holonet.

'Congratulations on the new job. Not that I helped you get it, pretty boy,' his cousin had told him with a big grin on his fat—and it must be said— ugly face. 'That, of course, would be unfair to all the other people who put in an honest job application.'

Paulo stopped moving gracefully through the park, then took an angry and wild swing with his sword. He was still young; he didn't have the experience to deal with bullying, and he let it get to him over the years—he let it change his personality for the worst.

Pretty boy!

Paulo felt the frustration and humiliation build up in his mind. He had the physique of a Greek Adonis, but even though his body was very masculine, he was a very effeminate-looking young man. For most of his life, he had been teased about his looks, girls always sniggering and joking on how he looked like one of them, boys wondering whether he indeed possessed a pair of balls or was just a girl pretending to be a boy.

'Pretty boy,' one of the school bullies would say as he sneered with scorn. 'You're just a big girl, aren't ya, Smythen, ya little cunt?'

'Dear God in Heaven,' his own father said scornfully to him, 'I have two pretty daughters already, what did I do to deserve a third one?'

'We had all the tests done when he was younger,' his mother said, embarrassing him even further. 'Everything is normal.'

His father grunted in disgust. 'He will be dressed up as a tranny when he's old enough, mark my words. Why couldn't he have been as rough as his cousins?'

His father had been bullied at school for the same thing. He had endured years of the same abuse. But instead of feeling empathy and compassion for his son, like he should have, he chose the other path of ridicule and derision.

He wasn't a nice man, in truth, and neither was Paulo. All that the bullying they both received really did was provide them with an excuse to be angry. The nastiness of their character had always been there, though, just like the feminine looks they shared. But unlike his father, Paulo's anger was very quickly turning towards years of physical violence. Paulo would soon be turning into a man who was not to be treated with contempt, a man who would indeed instill fear into a lot of people's minds. Sometimes Paulo's own father would give him a contemplative look, as if he knew what lay just under the surface in Paulo's mind.

'Bring me young women so I can cause them the same pain,' his cousin said. 'Let me disfigure them just as you like to disfigure yourself.'

His cousin knew. Somehow, the big man knew that Paulo cut himself on parts of his body nobody could see.

Paulo lifted the sword he cherished so much and ran the tip of the blade gently across his forearm. This would be the first of many cuts he would inflict on his own body that people would actually see.

Canberra, Mainland Australia

Jeff Brady was an average-looking man, an everyday sort of bloke I guess you could say. He was divorced, with an ex-wife he never saw anymore, or heard from for that matter, so you could say that he was legion. He had short brown hair and hazel eyes and was physically fit for a man of thirty-four years of age, but in his line of work, the years had taken their toll. The stress in his eyes, the wrinkles on his face, and the grey strands in his hair were marks that could be clearly seen. For Jeff was, up until this moment, a member of the Australian Federal Police Force and was part of major investigations into the corruption of some of the politicians in Canberra—until, of course, he made the mistake of finding some actual evidence that could put one of the Cabinet Ministers in jail.

"Yes, you did a good job there, Brady," Police Commissioner Rod O'Hara said, sitting behind his desk, but the expected smile was not on his face. In fact, he looked angry.

Oh no. What have I done? Jeff thought in a panic. *He knows the politician involved. O'Hara knows him personally.*

"Thank you, sir," Jeff replied unsteadily.

This place is so bloody corrupt!

"But I am afraid we have to transfer you to another department," O'Hara continued.

"What! The chemicals I found are dangerous in the wrong

hands," Jeff blurted in shock.

Shit, just keep your mouth shut, Jeff chastised himself.

He had found banned chemicals, which could easily be used as a biological weapon. They were bloody dangerous in the wrong hands, or even in the right ones.

"Yes, they are," O'Hara replied. "But we will look after it from here."

"But, sir—"

"You know how it is with politics, Brady," O'Hara said with a firm look. "We will handle this case from now on."

"Yes, I do, sir," Jeff replied to the police commissioner, and he did know how things were done in the Capital, he really did. He had seen what happened to lowly officers' careers who didn't play the game.

"Good man," O'Hara replied.

He resigned from the police force the next day. He knew his career was over after what he had found, and a part of him was worried that if he stayed where he was in the force, he may end up having an 'unfortunate accident'.

The 'worried' part of him was in fact correct, as minutes after Brady left the office, O'Hara was contemplating the very same 'unfortunate accident' and a plan for Jeff's murder was about to be arranged with an assassin known simply as Flowers.

Jeff made it safely out of Canberra the following night, but he was watched carefully from that day forward.

Flowers was forced to keep working part time in the bakery.

Sydney, Mainland Australia

The brain.

"What a fascinating organ it is," a strong, tall, handsome, and dark-haired middle-aged man named Henry Abel said as he looked at one of the hundreds of brains he kept in his numerous specimen jars in his laboratory. "To think of the control it has over the body, whether you are conscious or not. It controls body temperature, blood pressure, heart rate, and breathing; it accepts a flood of information from your various senses; it handles your physical movement when walking, talking, standing, or sitting; it lets you think, dream, reason, and experience emotions. It is truly a marvel, don't you think, Walker?"

His protégé, who really didn't like to be called by his first name of Biggus—who in their right mind would?—nodded his head in agreement.

"It is fascinating," Walker replied. His usually angry face was a bit nervous now, as he kept glancing at the people who were banging their heads against the cell bars behind him.

"They still worry you?" Henry asked, noticing his glance.

His trusted and well-armed security guard named Richards was standing nearby with three of his men, awaiting any orders that Abel was going to give, so he was not overly worried by the excessive anger displayed by the captives.

"Yes, they do," Walker said in disgust. "They are animals and should be put down."

"Animals, you say? Hmmm, they have children of their own you know," Henry replied with a wry smile. "So they must have some sort of . . . compassion. Some sort of . . . humanity."

"But isn't it a waste of time and resources keeping them alive?" Walker asked.

The four security guards shifted a little at this comment. Abel was paying them very well for what they did, and well-paid work was getting hard to find nowadays.

"Even though they are now useless," Henry replied with a glance at the captives, "the scientific studies of the effects of my operations need to be observed for a long period of time. The waste of resources is on the eight billion people living in our world today," he finished in disgust.

"You are right, Henry." Walker grimaced. "I apologise for my short-sightedness."

"That's quite all right, my friend," Abel replied kindly.

Their conversation was then interrupted by a coded message on Abel's Holophone, inviting him to that night's secret meeting.

"Looks like it's on," Henry Abel said to his protégé.

"You're going?" Walker asked, surprised. His teacher rarely ever went to one of these so-called secret meetings.

"Yes, I better go." Henry sighed. "I haven't been to one in

months. They may get suspicious if I don't show up every so often."

"Are they worth the bother?" Walker asked in contempt.

The Cabal was nothing but a bunch of lightweights in Walker's opinion.

"Yes, they are," Henry replied. "They have a great deal of influence in this country, even though they are not as *professional* as some we know."

"So how do you think you will get them to lean towards our way of thinking?" his protégé replied with another wary glance behind him.

One of the captives who was banging their head against the cell bars had now passed out. Or maybe he had died from a brain hemorrhage. Either way, Walker didn't care.

"Subtlety, I hope," Henry said with a tired sigh. "They must see where we are all headed as a society if they were honest with themselves, but unfortunately, they have their heads stuck in the political sand at the moment regarding the population problem. That means we, my friend, need to be subtle in achieving *our* ultimate goal. I have achieved inroads with converting Raller to our cause, and he has worked on a few others, such as young O'Sullivan and Wilkinson, and they are starting their very own Cabal, shall we say, with some members being in the ASIO department, as well as some being stationed at Pine Gap."

"Interesting," Walker said.

"Very interesting," Henry replied. "I think the ASIO members wish to be as politically *influential* as the other spy agencies around the world."

"So the Cabal could be usurped in the coming years," Walker said, surprised.

"It looks that way, or there may be two groups of influence in Australia," Henry said thoughtfully. "So we may need to keep a close acquaintance with Raller and his new allies."

Walker nodded his head in agreement. His mentor was usually correct with such things.

"Sometimes people need to be pushed firmly in the direction you want them to go," Henry continued thoughtfully. "Other times you need to wrap a comforting hand gently around their shoulder and walk with them to the destination of your choosing, whilst whispering comforting words to them."

"You can be gentle?" Walker replied with a laugh.

The younger man knew his mentor was a scientific genius, but had seen him on a number of occasions get involved in a full-on pub brawl and come out on top no matter how many men he fought, which was usually quite a few.

His security guard Richards had to wipe a small grin off his face as well.

"When need be," the strong man replied and grinned, knowing all too well how violent he could be. "I will inform you of the outcome of *that* meeting in the coming days. You keep working on your cryogenic project; it is important and may be needed in the days to come."

"Yes, sir," Walker replied politely. He had a great deal of respect for his mentor. His studies on the human brain were leading the field not just in Australia, but the whole world itself, and Walker had been overjoyed when Abel finally told him about The McKay Group and what their main objective was.

I'm going to see Natalie again, Henry thought with a touch of fear and took a deep breath and tried to mentally prepare himself for the night's meeting. Not prepare himself for the three-hour late-night drive to Canberra, that was fine, but for dealing with Senator Natalie Braiths, which was always an exhausting event. She was not only one of the smartest and most powerful politicians in Canberra but had confessed to him, when they were alone, to some strange sexual desire she had to spank him, of all things. Pub brawls and graphic scientific experiments were one thing, but Braiths was something else entirely. *I must remember not to be caught alone with her again,* Abel thought with a shudder.

Another coded message was received, this time from 'the real deal' when it came to secret societies.

"You may leave now," Henry said to his head of security, who would ensure that no other guards or servants would disturb them.

"Sir," Richards replied, and the big man with short blond hair left the room with his team at once.

Henry was sure of Richards's loyalty—he was the man who had obtained the human specimens after all—but he enabled the security system anyway, which would keep this conversation private.

"Get ready. It's probably her again," Henry said urgently to the younger man.

"The madwoman." Walker grimaced.

"I'm afraid so." Henry nodded.

All of Abel's servants who looked after the 'experiments' in McDermott's facility had been cleared out of the area half an hour earlier in preparation for this meeting. Like his security guards, the servants were loyal and paid well, and so they should be paid well having to deal with these 'experiments' every day. Walker now quickly put on his clown mask and became McLaren; Abel put on his own mask and became McDermott. The first of the clown masks now appeared on the huge Holoscreen they had installed in his laboratory for such meetings. As expected, it was her; she was always ten minutes early for their meetings.

"Oh, my dear boys, it is so nice to see you again," a woman's voice said in a delighted way. "Now, what have you good-looking men been up to?"

"Nothing, McShane," McDermott replied in a cold voice. "Nothing at all."

McLaren always let McDermott speak to her. Something about this woman, whoever she was, gave him the creeps.

"Oh, I know you lie." McShane giggled. "I can see those *humans* behind you."

McDermott's facility was very open. The laboratory where he performed his surgery looked out on where the subjects were kept in their cells. McDermott didn't worry about the captives seeing what he did, as they were probably too dumb to notice or comprehend.

Why does she always speak of humans as if they were a species completely different from her? McLaren wondered.

"They are just some test cases," McDermott replied gruffly. "We need to know as much about human weaknesses as possible if we are to succeed."

"Yes, we do, McDermott," McShane agreed. "And it is a shame the chip implant law did not eventuate. It would have been so easy to kill the population with that ticking time bomb under their skin."

The chip implant scheme involved waiting a few years after the law had been successfully implemented, and then suddenly, the elderly population aged over sixty, who numbered nearly thirty percent of the population now, would have started dying at a much higher rate than usual. Once the medical authorities became aware of the blood poisoning dangers of the chip, it would have been removed from all members of the public, but not before culling a large proportion of the retired folk who no longer worked. A few political and medical patsies were already marked out to take the blame. It was hoped that within a few years everybody would have moved on and forgotten about this tragedy due to the economic and socio benefits of not having to look after too many of the elderly.

Or at least in McDermott's and McLaren's heartless minds, they would have moved on.

"Yes, it would have been much easier," McDermott replied with a grimace, "but the fools in Canberra did not handle the subject very well."

"Politicians usually don't," McShane replied. "McCredie herself was especially disappointed that it didn't work. She had plans for some of the smaller countries in Europe to implement the same scheme."

So you are not a politician, McDermott thought. *Or maybe she is just saying that to give me that impression.*

McCredie seemed to be disappointed with every plan that McDermott came up with to kill large amounts of the population, but had no fresh ideas of her own. Some of the idiots of McKay were talking about nuking parts of the planet, of all things. McCredie was the one who had started this group thirty-odd years ago, but maybe someone else was needed to lead them now—someone like McDermott, perhaps? McDermott's own predecessor, another scientist known as McAfferty, had been implementing plans to remove McCredie and lead The McKay Group himself, until he was tragically killed in a hunting accident.

"You have a lot of *test cases* there," McShane continued as she raised her clown mask-covered face and looked again behind the two men at some of the captives.

"Yes, I need a big number so I can test—"

"Their brains," McShane finished off for him, and then she laughed. A laugh that was long, loud, and . . . insane.

Does she know? McDermott wondered. *Does she know what we put into the captives' brains?*

"Mad as a cut snake," McLaren muttered under his breath, and to gain a moment's respite from the mad lady, he looked behind him once more at what was kept in a secured prison.

McDermott's secret underground facility was part of a long abandoned train line called the St James Tunnels, which dated back to the 1920s and was hidden right underneath the CBD of Sydney. Inside the cells were approximately one hundred deformed humans—homeless people and drug addicts, people who would not be missed by society, and who were all presently looked after by Richards and his small security team, along with a few servants desperate enough for work that they would feed this madhouse. Scars covered their deformed heads from years of McDermott's surgical experiments and now, instead of being intelligent members of the human race, they were just empty shells of human beings, snapping and biting each other, causing many wounds all over their half-naked bodies.

Most seemed to have even lost the power of speech entirely, and some were so far gone that they were lying in their own excrement. They were all pitiful and seemed more animal than human now, except for one thing: In the midst of all these 'experiments' were four young children and a newborn child, who were all clean, healthy, and well looked after.

McDermott's servants did not need to feed these youngsters like they did the adults, the mothers and fathers of the babies, who spent most of their time staring aimlessly and eating like gluttons remembered one of the basic rules of nature even though parts of their brains were missing.

Look after your young.

"Dekker," one of the parents called out to a young boy who was standing close to the cell bars with the three other children. He had his fists balled up as if to fight and was deathly pale, due to never having seen the sun.

"Dekker," they said once more.

McLaren wondered whether Dekker was his name, or whether his parents meant that as a term of phrase like 'come here'.

He was about to turn back and face McShane when he heard a low growling noise from the cells.

He glanced back again at the boy and was astonished when the child then made a hissing noise like a snake.

More bizarre behavior, McLaren thought.

"You," the boy suddenly said. He seemed a lot more intelligent than his parents—a *lot* more intelligent.

"Yes?" McLaren replied curiously.

"You are dead."

The boy then ran his finger along his throat as if to suggest he was going to cut McLaren's throat.

The other three children looked at Dekker and started making the same gesture at McLaren.

What the hell is wrong with these kids? McLaren thought nervously. *These children of the experiments are just as mad as their parents.*

He was feeling more than a little discomforted at being so thoroughly threatened by a six-year-old boy when he felt something very strange and foreign enter his mind. It was almost as if something shifted involuntarily in his thoughts when the boy turned his gaze upon him.

It must be my imagination, the young scientist thought, pragmatic as ever. *I must be tired, that's all.*

This sort of thinking was a big problem for the scientists of today. Since they first began studying at university, they were told to look for evidence only, but sometimes that logic left them with a very narrow scope of understanding. The great scientists of the past were the ones who had always thought outside of the square. The great scientists thought with logic, but also intuitively.

"Parents who care for their young," McDermott suddenly said, causing McLaren to jump a little in fright. "A voracious appetite, and now the youngsters show extreme cases of anger."

"I just think he loves you, McLaren, that's all," McShane said, still chuckling to herself.

McLaren shook his head as he glanced at the madwoman but said nothing in reply. He had one young son named Sev who truly loved him; that was enough.

McShane kept chuckling madly in the background, but McLaren noticed from his peripheral vision that her gaze had now also shifted towards the boy.

Who freaks me out more, McLaren wondered, *the crazy kids or the crazy woman?*

"Why is it you always appear early for our meetings?" McDermott asked, turning back to face the most unsettling member of the McKay Group.

"To see your handsome faces, of course," McShane purred. McLaren felt like she was preening underneath her mask.

"The truth now," McDermott growled.

"Now, now, no need to be all snappish," McShane replied sulkily. "If you really want to know, I was excited by the news and needed to share it with someone."

"What news?" McDermott asked.

"You really don't know?" McShane said with a giggle.

"What news?" McDermott said, more firmly this time.

If McShane were a man and in this room right now, McLaren had no doubt that punches would have been thrown already. McShane said nothing in reply, just lifted a device in her hand, and a Holonews channel appeared.

Panicked investors have withdrawn a massive twenty trillion dollars from the money markets today as the US debt breaks what economic analysts say was over the fifty trillion-dollar mark. Some of the major US banks are no longer lending money to businesses, or each other, for any sort of loans, which economists say will affect businesses within a week, and even more US cities will become bankrupt in the coming months. Ordinary citizens now worried about these events have taken money from their local banks, and rioting has occurred in some parts of the country.

In the Middle East, all governments, on seeing this financial crisis, have immediately started selling Barrels of Crude Oil in Euros, Yuan, and Ruble, only causing further turmoil to the failing US dollar . . .

McDermott and McLaren both listened in a stupor for another

ten minutes as details of the US economic collapse was revealed. It was an absolute disaster for the US, as it was for the whole world.

This changes everything, McLaren thought in amazement.

McDermott also stood in a daze, unable to take in what had just happened.

"Chaos, boys, the balance of world power has now shifted, as was no doubt previously intended, judging by how quickly some of the country's oil currencies changed hands." McShane chuckled. "It was a house of cards and couldn't last forever; the old politicians must have seen that, surely?"

The old politicians were not the ones in charge, though, McDermott thought, trying to remember his history lessons.

"I wonder what delights are in store for us now?" she continued. McShane, on seeing the two men's stunned expressions, laughed all the more.

Eighteen-year-old Mercedes Radonculus sat on the expensive couch in a very expensive hotel and stared, nonplussed, at all the legal papers that were lying on the expensive lounge table in front of her. She was an attractive young woman.

With her long blonde hair, long legs, and hourglass figure, she definitely turned the heads of the boys, and made other women envious. One thing could make it all stop, however.

"Why should I sign this piece of crap?" Mercedes said in her usual high-pitched, whiny voice. Mercedes had been loved by her parents a little too much than was recommended, and she was spoilt, very spoilt. A lot of people referred to her as a cashed-up bogan, and a lot of other people referred to her only as an annoying little bitch.

"Because it is a contract, Mercedes, and if we are to be television stars, then some sort of binding arrangement is required," her twenty-year-old sister, Chardonnay, replied calmly as she read through all the fine print of the contract.

Chardonnay Radonculus, or Sharon as she liked to be called because she hated her first name, was also a very attractive young woman with an hourglass figure, but with short blonde hair. She also turned heads, and she continued to turn heads of the wise men out there, even after she opened her mouth, as she was also very intelligent.

"What's a contract?" a voice was heard from the corner of the room. This was the youngest sister, fifteen-year-old Mercury Radonculus, who was gazing out the window, looking at all the traffic, the bright lights, and the wonders of this big city. She had shoulder-length blonde hair and was as attractive as her sisters, but unlike Chardonnay, she was dumb; she was cute and adorable, but she was painfully dumb.

"A contract is required if you are to be a star," their new manager, Remi Hiller, said.

When Remi said the word 'contract', Mercury frowned at him in incomprehension, but when he mentioned the word 'star', her vacant eyes lit up.

"You mean it, Remi, are we going to be *famous*?" Mercury said excitedly in a voice that sounded a lot like Marilyn Monroe's pretend sex-bomb voice, only hers was her regular voice.

"Yes, Mercury, you will," Remi replied with a false smile. Remi, like his brother, Frank, who managed boy bands in the music industry, was the man who would make these girls famous, make a mint of money mainly for himself, and then abandon them just like all the other washed-up has-been reality stars in the past.

"Will I have money to buy the most expensive clothes?" Mercedes asked keenly.

"All that you want, Mercedes," Remi replied, still maintaining that soulless smile of his.

"That's so awesome."

"That's so super cool."

The sisters giggled like a pair of twelve-year-old girls, which mentally, they still were.

"Are you sure about this, Remi?" the third sister asked. "Are you sure all this will work out as planned?"

Remi's fake smile disappeared.

He swept his black greasy hair back from his face, as he contemplated the oldest sister, Chardonnay. Doing so exposed the widow's peak hairline, which some said made him look like a vampire—and he kind of was, if you thought about it for a while.

He couldn't lie to this girl. She was way too smart for that.

I am now going to do something completely out of character, and something that only my dear mother has ever seen, he thought.

"I think I can make you and your sisters filthy rich when all this is said and done," he replied in all honesty. "You were picked only for your looks and your looks alone. You have no talent to speak of, as you are well aware, so in the coming months, I will only require you to simply behave as you normally do whilst you are filmed. A Reality Show is nothing but a joke; there is nothing at all *real* about *anything* that you do or say. I mean, how could there be when there is a camera shoved in your face every day? But my own cameraman and producer will edit the final product in such a way that it makes you look more than just average, for which the public will love you by either wanting to be you or to have sex with you." Remi now shrugged his shoulders. "Or maybe both."

Sharon flinched at this analogy, but Mercedes looked quite pleased. Mercury wasn't bright enough to really know what was going on.

"During this time," Remi continued, "with additional clothes and product endorsements, you will end up with enough money that it should set you up for life. However, there is a downside to all this, as some people will think you are all fake, which, of course, you are, as well as being plain dumb." He didn't look at Mercury when he said this, but Sharon did for just a split second. "Over a period of time—hopefully it will be after more than just two seasons—the viewing public will eventually get bored with you, and the show will be cancelled. Then those same people who initially loved you will turn against you viciously and begin to despise you. This is not because of anything you have done wrong, mind you, but for two reasons:

One, the public's own embarrassment as to why they were so easily hoodwinked into putting three attractive but basically talentless young women so high up on a pedestal. And two, when you are no longer deemed cool and trendy by the so-called movers and shakers of the TV world, the viewers, who blindly follow their opinion, will have moved on to the latest 'it' people, whom we have already manufactured and have waiting in the wings to take over your role in this strange entertainment industry we have today. The public will deem them to be much more talented, which they are not, and more worth watching on TV than you . . . which, again, they are not. Then, a few years later, this latest TV sensation family will also be thrown out and discarded, just like you were before them, and the cycle will continue on to the end of time. Is that clear enough for you?" Sharon looked at their new manager for a long moment and took in all of what he had said. She had only agreed to both of her sisters' demands that she do this show because the money they would make *would* set them up for life. She knew that whilst she loved her sisters dearly, they really weren't the sharpest tools in the shed, as the old saying went, and after both had dropped out of school at an early age, she was well aware the struggle to make a good living in these turbulent times would be that much harder. And since both of their parents had recently passed away, she was the one left with the responsibility of taking care of them.

"Thank you for being honest with me," she replied with a look of gratitude.

"You're welcome," Remi replied with a nod.

Well, what do you know, Remi thought, surprised, *honesty does work sometimes.*

"So we still get to buy lots of clothes, right?" Mercedes asked, who, like Mercury, really didn't fully grasp much of what Remi had just said.

"Yes, you do," Remi replied, giving her his best heartless smile. *Fame and clothes for the younger ones, but what does the eldest sister want?*

"That's so awesome."

"That's so super cool."

Remi Hiller looked on as Sharon signed their new contract deal on behalf of her two beautiful younger but talentless sisters. The Radonculus Reality Show was now born.

The Year 2034 – ten years before The Collapse
Canberra, Parliament House, Mainland Australia

The rain poured down outside the building in which the Federal politicians of Australia went about their daily business. A lightning bolt hit the ground in the distance, followed by a massive sound of thunder that made most of the politicians and public servants flinch when they heard it. They didn't flinch as much as they used to, though. This sort of wild weather was happening way too often nowadays.

"I wish it would rain where it was needed," a woman muttered as she strode towards her office.

Senator Natalie Braiths was a very tall and strong-looking woman in her mid-forties with brownish-grey hair pulled back into a tight bun, a misshapen head, angry face, and a square jaw. Most of the tactless men in parliament believed that she had balls. But they didn't believe, in their stupid, small-brained male way, that she had balls because she was a strong woman; they thought Braiths had balls because she looked like a man.

It was insulting, very insulting, actually, but she didn't really care, as she had put up with that nonsense for so long it was now like water on a duck's back; she also knew from experience that some men in this building liked women who looked like men, and they also liked to be dominated verbally and physically by a manly woman. This was something Natalie was more than happy to do, eager even, you might say.

Parliaments across the globe today, and back throughout the pages of history, always contained a number of powerful men with very strange sexual fetishes. This place was no different; it was no different at all.

They are still ignorant scumbags, though, she thought, clenching her huge hands into fists and glaring at the men in their suits and ties, wandering around the parliament corridors. *They think they were the real power in this land, the bloody idiots. They still have no idea of the truth. They have absolutely no idea that the real power lies not in being the so-called elected politician, but in the more subtle rule of The Cabal, and it had been that way for a very long time.*

The Cabal.

Yes, it was stupid and pretentious to call a group The Cabal, and various members of the group, current or retired, had mentioned this many a time. But it was something that she, as the de facto leader of the group, and her predecessors had encouraged because of its obvious implications. The obvious implications being it *was* indeed a ridiculous name, and the more ridiculous the name, the more people dismissed you.

The Illuminati, or The McKay Group, were just two of the many mythical secret societies who were meant to dominate the world through political espionage. But anybody who mentioned they believed that such a group even existed would either be met with instant derision, be completely ignored, or considered thereon to be a delusional conspiracy theorist fool. However, if that same person was to state simply that there was a group of rich politicians, bankers, and media moguls who wanted more money, control, and power, then the public would instantly believe them because that sort of thing had been happening for centuries.

So, The Cabal was the name they were stuck with, and anybody in the public who said they believed this group existed would be instantly classified as a lonely person with a tinfoil hat who didn't have a girlfriend and lived in their mother's basement. The people who made these insults, on the other hand, strangely never really bothered to do any thorough research on these subjects, so the conspiracy theorists would label them all 'mindless sheep'.

Both of those derogatory stereotypes kept these people focused on each other only and had done wonders in protecting the hierarchy of many of the ruling elite around the world. Indeed, their very own Cabal member Johan Franz was a well-known Radio and Holonet Conspiracy Theorist, who had been hired by their group to promote the craziest theories out there. He did a wonderful job in broadcasting the dumbest and most illogical conspiracies that he could find; he even mentioned The Cabal a few times in his talks. Natalie believed Johan was invaluable in keeping the public's attention away from their group by muddying the waters so to speak, so that the real truth was very hard to find.

'Make the public embarrassed of seeking the truth, Johan,' Natalie had told him. 'Make it personal; make each of them feel that they would be labeled a conspiracy nutjob if they asked too many questions.'

'Really! It's as simple as that, Senator?' Johan asked.

'Yes, it is,' Natalie said to him, looking him up and down and thinking how easy it would be to smash his face in. 'It's funny how easy it is to keep people on track when you target their ego.'

'Their ego?' Johan asked nervously.

'Yes, their ego, Johan. It is one of the keys to controlling the public; the other, as we all know, is, of course, fear.' Natalie then smiled, making Johan flinch. 'My, you are a handsome young man.'

'I better go,' he had replied hastily.

Natalie had chuckled as the young man ran away from her.

'Fear,' she had said again and chuckled some more.

But the real mainstay of keeping the public's focus safely in the realm of dumbland was undoubtedly the Cabal member, TV presenter, and all-round hunk and spunk Brad 'Sparkles' Hoffington. Just thinking about him made Natalie want to throw him against a wall and hit him. His Reality Shows were a godsend for the ruling Cabal, as they mesmerized the public's imagination in inane, useless, and utter shit. Nobody in human history could take the public's attention away from the new laws and the world's political, environmental, and economic woes like that man. Even the evil Goebbels himself would have been envious of the way Hoffington pulled the wool over the public's eyes.

'I want the public to be mesmerized by these people,' Natalie said to him, looking him up and down, thinking he may be a bit harder to beat up than Johan. 'I want the public to want to be these people, to see how rich and hot they are. I want them to follow them in the news, to be so focused and jealous about what a great life they lead that they don't have time to think of anything else.'

'Will they do that?' Brad had asked.

'Of course they will, Bradley,' Natalie had all but purred. 'They have been doing that for decades now. She looked at him for a long moment. 'My, you are a handsome young man,' she continued.

'I better go,' he replied hastily and ran away.

Natalie remembered a young woman from the Middle East, who

risked her own life numerous times years ago, in trying to promote equal education for young women. She received very little media attention in the West, even though she was a true role model for all young girls all over the world. Around the same time, there had been a young teenage celebrity, a girl who was talentless and had rich and famous parents and received a million-dollar car for her birthday present. The spoilt brat got one hundred times the amount of media coverage and adulation from the youngsters in the West than the young woman of real substance from the Middle East.

It was a weird world they lived in, to say the very least.

Another lightning bolt hit the ground very close to the building, followed by an even louder roar of thunder, causing a few people to cry out in fear. But Natalie still didn't flinch; she was too focused on wanting to bash someone up now as she dwelt on Hoffington and his dazzling smile.

And by what other means did their group truly rule the everyday people of Australia? Was it money? Of course, money was a means of controlling people, but that was not it. Religion, then? No, religion had been on the decline for years in Australia. Although it did control maybe five percent of the voting public, which was handy if you needed a small minority of voters to help get you over the line in an election, so long as you were prepared to be seen by the media going to church and lying a lot about believing in God.

Subliminal messages or chemicals in the air and water, perhaps? No, that was the works of science fiction, although a scientist in their group named Henry Abel could possibly help them with that. No, Natalie thought once more in amazement. The Cabal's power came from something that scared everybody into absolute silence, something that frightened people to their very core. It came from political correctness.

Yes, the movement that had initially had very good intentions in fighting prejudice had now become a weapon of oppression. Over the last two decades, as the older people who remembered the pre-days of political correctness passed away, the general public had now grown up believing this was the normal way to behave, and had now become more and more frightened of saying or doing anything that would upset anybody in any way. By controlling the political correctness agenda, along with the dumbing down of people's intelligence through mind-numbing reality television shows, and with promoting the so-called 'Nanny State', The Cabal gained more control than they could possibly have imagined.

Natalie laughed to herself as she contemplated her secret group of elites and the self-righteous people who did their bidding without ever knowing they were.

Her laughter sounded like a growl from an angry dog, which made a lot of the passing men flinch in fear. She loved that reaction and laughed all the more.

"Senator Braiths," a young, straight-laced man named Aiden Wilkinson said as he tentatively walked up and stood before her.

"Yes, what do you want?" Natalie replied gruffly, looking the young man up and down.

Hmm, I wonder if this young boy likes to be slapped around a little? she thought curiously. He was the advisor to Cabinet Minister Mark Howles, who, along with Wilkinson, was also a member of The Cabal, so he was used to a little groveling at the very least.

"There is movement," Wilkinson said quietly, in what he hoped was a mysterious and secretive way.

Dick, she thought.

"In your bowels perhaps," she replied sarcastically.

Wilkinson flinched.

"No, ah . . ."

It was so enjoyable making some people squirm, and she was the leader of their group after all.

"Midnight it is, then," Braiths barked. That was the time her group usually met. "Send the message out."

"Yes, ma'am," Wilkinson replied a little nervously.

Ma'am?

Natalie Braiths liked his respectful nervousness and now found him to be very intriguing.

"You know you could stop by my office beforehand, Aiden, for a . . . drink," Natalie said, smiling at him in a way that most people believed looked like a wolf baring its teeth at a lamb.

"Um, no . . . I'm busy . . . arranging . . . uh, stuff," Wilkinson stumbled, his face going very pale, and then he ran away from her.

"Pity," Natalie said to herself as she watched him leave.

She looked around and saw one of the young advisors in her own political party named James O'Sullivan smiling hopefully at her.

Yes, you will do, little man, she thought, clenching her huge hands again. She nodded and smiled back at the skinny man, then walked towards the Senate for today's political haggling, but tonight was when the real debating would begin.

Axel Rigozzi was a tall, slim man with short blond hair. He wasn't a tough man as such who fought in pubs and on the street, nor was he a coward who ran away from conflict, but he involuntarily flinched as the powerful senator named Natalie Braiths strode passed him. She was bloody awful in Axel's opinion—she was the tyrant of the parliament; she reminded him of the school bully at his old school, who used to beat him up all the time, except Axel's school bully had been a boy.

"Axel," his colleague Fred said.

Fred was a short, middle-aged man with dark hair and a constant look of worry on his face.

"What, mate?" Axel replied with a wary glance to see if the nasty harridan Braiths had finally gone.

"I think we may have a problem," Fred replied.

Axel was in charge of the IT department for the government. He held great responsibility to make sure all the government computers worked perfectly, or as perfectly as the old clapped-out machines could.

"What sort of problem?" Axel said in a mild panic.

What is it, what is it? What has stuffed up now?

"Well, everything went well with the weekend updates," Fred replied. "Except . . . the Enter key on the side of the keyboards no longer works."

Oh, Jesus, is that all?

"Bloody hell," Axel growled, "you almost gave me a freaking heart attack."

"Sorry, mate, but I thought it may have been a big deal."

"Well, it's not," Axel replied. "The keyboard has another Enter key, and you can use the mouse as well."

"Yeah, I guess." Fred frowned.

"It will be fine," Axel replied. "We will fix the error in our next updates, okay?"

"Yeah, I guess," Fred replied, frowning all the more.

Hobart, Tasmania

"Geez, it's so freaking cold," Jeff Brady muttered as the cold winter's morning wind blew strongly, almost knocking him off his feet. But he had worked in Canberra for a while, and their winter mornings were much colder than this.

He did miss Canberra, but Tasmania was a good place to live, he conceded. As the population of the world grew at an alarming rate and the environment was slowly destroyed, Tasmania had a relatively livable environment, due to some passionate work of environmentalists of the past. Clean and green some used to call it. Well, it did have some polluted places, the big industries saw to that in their short-term quest for profit, but on the whole, it was one of the best places to live in the world today.

He kept on walking down the main street of his hometown, taking in the same old sights of the place he was born and lived in for most of his life.

The place is still there, he noticed as he walked past the pub at Salamanca Place, which he used to frequent nearly every weekend for many years in his youth. Different name, but it still looked the same.

"Hmm, I spewed there, there, and also there," he said, reminiscing about his youthful drinking prowess, or lack of, as he walked along the surrounding streets and the public garden just outside the old building of the Tasmanian parliament. "It's a wonder I didn't bring up my stomach lining as well," he continued with a shake of his head. "So many good three o'clock-in-the-morning kebabs gone to waste."

I even spewed on the doorsteps of Parliament House itself and didn't even realise it, he suddenly remembered. *Nowadays, that would be seen as an act of rebellion, but back in the day, I didn't even know where I was or what the building was used for.*

"Tassie," he said with a half-laugh as he kept walking past the parliament house.

What would have happened to him had he somehow thrown up on the front doorsteps of the Canberra parliament?

Prime Minister Laughlin would have come out and beat you up, that's what would have happened, he thought, smiling to himself. Tough as nails that man was, which was needed in these tough economic times. And he had a bit of charisma that had been so lacking in leaders since way back to the days of the twentieth century.

"And now I'm just a private dick." He sighed as he made his way towards his office. "I'm no longer a copper."

He had loved his job as a policeman.

But then again, my new job does pay the bills, he thought, trying to consider the positive side of his new business and to dominate the dark cloud of negativity that flooded his mind so often nowadays. *Yes, and being my own boss is pretty good, even though most of my new work is spent on surveillance, watching to see whether some wife or husband was screwing someone else's wife or husband.*

Another blast of the wind made him shiver a bit more.

Yeah, it's good being my own man, nobody around to tell me what to do, he thought, trying desperately to cheer himself up and ignoring the fact that his secretary, Susan, told him what to do quite often.

He walked a few more steps.

"No, it's not good; it's *bullshit*," he said loudly, which caused every passerby to jump in fright and look up from their mobile or new expensive Holophones.

I made them look at the real world. How could I be so rude?

"You, right there, mate," one man said with a wary frown.

"Calm down, all right? You almost made me drop my phone."

The universe itself would have collapsed if you dropped that phone, Jeff thought sarcastically.

"Sorry, mate. I have . . . Tourettes, yes, Tourettes you . . .you prick-faced dick," Jeff replied and started walking a bit faster.

Hmm, he was probably regretting that he didn't film the incident so he could download it on the Holotube and be famous for fifteen minutes like the rest of them. Or maybe he was just simply nervous of me, he thought as he glanced quickly behind him to see that the man was still frowning at him.

The whole world was in a state of nervousness, though. Ever since their economy had crumbled, the US had withdrawn in on itself, and it seemed a lot of countries were now flexing their military muscles that had lain dormant for so long.

His stomach rumbled loudly, really loudly.

I have to get rid of my hunger pangs.

He knew just the place.

"G'day, Jeff," the man behind the counter said as he walked into the takeaway shop situated next to his small office.

"G'day . . . mate," Jeff said back. The takeaway shop owner had told him his name once, which Jeff quickly forgot—not a good trait for a private detective. "The usual, thanks . . . mate," Jeff continued as he handed the money over, and the shop owner handed over his breakfast.

Money, Jeff thought, *actual real money, not the card the politicians are trying so hard to promote.*

"Bacon and egg sandwich." The shop owner smiled.

"Grub fit for a king." Jeff smiled back. And it was, in his opinion. None of that bird food crap that everybody else ate for breakfast. Jeff ate what he thought humans had been eating for millennia. And besides, he couldn't be arsed making breakfast for himself anyway.

"Catch ya, Jeff," the shop owner said.

"Yeah, see ya . . . mate," Jeff replied.

He really needed to find out that man's name.

Perhaps I could do some detective work, he thought ironically.

Susan Milligan sat at her desk, on time as always, and waited for her new boss to arrive, late as always.

He wasn't really her new boss as such; she and Jeff went way back to their high school days. She had lost contact with Jeff for years when he worked for the Feds on the mainland, but when he returned to his hometown, he had called her to ask if she would be interested in working for him.

She laughed long and hard at the irony of working for this man and was also delighted and relieved, as full-time work was so hard to find nowadays.

Susan was a single parent with two kids to support, as her useless husband was currently languishing in jail. She would do anything at all to see her daughters well cared for.

She looked at herself in a small mirror she carried in her purse to make sure she was presentable, checked her dyed black hair—which went really well with her blues eyes, if she did say so—to make sure none of those pesky grey hairs that started when you reached your thirties showed and double checked her make-up to make sure those bloody crow's feet didn't appear.

Not that he would care, she thought. *I could turn up in my pyjamas and fart all day, and he wouldn't notice. In fact, if he did notice, he would probably be jealous that he couldn't do the same thing.*

But she did take pride in her appearance and could still make some men's heads turn to have a second look. Not that she really wanted them to, as her husband would kill them, but it was good for her ego when they had a look sometimes.

She heard the usual slow, trudging footsteps coming up the stairs and prepared for the day.

"Morning, Susan," Jeff mumbled as he wolfed into his usual bacon and egg sandwich.

"Good morning, Boss," Susan replied.

"Did you have a good night last night?" Jeff asked.

"Yes, I did, thanks, Jeff." Susan smiled. "And you?"

"Just watched the football on TV," he said.

Oh, goody, here it goes, Susan thought.

"And which football would that be, Jeff? League?"

"Nah."

"Union?"

"Nah."

"Gaelic?"

"Nah."

Jeff's face was getting redder.

"Soccer?"

"Nah."

"American."

Here it comes.

"AFL, for fuck's sake, Susan!" Jeff snapped, spraying parts of his sandwich all over her desk. "We are from Tassie; we watch the

Australian Football League down here."

It was so much fun making him angry, Susan thought, trying to suppress a grin. She shouldn't do it, she knew, as he was her boss, but it was so funny that she just couldn't resist.

"Of course, Jeff." She nodded. "Oh, *look*! This piece of bacon was overcooked; perhaps you should take it back." Susan smiled, bringing out a sanitary wipe to remove egg and bacon from her desk, and also not mentioning that soccer was the most popular 'football' code in Australia and had been for decades.

"Sorry," Jeff muttered as he wiped the egg from his own shirt, with his hands.

"And the team you follow would be the Southern Kangaroos, of course," she continued.

"No, I go for the Western Bulldogs."

Although, the way the recently retired Southern Kangaroos' ruckman Ray Beasley went about punching other players in the head was truly an inspiration, Jeff thought, *even though he did spend most of the time suspended on the sidelines.*

Bring back the biff; the fans have been calling that out for many years now. But violence was quelled by the 'powers that be' and the game of AFL and even Rugby League was very tame to what it used to be. The 'Nanny State' rules had been in place for so long now that the younger generation just took it as the way things had always been. Jeff thought the new 'Nanny State' mentality made young kids dumber and less self-reliant, but what did he know? He was just an ex-copper, not someone with a professional degree.

"The Western Bulldogs, that would be the team from the western suburbs of Melbourne, Victoria," Susan continued.

"Yes," Jeff replied.

"And you are born and raised in Hobart in the state of *Tasmania.*"

"Yes," Jeff said, frowning.

"Which now has its own team," Susan continued.

"Look, we don't change clubs, Susan." Jeff sighed. "It's an unwritten rule that the team you support when you were a kid, you support until the day you die."

Or they fold, Jeff thought, *thinking of the number of teams over the years that had disappeared. Fitzroy, South Melbourne, North—*

"Of course," Susan said, interrupting his thoughts. "Men in tight shorts chasing a leather ball around an oval and making more money in one game than you make in a *whole year* of hard work must be followed like a religion."

"Exactly," Jeff said in agreement.

I was being sarcastic, Jeff, Susan thought. *Didn't you pick up on that?*

"Anyway, back to business: do you have any interesting new jobs for me?" Jeff continued. "And no cheaters! I'm sick of watching people's affairs. I feel like Uncle Pervy."

"You love it," she replied. What man would not like watching people have sex? It was just like the Holoporn, but more real.

"No, I don't," he replied.

"Oh, go on, admit it," she chided.

"No, honestly, I don't," he insisted.

"Really?" she said, surprised.

"Yes, really."

"Well . . . well, I'm proud of you, Jeff." Susan was almost in a state of complete shock. "Most men would like to cop an eyeful and get paid for it."

"Not with the couples I get to see," Jeff said, shivering. "Fat lumps of blubber banging up against each other, grunting like pigs and causing minor earthquakes. It makes me feel ill."

He was looking at his half-eaten bacon and egg sandwich as if considering whether to throw it out.

"Oh, I see." She sighed, regretting saying she was proud of him now and realising again he was a dirty perv like most men. "So if you had to watch a hot young woman, you would think differently."

"Yes, yes, I would," Jeff replied simply. He looked a lot happier now and started finishing off his sandwich.

Typical, Susan thought.

"Well, you *do* have an interesting prospective new client as it so happens, Jeffrey. But, unfortunately, it doesn't involve watching some hot young university chick with a big pair of norks bouncing up and down naked, so you might find it all rather boring," Susan replied sarcastically.

"Oh," Jeff mumbled in a disappointed tone.

Susan's eyes widened for a moment. *Does sarcasm just go straight over his head?*

"He left a message on our answering machine," Susan continued in a tight voice.

"We have an answering machine?" Jeff said, surprised.

"Yes."

"Who left a message, then?" Jeff asked.

"Bill Cooper," Susan replied.

"Who?" Jeff frowned.

"You don't know him?" Susan frowned back.

"Nope."

"Really!"

"Really."

If he was a dumb footballer, Jeff would know him.

"You don't watch the Holonews at all?" she asked.

"Nope, nor do I read the Holonet," he replied.

"Well, I'll give you a hint. He is involved in politics."

Jeff just stared blankly at her.

"His brother is Michael Cooper."

Jeff continued to stare blankly at her.

"Michael Cooper, you know, the Premier of Tasmania!" she said, sighing.

"Oh, yeah, I know him," Jeff replied with a nod.

Hallelujah! Susan thought.

"I think," he added, frowning.

Bloody hell!

The very large and imposing figure that was Bruce Cunnington strode down the street from the parliament car park with a cigarette hanging out of his mouth, deep in thought over what latest economic idiocy the Premier Cooper was going to bring up in parliament today. He was also panting and sweating very heavily, as exercise was definitely not his forte, which was very ironic as he was the current Health Minister.

Premier Cooper's plan was economic idiocy in Bruce's mind, only because it just might be a very good plan for the state's financial debt.

We can't have that, Cunnington thought frantically as he barged past and almost knocked over one of the reporters who were setting up their equipment outside the parliament to interview one of the politicians after the economic stimulus package was announced.

How am I to become Premier if the current one keeps doing a good job? Cunnington thought with a frown on his face.

Michael Cooper had been Premier for six years now, and judging by the historical records of past Premiers, he had done a fair job so far. Bruce Cunnington was insanely ambitious, and he desperately wanted to follow in Michael's footsteps, but he knew he had to wait his turn. The only problem with that was that Bill Cooper, Michael's brother, also wanted to be the Premier's successor, even though he had taken a massive beating by the media and in the opinion polls, due to his political donations gaffe.

I have to be Premier, Bruce thought desperately. *It's what I have wanted for so long.*

"Hey, watch where you're going, fatso," the reporter Bruce had elbowed called out to him.

What!

"Who said that?" Cunnington growled as he turned around, clenching his big hands into fists.

"I said it, barge arse," the elbowed reporter replied.

"*Who* do you think you're talking to, young lad?" Cunnington said with a red face, his chins quivering his outrage. "Don't you know who I am?"

'Don't you know who I am?' was probably the most irritating thing a famous person could ever say. Nothing could annoy the average everyday person more than this comment. Except, of course, the everyday person realising what they get paid as compared to themselves.

"Oh, I am *so* sorry, Your Royal Highness," the reporter replied. "I was just so overjoyed the way Your Rotundness elbowed me in the ribs like that, the bruises or nay, maybe the cracked ribs, I shall cherish forever, believe me. But please, don't let me, your humble peasant, nor my cracked ribs keep Your Eminence from his royal duties."

And then the reporter bowed with one hand, making a mocking

flourishing gesture.

The other gathered reporters looked away quickly, either to hide their sniggers or to escape Cunnington's wrath.

Cunnington glared back at the reporter, then turned and entered parliament. He was grossly overweight, there was no doubt about that, but he didn't like being called out on it.

Let's see if I can make a few phone calls, Cunnington thought nastily. *Perhaps that smart arse young prick will think differently when he is on the dole queue.*

As always, he superstitiously stepped over the step he had spewed on when he was a youngster.

"You know, you really can't talk to the Health Minister like that," the cameraman said as he adjusted his equipment in preparation for the budget announcement.

"Yes, I can." Terry Tyson, the twenty-one-year-old Channel 12 political news reporter grinned. Young and handsome he was, but as his deceased father would often say: 'the boy shows no respect for his elders'. His Uncle Roger was inclined to 'clock him one' when he showed such disrespect.

"For we live in a democracy," Terry continued, "not in North bloody Korea, and if someone attempts to break my ribs with his huge gut and pointy elbows, no matter how high-ranking, then I, as a member of such democracy, am entitled to tell him to piss off."

"But we're not entitled, Terry," the cameraman said quietly with a look around him, as if he was telling some national secret. "We have to play the game."

"So we do, I agree," Terry replied. "And if someone were to tell me off for this, then the newspapers . . . well, the newspapers who don't support the government, would soon hear about it. Votes, it's all about the votes. It's the only thing that scares the pollies."

"Still, it is a dangerous game you're playing," the cameraman said worriedly. "The powerful always tread all over people like us."

"Not in Tassie," Terry scoffed. Tasmania was so poor compared to the bigger states. Terry doubted there were any powerful people down here at all.

"Yes, even down here," the cameraman replied. "We are small, yes, but the 'game' is still played down here."

"You sure?" Terry frowned.

"Yes."

Terry pondered this for a moment. *Tasmania? Maybe he was right; maybe I should play the game . . .*

"Nah, stuff him," he said as he waved his hand in a dismissive gesture and his big grin returned.

If Terry's father had seen this response, he would have shook his head in displeasure, but would not have been even remotely surprised.

The other reporters who had avoided Cunnington's gaze did shake their heads as they listened to this young reporter.

They think he is an upstart, the cameraman thought, *and after today, I don't blame them.*

Terry then began to fuss with his suit and tie and his well-groomed hair as he kept talking. "It's the convict streak in us Aussies," he continued to the cameraman. "It's the tall poppy syndrome. So fuck the high and mighty, bugger the whole bloody lot of them."

It was now the cameraman's turn to shake his head in resignation. This young man was destined to end up in hot water someday. And besides, Australians didn't bag the high and mighty anymore; the 'tall poppy syndrome' psyche of Australian culture that had been around since the convict days had died decades ago. Today, the majority of people wanted to be rich and famous, and some sought the limelight, as they believed fame was the ultimate achievement in life.

"So how do I look?" Terry asked when he thought he was all ready.

"Boring and conservative," the cameraman replied.

"Perfect." Terry smiled and then winced.

"What's wrong?" the cameraman asked, concerned.

"Um, nothing." Terry grimaced.

Maybe that bastard really had cracked his rib.

The immaculately dressed man in his Armani suit stared at the detective from across the bar. Some people gave him a curious look, a few an angry one, but most people didn't give him a second thought, as they were used to politicians frequenting establishments around this area. The well-dressed man hoped the detective was as smart as he was said to be. He had heard rumours of why he had left Canberra, so that gave him the belief that he was indeed intelligent.

The building where they had decided to meet was near the parliament. It was almost two hundred years old now, harking back to the Colonial Days, but it had been a pub for generations, which most people tended to revere more than any other building, especially the building he worked in.

"Drink, mate?" Bill Cooper asked as he approached the detective and shook his hand.

"Yes, thanks, Mr Cooper," Jeff Brady replied with what he hoped was a pleasant smile as he appraised the middle-aged man and noticed his serious demeanor. He was a smartly dressed man, Jeff noticed, and would have looked younger than his years, if not for the hair he had lost on the crown of his head. Bill Cooper was a politician, and could have been a good one at that, but Jeff didn't really mean that as a compliment. Cooper had been the Police Minister until he was caught out receiving a suspect political donation. It took all of his, and his brother's, political clout to even keep him in parliament.

Jeff knew all this before Susan told him, he just liked stirring Susan up a little by playing dumb—well, sometimes he did, other times he really didn't know what she was talking about.

The two-headed beast, Jeff thought, reminiscing about what his dad always said about the political system.

'We don't really live in a democracy, Jeff,' he had said. 'We live in a two-party dictatorship. They are not political parties anymore but purely business aligned organisations who share power by turns. We are just dumb enough to believe that it is democratic because that is what we have drummed into our heads from when we are youngsters.' He then chuckled ruefully, which was what people did when they faced a problem that could not be fixed. 'But what a generous dictatorship it is, Jeff, where, if you're prepared to get down on your knees and kiss some political committee's arse to get the candidacy, you will indeed have a good life ahead, with good pay and perks beyond your wildest dreams.'

'Really, Dad?' Jeff grinned. 'You really think that?'

'Oh, yes, Son.' His father laughed now. 'Buy trousers with extra padding over the knees, Jeff, and you will go very far in this world.'

"Call me Bill, please," the politician replied, glancing at Jeff's egg-stained shirt with a slight grimace and then giving a smile that was clearly not sincere. "Two Boags, Bartender," Cooper said, then flashed him the money card that everybody carried nowadays.

They are trying so hard to get rid of real cash, Jeff thought as he remembered the politicians' last attempt at getting rid of paper money and coins. *Let's see how he likes this question.*

"Glad you have no chip implant?" Jeff asked.

Bill Cooper turned his cold face towards Jeff, obviously surprised by the question, and then, to Jeff's shock, he laughed in an almost warm way.

"Dumbest idea, since the invention of dumb ideas," he replied, smiling. "Nothing says 'I am your evil overlord' more than requesting the everyday population wear an implant under their skin."

The public hated the idea. The population was so docile in nearly everything, but an implant under your skin made the people very scared, and the federal government who came up with the idea had suffered greatly in the polls and had to give up on the idea.

The idea really worried Jeff too; who knew what the implant was really made of? There could be anything contained within that chip. But again, the public, even though they were scared, still didn't show any sort of pro-active behaviour. They still couldn't be bothered breaking their gaze away from the Holonet or their Holophones to actually physically protest.

The people should protest, Jeff thought. *The everyday person, not the rent-a-crowd protesters of today. They used to all the time, so I have been told. But not protest in an undisciplined, violent way, which achieved little and made the protesters look like brainless thugs, but in a focused and planned way that made the pollies worried that they would lose their seats of power.*

The politicians with the chip implant idea had broken the basic rule of power. They created fear in the public, which was what they were good at, but they made the critical error of making the people scared of them, instead of an unseen or outside foe. "Is that a politician's response due to the unpopularity of the idea, or do you genuinely believe that?"

Jeff tried to make the question lighthearted but couldn't. After being booted out of Canberra for catching a high-ranking politician involved in the importation of very dangerous biohazard chemicals, he had very little time for his ilk.

Bill Cooper's face now turned serious.

"I wouldn't have that implanted in me, or my late wife, Nadine, or my son, Carl, so I don't expect anyone else to. No matter what the security issues are with credit card fraud, it's just plain wrong."

Interesting response, Jeff thought. But does that mean he would have approved of the idea if he didn't have to have one implanted in him, though? Would the billionaires of Australia have a chip placed under their skin, or would they be exempt somehow? He couldn't imagine the media mogul Brandon Townsworth having one.

He was being too cynical again, he realised, so he nodded his head, making out as if he believed him, and drank half of his beer.

At least beer had never let him down, he thought, quickly falling back to cynicism.

Cooper was only sipping his beer, he noticed. No doubt he wished he had the most expensive bottle of red available, but had to maintain the charade that he was just one of the everyday blokes in a local pub.

Stop being a cynic, Jeff told himself once more. *There are some politicians who care . . . I don't know where they are, but they must be out there somewhere.*

This whole 'trying not to be a cynic' thing was clearly failing.

"But most of the small countries in Europe have converted and have no physical money now," Jeff continued. "It's only—"

"A matter of time, I agree," Cooper finished off for him impatiently, "but this is not what I came to talk to you about."

I pissed him off already, which is almost a record for me, Jeff thought.

"And what do you wish to talk to me about?" Jeff asked. "I must admit that up until now, I have only been providing proof of some people's extramarital affairs."

Jeff shivered again. *C'mon, they weren't that bad,* Jeff the Positive thought. *Yes they bloody were; their beds must have been made out of bloody steel,* Jeff the Cynic replied.

"No marital affairs this time," Cooper replied with a deadly serious face. "This time it is murder."

What!

"Are you serious?" Jeff said, which was clearly a stupid question, as anybody could tell that this man was serious in all things that he did, simply by looking at Cooper's face.

Especially if it would advance his career, Jeff the Cynic thought.

Cynic or not, he was just about to find out how right he was.

"You're joking, right?" Susan said when Jeff had returned from the meeting.

"I'm afraid not," Jeff replied, still in a state of shock.

Bill Cooper had sat next to him in the pub and told him with that hard face of his that he believed Bruce Cunnington's own brother was killing prostitutes and burying their bodies.

"But how does he know this?" Susan replied.

"He wouldn't reveal his sources," Jeff replied.

'Follow him, Brady,' Cooper said. 'I want to know if he is a suspect.'

'But who told you this?' Jeff asked.

'Someone anonymous and very high up,' Cooper replied.

'You need to tell me,' Jeff insisted.

'No,' Cooper replied angrily. 'You of all people know not to step on the toes of the powerful.'

'You know of my history,' Jeff said, surprised.

'Yes, only a little, but enough I think, Brady,' Cooper replied with a ghost of a smile crossing his lips.

"He may be protecting his own ambition to still be the next Premier, so this could all be just lies," Susan said. "There are no other real leadership candidates in his party, apart from Bruce Cunnington."

"I have thought of that, but if it is lies, then we still get paid for it," Jeff replied with a sigh, rubbing his hand wearily across his face. "Cooper wants this kept between me and him. No police are to be involved; he just wants to know if Cunnington's brother is doing this foul act."

"That's strange," Susan said.

"Not when politics are involved," Jeff replied.

"So he wants proof so he can bribe Bruce Cunnington into resigning, not for justice?" Susan replied.

"That's what I thought," Jeff replied, thinking once again how lucky he was to have his old friend as his secretary.

Cunnington acts like a man who wants to be Premier, Jeff thought. *He seemed to be one of those pollies who were in it for the long-term.*

"I don't like this, Jeff," Susan said.

"Me neither," Jeff replied. "But the money he has offered . . ."

Susan looked at Jeff for a long moment, then finally nodded in agreement. Their new business was just struggling to stay afloat, and both had their own bills to pay. The financial collapse of the US had hit everybody hard.

But now, like a white knight coming to their rescue, Cooper had offered him lots of cash to investigate Cunnington's brother, which could set them both up for the next few years.

It was worth the risk. Wasn't it?

Victor Cunnington had just been to the toilet. He missed the urinal and pissed on the floor yet again. But he also didn't care, yet again, which would surprise no one who truly knew him.

He didn't care partially because he didn't notice he was peeing on the floor due to his enormous gut blocking his view and aim. The rest of him didn't care because he was Bruce Cunnington's brother and could do whatever he wanted and still not get the sack. In fact, all that ever happened to him when working for the government was that the managers who thought he was a lazy, useless bastard—which he was—did everything they could to move him out of their department. The result being Victor Cunnington, due to his increasingly wide range of obtained knowledge from all those job moves, was now one of the most experienced workers in all of the government departments and had, to everybody's disgust, slowly made his way up the management chain.

Bruce has got my back, he thought smugly and slapped a few of his workmates on the back as he made his way back to his desk, not realising or caring that he had not washed his hands after doing his business. *If they cause trouble with me, they cause trouble with my brother.* That was his motto.

It is good being untouchable. Victor yawned over what boring government rubbish he had to do today. He tried to focus on the crap he called work, but his mind drifted back to the night he had cut up yet another prostitute.

His 'scouts' had done so well in finding yet another victim, another young girl who would not be missed if she disappeared. He felt his cock grow hard in his trousers at the memory of her screaming in agony, but again, he didn't care or notice this embarrassing moment, as his gut was so big, nobody was likely to see a thing. Anyway, he wouldn't get in trouble if he did walk around with a noticeable hard-on, as he was Bruce Cunnington's brother after all.

It's good to be the king, he thought as he gave up on this morning's work, grabbed his cigarette packet, and walked outside without notifying anybody, to have another half-hour smoko break.

It's good to be the king.

"Another murder, Rizo," Constable Eric Woods said worriedly.

"Yep, looks that way, Woody, old mate," Constable Razan Hussein replied.

Both policemen were looking at the dead body found in the dense bushlands in the south of the state. It looked to be another young woman, possibly a teenager, but it was so hard to tell straightaway, due to the body's badly decomposed state. This was the third body they had found in the area in the last few weeks, and after forensic testing, it seemed the first two bodies had suffered horrific injuries before death. Almost as if someone had skinned them.

"Bastard," Razan growled and looked around the area with his usual harsh expression. "If I can just catch the fucker who did this."

Violence disgusted him, violence against women enraged him. Razan Hussein was a first-generation Tasmanian. His parents had fled the Middle East due to persecution, and instead of settling in the bigger cities on the mainland, they had decided to live in the peaceful southern island capital of Hobart.

But the Hussein family had done it tough. Due to the decades-long terrorist war between Islamic Extremists and the West, anybody from the Middle East was looked upon with suspicion and mistrust. Razan himself had to not only endure years of harassment at school from the worldwide clan of dickheads known to one and all as 'the school bullies', but even today, as one of the best cops in Tasmania, who had served his State proudly, he still had to endure people's silent prejudices simply because of his ancestry.

"We will get them, mate," Eric Woods replied, concerned at his friend's anger.

Eric had come from a long line of Tasmanians going way back to the convict days. He suffered no prejudices, apart from being called a 'pig' by all the bogans and criminals out there.

"I hope so, Woody," Razan replied, still glaring at everyone around him, causing a number of fellow officers to flinch. "I really hope so."

The Cabal, Canberra, Mainland Australia

"Ladies and Gentlemen, thank you all for coming at such short notice," Environment Minister Mark Howles said as he looked around the table at what he believed was the gathered elite of Australia.

Howles was a powerful senator in Canberra at the moment. He was also the leader of the republican movement, whose goal was to install an Australian as their Head of State. Not because he wanted an Australian president as such, he really didn't care about that, it was just that he wanted to be named in the future history books as the man who led Australia to becoming a republic.

'They will never forget me if I do this,' Howles had been overheard saying on many an occasion.

Thunder was now heard overheard as the rain continued to pour on the roof, giving the meeting a more sinister edge.

Florian will love this weather, Howles thought, looking over at the Water Corporation executive. In fact, the greedy-looking man with dark hair and almost black eyes was gazing out the window in awe.

"Too short of notice, Mark," Senator Braiths growled back, but not before she looked suggestively up and down at his young advisor, Aiden Wilkinson, who nearly squealed in fear.

"My apologies, Natalie," Howles replied with a nervous nod of his grey head. He was a little scared of her as well.

"It's fine by me," the fat man Bruce Cunnington said over the Holophone from his home north of Hobart. He was lounging on an armchair with a cigarette in one hand and a beer in another.

"And by me," Florian said, tearing his gaze away from the window.

"I enjoyed the drive," the muscular scientist named Henry Abel said mildly.

Senator Braiths now started looking him up and down.

What I would give to slap that man. He refused me once, but maybe if I try a little harder next time . . .

"So what is the agenda tonight?" ASIO member Brook Raller asked. "And there is no need to fear; my people have checked for any surveillance, and we are quite safe here."

My people, Henry Abel thought curiously. *I wonder how many of 'his people' there are now.*

'Here' was a small house in the outer suburbs of Canberra. This group of so-called elites thought that meeting in a normal suburban house was being subtle in the world of political spying and intrigue.

"Are you sure?" Natalie asked, frowning.

"Yes," Raller replied with a frightened look at the senator. "The only people who are listening are a few of my chosen men." His eyes quickly flickered to Henry Abel, then back to Senator Braiths.

"You better be bloody right, Raller," Natalie growled.

"Yes . . . yes, Senator, I am," Raller replied and then took a quick swig from his glass of wine to steady his nerves.

Natalie chuckled under her breath.

They're all terrified of me, she thought with great pleasure.

"A few of my people have the streets protected as well," Police

Commissioner O'Hara added.

"Well, let's hurry it up," Banking Cartel leader Phil Miller said in a brisk tone. "Time is money."

His son, Gary Miller, sat beside him and nodded in agreement. Normally, a 'time is money' comment from a Banker may have been seen as a joke, but Phil and Gary Miller were very serious in everything that they did. Their clear blue eyes shone with the signs of impatience.

"I agree with Phil here. Fucking hurry it up, will ya, ya flog," someone barked. "I had a long day at work, and I'm completely fucking knackered."

This was Brandon Townsworth, the large, bald-headed sixty-year-old media mogul who owned all of the major media outlets in Australia. There used to be a number of people who owned the numerous major media outlets. This number had been whittled down to only one over the last fifty years. The public, in their apathy, didn't notice or care, and the politicians who strangely agreed to this change now had to kiss Townsworth's old and spotty arse to gain favourable coverage. Townsworth's opinion was Australia's opinion.

Thunder was heard again, and the windows rattled. Gary Miller frowned and got up from his chair and checked the window locks were secure. "Bloody weather," he muttered.

Florian was gazing out the window again.

"Well, c'mon then!" Townsworth barked once more.

Townsworth was also the leader of the Change the Australian Flag movement. Not because he wanted a new flag as such—he really didn't care about that—it was just that he wanted to be named in the future history books as the man who changed the flag.

The floggers will never forget me if I do this,' Townsworth had been overheard saying on many an occasion.

"Yes, Mr Townsworth," Howles quickly replied and wiped the sweat from his forehead.

Natalie sniggered at Howles's nervousness. She wasn't scared of Townsworth; she wasn't scared of anybody—well, apart from one unknown entity in this group known as Flowers—and not even the voters made her sweat, as she was a senator after all and had bullied her way to the number one placing on her party's voting ticket. She had been in Canberra for twenty years now; she was content with her lot and wasn't going anywhere anytime soon.

"The people are starting to worry about the Resource Wars," Howles continued. "There has even been—"

"Money taken from my banks," Phil Miller interjected with a grimace. "All this talk of Satellite Wars and lack of resources has made the public nervous, and some of them are withdrawing as much money as they can."

Florian's dark eyes lit up at the mention of the Resource Wars.

"The ATM machines are nearly always empty today," Senator Howles said knowingly.

"ATM machines, you dickhead, Howles?" Townsworth growled. "You do realise you just said automatic teller machine machines, ya moron."

Howles made a small noise in his throat, and then his face went a very deep shade of red.

Is it automated, or automatic? Natalie wondered.

She doubted whether the billionaire Townsworth knew what an ATM looked like, not just whether he actually used one. She knew she didn't; she hadn't been near one in years.

"Perhaps this is more reason to push onwards with our cashless society agenda," Gary Miller said firmly as he sat back down. "If we can remove cash from society, then maybe we can help stop any future crashes from occurring."

"The people will go crazy if they cannot get to their money," Howles said without thinking.

"What the fuck are you talking about, Howles?" Townsworth growled again, making the senator blush *again*. "The people don't get upset about anything anymore; they are too fucking lethargic. The only people who really protest are the racist Extreme Right and the righteous Extreme Left, and their little flare-ups and abuse on the streets make the majority even more lethargic."

"The good old ever-reliable rent-a-crowd protesters." Natalie smiled. "You have to love their enthusiasm."

And the Righteous Left sounds very stupid, Townsworth, Natalie thought.

"They should get a bloody job," Townsworth growled.

"Hear, hear," Bruce Cunnington added, then leant forward a little and looked curiously at his fingernails in a very weak attempt to distract attention from the fact that he had just farted on his couch.

Does he think we are all deaf? Natalie thought incredulously.

"With a cashless society, the cyber money could be more easily controlled," Phil Miller said thoughtfully. "We can make any old excuse for not giving people all of their money in a financial crisis if they demanded it."

"What excuse, Phil?" Natalie said, intrigued.

"National Security, perhaps," Henry Abel interrupted with a grin, which made everybody break out into loud gales of laughter.

"That never fails," Howles said as he wiped a tear from his eye. Townsworth almost choked to death he laughed so loud.

After they stopped laughing, Phil and his son, Gary, again looked thoughtful. No doubt they thought national security *was* a good idea to inflict their will.

"Ooh, you are a bad man, Henry. You so deserve to be *disciplined*," Natalie said with another appraising look at the man who rarely appeared at their meetings. Her gaze stopped the famous scientist from smiling pretty quickly.

"A-anyway," Abel stammered with a wary look at the senator, "can we get on with what we are here for?"

"Of course, Henry," Natalie purred.

There was something soulless about a cashless society, though, Natalie realised after Abel had turned his handsome face away from her in fear. When you had your hard-earned cash in your hand—not her hand exactly, but someone who actually worked hard for a living—there was a feeling of achievement. If Australia converted to a cyber money society, then the people just may start to wake up and realise how much of financial slaves they really were.

"Yes, indeed," Bruce Cunnington grumbled as he sculled down another can of beer. "Even though I'm not sure that I can achieve *anything*, as Bill Cooper is still sniffing around after his brother's job."

He then gave a loud belch.

Charming man, Natalie thought.

Thunder rattled the house once more.

That was probably the butterfly effect, Natalie thought smugly.

"We did our best, ya fat flogger," Townsworth said with an angry frown. "I gave the recording to Pratt, after all. That bastard Cooper just has some resilience; he has some ticker about him, unlike your fat heart, which looks like it is about to burst at any minute. And even though the public hate him, they respect him at the same time."

There were a number of cases where politicians had long careers even though the public didn't like their personality. Some pollies, rare though they may be, could behave like bastards and people would like them anyway, as they believed them to be strong and forthright.

"He was caught taking a bribe," Cunnington said with a wary look at one of the most powerful men in Australia. "We need somebody else to take over from his brother."

"Like you, you mean," Abel replied in disgust.

Abel liked to spend as much time at the gym as his schedule allowed. The huge man sitting on his couch was repugnant to him.

"Yes, me," Cunnington replied with a glare at a scientist who had no political power. "Unless, of course, you don't want a Cabal member as a Premier."

"Of tiny and insignificant Tasmania," Abel said flippantly. "I can take it or leave it."

The Senators Howles and Braiths tried not to snigger.

"Piss off, Abel." Cunnington growled.

The whole room went deathly still.

This could be interesting, Natalie thought.

"You would be wise not to talk to me that way, Cunnington," Abel replied angrily as he sat up a bit straighter in his chair. "I may have plans to visit you and your state very soon."

Cunnington's face went pale. He had forgotten for a moment about Abel's talents in regards to beating people up. Abel wasn't a complete science nerd, that was for sure; he was more like a cross between Albert Einstein and Mike Tyson.

"Now, boys," Natalie interjected breathlessly, "if there is to be any violence going on . . ."

These two men were really turning her on with all their testosterone flying around. Even chubby Cunnington with his flabby chins and cigarette hanging out of his mouth was starting to look good.

"Why would you be visiting that state?" Howles asked curiously.

Henry Abel's body stiffened for a moment as he realised his subtle plans had been dashed by Cunnington. He would have to lie to his protégé tomorrow to save face and say he had a change of mind as to how to implement his plan.

"Because I am looking at purchasing some land in a quiet place, and the southern island would do quite nicely," he finally said.

"Fuck me—where?" Cunnington said in surprise, with more than a touch of anger.

"I will show you when you drive me there," was all Abel said.

Everybody was silent for a moment, except Cunnington, who kept muttering the word chauffeur. They knew if Abel was buying some farmland then it had to do with some experiment.

"Are you going all *scientifical* again?" Howles asked curiously with a small smile.

"Yes, I may be going . . . *scientifical*," Abel replied with a grin.

"Is it dangerous?" Gary Miller asked. He was actually quite keen to know, as he was mildly interested in science. His 'little' brother James was mad for it, to their own father's disgust.

"Yes, I am going to create an epidemic that makes people more lethargic," Abel said simply.

"Television has already been invented." Howles smiled.

"No, even more lethargic than that." Abel chuckled.

"And create a cure, of course?" Townsworth asked immediately.

"Yes, but that would only be *discovered* months later," Abel replied.

"And I would promote it," Townsworth said.

"Of course," Abel confirmed.

"And we would obviously have foreknowledge of the pharmaceutical company who would provide the cure so we can buy some shares beforehand?" Natalie asked, already knowing the answer.

The shares purchased were always arranged through shady business deals that kept their names anonymous. The pharmaceutical industry was worth billions. The public obviously believed that the industry was there to help them, which, of course, it was, but behind the good intentions were underhanded deals and massive profits. Rumours of all sorts of cheap illness cures being repressed were rife in the industry. It was good business to keep the population as sick as possible.

"And you will take the necessary precautions?" Phil Miller asked on top of Natalie's question. "The epidemic will be controlled?"

Yes, but not the sort of control you think it will be, Abel thought smugly.

Raller was looking at him very curiously; he may have had an idea already that there was no cure for what Abel intended.

"Of course," Abel replied to both questions. "I will provide you with all of the details once the produce is grown and in the marketplace. And my disease will not be caught out like the chemicals that were seized last year," he finished with a meaningful look at the police commissioner.

Nice deflection, Abel praised himself even more smugly.

"It was taken care of," O'Hara replied, going red in the face. "The policeman who found them resigned the next day. The chemicals are safe and will need a decade of testing before it is an effective disease."

"And the cure, of course?" Townsworth asked immediately.

"Yes, of course," O'Hara replied, almost bowing at the media mogul. He didn't know that in ten years' time the biological disease would be set on the public with the approval of Raller and his ASIO associates and have no known cure apart from a very healthy immune system.

"Well, mine will not take that long," Abel replied confidently. The gathered elite all looked at each other for a moment, then nodded their heads in agreement.

"Well, keep us informed on your progress, Henry," Senator Howles replied.

"Of course."

Well, that was easy, Abel thought. Subtlety was not required with these people, so long as money was involved. He would need to remember that.

Cunnington was still muttering angrily, but he did not have the courage to ask whether Abel was buying some lands in his home state electorate of Lyons.

"If I may speak?" the weasel known as Florian Grainger asked.

"Of course," Townsworth said before anybody else could reply.

He is going to try again, Natalie thought in amazement. *Doesn't he realise how difficult his plan would be to get through parliament?*

"It is to do with privatising the water supply," Florian continued, raising his hands as if to emphasise the point. "With public water in my corporation's hands, we can begin to make people more responsible with their water usage by charging them a higher cost. The effect on the public's hip pocket will reduce all the water wastage that goes on nowadays."

Well, at least he is honest, Natalie thought, *and people in other drought-ridden countries can't believe that we poop in our own water to wash it away.*

"We have been through this before," Natalie replied. "The public would not stand for the water that falls from the free sky being owned by a corporation."

"But with the climate changing and droughts lasting for longer—and yes, I know some of you politicians don't like to admit anything about climate change—it is imperative that this resource be controlled and managed by the private sector."

"It is an interesting idea," Henry Abel added.

I could put anything in the water if it was privately owned, Abel thought with a touch of anticipation. *A mass culling of the population could occur, or maybe something to make the people even more lethargic?*

"No, it is not an interesting idea, Henry," Natalie said firmly. "If water were privately owned, the whereabouts of the majority of water would go to the highest bidder, and we all know who that is."

"But with private finances, we can provide the necessary infrastructure to send the water evenly all around the country," Florian argued, gesturing with his hands again. "You know how uneven the rainfall has become."

Thunder crashed against the house again, as if to emphasise his point.

Natalie raised a disbelieving eyebrow at him.

"The water would still go to the people," Florian lied.

"You must know I don't believe *that*." Natalie growled.

"Well, what about control, then?" Florian shot back, starting to get desperate. "The droughts *are* getting worse, the population is rising at an alarming rate, and the water usage needs be controlled. Would you prefer the public's anger to be directed at us or at you, Senator?"

Hmm, he has you there, Abel thought.

Natalie paused for a moment, confirming Abel's assessment.

Control, Natalie mused.

"I will give it some consideration," she said, looking over at her work colleague Senator Howles, who nodded his head a fraction.

"Some shares, perhaps," Florian instantly replied, latching on to the softening of her views. "A lobbyist job for life after politics or a high-paid position on our Board?"

"Again, I will give it some consideration, Florian," she replied.

Florian looked quite smug now. No doubt he thought he had made some inroads tonight into achieving his goal.

"Well, getting back to the matter of why I asked you all here," Howles finally said, "we have a vote next week in the senate in regards to ensuring the public's safety."

"Taking people's rights away again?" Townsworth asked.

"Yes, by spying on them," Howles replied honestly.

"To make them safe and free?" Phil Miller asked with a small smile.

"Yes, exactly," Howles said simply. "It is a legislation that comes in five parts so as not to arouse suspicions from the public."

Townsworth chuckled at that comment and muttered softly the words, 'but they don't care'.

"And it will pass the senate, I assure you, and become law," Howles continued. "But to be safe, we need the public's eyes to be looking elsewhere."

"You want me to focus them on something else?" Media Mogul Townsworth asked.

"Yes, I do, Mr Townsworth."

"Well, on what then, Howles?" Townsworth said gruffly. "What do you want the public to see? It better be good."

"It is," Howles replied with the beginnings of a smile.
"What, then?" Townsworth asked, impatiently.
"Oh, the usual." Howles grinned.

Sydney, Mainland Australia

The weather was unusually hot for this time of year, and the whole state of New South Wales was in a drought. Water Taxes were being considered by the state government, and heavy fines were to be issued for those who wasted too much water. Scientists were worried that within a couple of decades, the people of New South Wales would have no water left.

But that didn't matter to the media and the public at all, as today, much more important news was about to be announced.

"An Australian Tour, really?" Mercury Radonculus cried out as she and her sisters all sat in their very expensive hotel room. Mercury had loved all the fame that their reality show had showered upon her. She was twirling her shoulder-length blonde hair in her fingers, which usually meant that she was excited, or that she had met some young guy she thought was hot.

Sharon, her eldest sister, just groaned as she sat cross-legged on her bed. The last year had been a nightmare for her.

I have to get away from here, she thought desperately, *somewhere quiet, where nobody would stare at me and take photos.*

"That's right, Mercury," Remi Hiller replied with a warm smile this time. Warm because this tour was outside of the original TV contract, and he was going to make sure his percentage of the profits was a lot bigger this time.

"You mean we are going to Wellington and Christchurch?" Mercury said breathlessly.

Sharon groaned some more.

"Um, that is New Zealand, Mercury," Mercedes Radonculus said in her usual whiny voice as she brushed her long blonde hair and adjusted her black dress so her big boobs stuck out a bit more, then went back to taking photos of herself for the Holonet website.

"Yes, so?" Mercury replied, her vacant but pretty eyes fluttering in incomprehension.

Sharon was really groaning now. She was still in her pyjamas and had been eating crisps and chocolate all morning.

"We will be going to Perth, Adelaide, Darwin, Brisbane, Sydney, Melbourne, and Hobart, Mercury," Remi Hiller replied. "Those are cities in *Aus-tra-lia*."

She can't be that dumb, surely?

"But why not Wellington and Christchurch?" Mercury replied. "I have always wanted to go there."

She is.

"No, Mercury,"—Remi was starting to lose his warm smile now—"those cities are in *New Zealand*, and we are going on an *Australian* tour."

"I don't understand," Mercury said, still confused.

Far out!

"I give up," Remi muttered and walked towards the window to take in the views.

"Look, why do we have to do this tour?" Sharon asked frantically. "I mean, we are doing well in the TV ratings, so why is this tour necessary?"

The paparazzi and their endless stalking for photos, she thought in dismay. *And the tabloids always wondering who I am dating, wondering whether I am gay because I am single. Who cares if I am gay or not—it's none of their bloody business.*

"For money," Remi replied, still gazing out the window.

Why does this girl not love money? he thought in puzzlement. *Her sisters definitely do. Mercedes spent it like it would never run out.*

He looked over at Mercedes and noticed she was still making duck-faces at her Holophone. Her followers over the Holonet loved every seductive moment and sometimes watched it live at preplanned times, which was quite the money-earner. No doubt there was a fair bit of 'teenage happiness' going on around Australia when it happened. Speaking of money-earners, there were even rumours of her making a sex tape with Grantee-Grant from the recently dispersed boy band Loyal Angel Memory Eclipse. He needed to get his hands on that tape; it could make him a small fortune.

"Well, I am not doing it," Sharon suddenly said.

What!

"But you have to," Remi replied, turning back to look at the eldest Radonculus sister in shock. "We have already signed up Street United Cat Kings for the tour, along with international singing sensation El Froggo."

"Yes!" Mercury squealed. "Froggo File. I love that song, it's so original and fresh."

Original! You've got to be joking, Remi thought.

Mercury then started leapfrogging around the room. The gimmick of the Froggo File song was for everybody to start playing leapfrog instead of dancing, and the public amazingly did just that, once more proving to Remi that the public would do anything, no matter how lame, so long as you convinced them that it was cool.

"Mercury, the Froggo File can only be done when you leapfrog over another person," Mercedes whined. "You look like you have something shoved up your bum and you're trying to get it out."

"Oh, sorry." Mercury blushed.

"Well, I don't *have* to do anything," Sharon snapped.

"But the money," Remi said, frowning and starting to look just like Mercury when she was having difficulty understanding something. "We live in such hard economic times . . . and . . . and the people need to be entertained to take . . . to take their worries away. . . from the weather . . . peace of mind . . . and global warming . . . stuff."

Jesus, Remi, he chastised himself. *Why didn't you mention that it could bring world peace as well?*

But Brandon Townsworth himself had insisted on this tour, and it had to be on a certain date. If he disappointed that man his career could be over.

"But we don't do anything!" Sharon wailed. "We have no talent." *Photos and screaming fans, I don't think I can take much more of this.*

"Oh, bloody hell, *Chardonnay,*" Mercedes whined, tearing her gaze away from her Holophone for a moment. "You are *always* such a spoil sport. Stop thinking about *yourself* all the time. *You're so selfish.*"

She then went back to gazing at herself in the Holophone and taking more cleavage photos. No doubt a lot of teenage boys would be pleased by that.

Sharon glared at Mercedes. She had never hit one of her sisters before, but she was seriously considering doing that right now. *And my name is Sharon, not bloody Chardonnay*, she thought angrily.

"Oh, please say yes to this, Sharon," Mercury begged. "I have always wanted to visit the city of New Zealand."

"Listen to your sisters," Remi begged with a disbelieving frown at Mercury. But Remi had just remembered a way of making her go along with the tour.

Nobody could say no to this.

"And just so you know," he continued, "the man who will be accompanying you for the interviews all around Australia is none other than . . . Brad 'Sparkles' Hoffington!"

Mercury squealed like she had just been attacked by a knife-wielding maniac. Mercedes adjusted her dress even tighter, making one of her boobs pop out, which she would no doubt learn to perfect once she was alone with Hoffington, or maybe the live Holonet feed.

"It will be fun. It will be . . . fun . . . and you will make enough money—money to never work again," Remi said, trying to take his eyes off Mercedes' exposed boob.

"I think I already have enough money," Sharon replied, plucking at some crisps that were stuck to her pyjamas. There was even some chocolate in her hair.

"But-but have you made enough for the three of you?" Remi asked, finally tearing his gaze away from Mercedes, who still hadn't addressed her exposed-boob problem.

Sharon frowned for a moment in thought.

She and her sisters were still young, and Mercury and Mercedes had been spending money lavishly. It was such an irresponsible thing for an individual to do in these bad economic days, even though capitalism said differently.

What am I to do?

Mercedes was now glaring at her with her hands on her hips, her boob still hanging out, and Mercury was looking at her with those puppy dog eyes of hers, which always made Sharon give in to her whims.

She had to make the hard decision.

"I will do it on one condition," she said firmly.

What, that Mercedes puts her tit away? Remi wondered.

"And what is that?" he asked instead.

Across town, in a small radio station, another, well, not a member per se, but a valuable contributor to The Cabal was again hard at work in the land of the conspiracy theorists.

"A flying spaceship landed on your front lawn, and the aliens came out and talked to you! No way!" Johan Franz said in mock horror to one of his radio callers.

"Yes, they did," the caller replied.

"And what did you say to them?"

"I said, 'Get off my lawn, I just mowed it'."

"Ha-ha, that's awesome and so forthright, bro. I love my garden too. And, dude, do you have any video footage of this *creepy* alien visitation?" Johan asked, already knowing the answer.

"Um, no, no, the alien zapped my Holophone, and . . . and it erased all footage," the caller replied.

"Oh, that is so unlucky, dude," Johan replied. "You saw an actual live alien, not those things flying in the distant sky, but the footage was lost. Why does it always happen that way?"

"Yeah . . . just bad luck, I guess," the caller replied.

"Well, thanks for calling, dude, and have a nice day." Johan disconnected the caller and adjusted his seat so he could reach the microphone better.

Johan Franz was a short-statured man of twenty-two years of age with wild, curly dark brown hair and hazel eyes. He was presently at University studying law, but to help pay his fees, he had gotten a part-time job as a conspiracy theorist shock jock in one of the small and obscure local radio stations. It was a very embarrassing job to have for someone who was supposed to be an educated and learned young man, so John France, which was his real name, put on a fake accent over the radio so his friends at Uni would not recognise him. His dad, on hearing this accent, laughed so hard he almost cried and kept telling him to have an *'excellent adventure'* every time he went to work.

He was good at lying, which was required in this job, and as he was studying to become a lawyer, he thought that was a good thing for his long-term career prospects. Lately, though, he wasn't really sure he should be doing this job at all, as some of the people who contacted him were a bit dodgy, to say the least. It wasn't the callers who were dodgy—they were just mad. It was the people who were in high places of power that made him uncomfortable.

Senator Natalie Braiths of all people, who was the scariest woman he had ever come across, had contacted him and offered him extra money if he would promote conspiracy ideas of hers. Johan didn't mind, as the extra money was very welcome, but once she had entered his life, his radio station had all of a sudden become a lot more popular. Advertisement of his show, which the manager knew nothing about, started appearing on street billboards and all over the Holonews and Holonet, and Johan, to his dismay, had somehow become a minor sort of celebrity, not just in his hometown of Sydney but all across Australia.

'Are you doing this, Franzie?' the radio manager had said angrily.
'What!' Franz replied, astounded. 'I can't afford to pay my own rent, let alone put advertisements all over the city.'

Johan was in a serious bind because Braiths had made it crystal clear that if he revealed their connection she was going to make his life a living hell, and she smiled almost eagerly when she said this, which made the threat seem a lot worse.

"And we have another caller," Johan continued, getting back to his job. "What happened to you, man?"

"I was visited by aliens too," the new caller replied. "They came into my house and possessed my soul because they were demons from the Underworld."

"Wow, demons from the Underworld, and I thought they came from the sky! Far out, man."

"Yes," the caller replied. "My body levitated, and things were thrown around the house."

"Oh, no way! Did anyone see this, dude?"

"Yes, my whole family, the local priest, my psychiatrist, and even my neighbours saw the exorcism."

"And did they video it?"

"Um, yes, they did."

"So we have proof at last!"

"Um, no, no, we don't, because the alien demons zapped all of their Holophones and, and . . . it erased all footage," the caller replied.

"Oh, that is so unlucky, dude," Johan replied. "People once again saw an actual levitation, but the footage was lost once more. *Why* does it always happen that way?"

Hobart, Tasmania

Jeff sat in his car and continued his surveillance of Victor Cunnington. He did not have any of those Holographic Scans that the police in Canberra had, and Cunnington was not having any affair—thank the Maker—so he did not place any video surveillance equipment in anybody's bedrooms.

No, Jeff had to watch Victor Cunnington's comings and goings through listening devices and in the old-fashioned way, with his eyes.

And what had this strange, fat man done so far? Well, not that much. He worked in the public service in a managerial role, although he did spend most of his time outside puffing away on cigarettes, but he did have some interesting close work friends. Paulo Smythen, an effeminate but strong-bodied teenager with longish blond hair, Reginald Yeasmith, an intense-looking, grey-haired, balding middle-aged man with glasses, and Colin Wise, an almost anorexic man with greasy brown hair. Normally Jeff wouldn't have thought anything of those four being friends, especially as Paulo Smythen was Victor's cousin, but well, to put it honestly, together they all looked kind of odd, and his policeman instincts went on high alert.

His phone now rang, not his Holophone, which he barely used, but the good old-fashioned, easily hackable mobile phone.

It's not her, is it?

"Yes?" he answered.

"Watcha doin?" she asked.

It was her.

Jeff had trained Susan to be his back up, which she was very keen to learn and amazingly fast at picking up what it entailed. So whilst Jeff was watching Victor Cunnington, Susan was watching Jeff, or watching his back, to be precise.

"Watching fatso and the creeps; what are you doing?" he replied.

"Our employer," she answered, "wants to know if you found anything. He says you should get your lazy arse into gear or he will hire someone else."

"For fuck's sake, it's only been a week," Jeff growled, spitting his bacon and egg sandwich all over his mobile phone.

Fucking Bill Cooper, fucking politicians!

Jeff could hear Susan laughing now.

"What are you laughing at?" Jeff asked, bewildered.

"Oh, nothing." She chuckled. "I lied the last bit; he just wants to know how you are going?"

"That's not funny." Jeff wiped the bacon and egg from his phone.

"I know." He could still hear her laughing.

"You shouldn't be laughing," he said, still a bit annoyed at her strange sense of humour.

"I know, and I'm sorry," she replied.

"Well, that's okay, then," Jeff allowed, feeling a bit mollified.

"Oh," Susan suddenly said, "and you're being watched."

"What!"

"Yeah, some guy in one of those fancy new cars."

"What!"

"Yep."

"You're kidding."

"Nope."

Jerry McGuiness sat in his car and kept his usual watch over Jeff Brady. Brady spied on people just like he did, but Jerry had the advantage of spying technology, which Brady could not afford. It was pretty boring, for the most part. Jeff seemed to spend most of his time watching people having affairs and trying not to gag on whatever he was eating at the time he was doing it, but this time, he was doing something that shocked Jerry to the core. This time, the person Brady had under surveillance was Victor Cunnington, which was the man Jerry was supposed to be watching as well.

"He is here again," Jerry said in an official tone. "I can positively confirm that Brady is watching Cunnington."

"Why the hell is Brady watching that fat lump?" ASIO Chief Brook Raller said quietly over the phone.

"I don't know, Boss," Jerry replied nervously.

Jerry thought it was a coincidence the first day he saw Brady hanging around outside of the government building where Cunnington worked, but late last night, he was seen outside of where Cunnington lived.

"This doesn't make any sense," Raller said, obviously confused.

"What do you want me to do?" Jerry asked.

"Just . . . just keep watching them," Raller replied.

"Well, I guess it will be easier watching both Brady and Cunnington since they spend so much time together," Jerry replied in a light tone.

"Not funny," Raller said firmly. "Now do your bloody job."

"Yes, sir," Jerry replied formally and went back to listening in on Brady and was startled that he was now on a phone call.

"Yes."

"Watcha doin?"

"Watching fatso and the creeps; what are you doing?"

"Our employer wants to know if you found anything. He says you should get your lazy arse into gear or he will hire someone else."

"For fuck's sake, it's only been a week."

"Are you hearing this, sir?" Jerry asked his boss.

"Yes, I am," Raller said thoughtfully.

"You shouldn't be laughing."

"I know, and I'm sorry."

"Well, that's okay, then."

"Oh, and you're being watched."

"What!"

"Yeah, some guy in one of those fancy new cars."

"What!"

"Yep."

"You're kidding."

"Nope."

"What!" Jerry said, quickly looking around him and seeing

nothing but the usual busy city traffic.

"What!" Raller said, also in shock.

"Should I track that caller?" Jerry asked urgently.

"No. No, get the hell out of there, now!" Raller said.

"But—"

"Now, McGuiness!" Raller yelled.

"Yes, Boss," Jerry replied. He had a brand-new self-driven car, which only recently came out of China, but he kept the car in manual control, slammed on the accelerator, and gunned it down the street as fast as he could.

"Yeah, he is going now," the female caller continued. "He is driving like a maniac in one of those rich tossers new cars—must be having a mid-life crisis or something."

"Bitch," Jerry muttered. "I'm only in my early twenties."

Jerry was young and inexperienced in this field of work, so in his haste to get out of there, he failed to notice the police car in front of him, until he had totally rear-ended it that is.

"Ahahaha, he just ran into the back of a cop car."

"We better go," Brady said.

"But don't you think that was funny?"

"Yes, I do, but we better go; we don't know who else is listening," Brady said in a much tighter voice.

"Okay, then. See you back at the office."

"Oh, fuck!" Jerry shouted.

"McGuiness, what are you doing?" Raller asked.

"Nothing, sir, just getting arrested, that's all."

"What! And what was that they said? Did you just hit a cop car?"

"Got to go, sir," Jerry replied.

Jerry frantically disconnected the communication system and tried his best to hide his equipment in the back seat and hidden dashboards.

I don't have enough time, he thought in a panic.

Two policemen now groggily got out of the car. One was a man with short blond hair, the other—well, he was a man with dark skin and had the angriest face Jerry had ever seen.

"Good day to you, sir," the angry man said as he walked up to Jerry's ruined vehicle. "My name is Constable Hussein, and this here is Constable Woods. Now was there any reason you decided to drive like an idiot?"

"Rizo," the other constable said before Jerry could reply. His attention was inside the car, with a look of amazement. "Look at all of his equipment. There's some pretty expensive stuff here." The hard-looking policeman took in what equipment he saw and looked back at Jerry.

"I think, young man, that you best be coming along with us," was all that he said, but with a look that made Jerry flinch.

Victor Cunnington sat outside his work building having a smoke and watched as some idiot raced his new Chinese-manufactured self-driven car down the middle of Harrington Street and then plowed straight into the back of a stationary police car.

"What an imbecile," Paulo Smythen said by his side.

Victor took another long drag on his ciggy and nodded his fat head. "Idiot," he mumbled.

"Dangerous," Colin Wise added.

"Crazy," Reginald said in his soft-spoken voice.

None of these three men smoked, but as they were his friends, or brown-nosing suckholes as some people in their office called them, they were allowed to spend as much time bludging outside with Victor Cunnington as possible.

"Some people are just dangerous." Victor smiled, watching some young man get out of his damaged car and being handcuffed by two policemen. "They cause trouble wherever they go."

"That they do," his young cousin Paulo said and smiled as he swept his blond hair out of his face.

Colin laughed so hard he almost fell over doing it, as he was so skinny and frail. His laughter sounded as if everything was loose in his chest, and Victor kept expecting him to cough up his lungs. But whilst he looked weak, Colin could be as nasty as they come, and what he would lose in a fight through his lack of strength, he would win through pure cunning.

Reginald said nothing, just stared with those intense eyes of his and tried to place his pathetic comb-over back on top of his head.

All three men, except maybe his cousin Paulo, didn't like to be directly involved in Victor's violence, but they liked the fact that the women they set up were killed by their own machinations. It was a hobby of theirs you might say, and was something that Victor truly didn't understand but was grateful that they did.

They also enjoyed getting rid of the bodies, even though three of the deceased had been recently recovered, to Victor's immense displeasure.

Victor now looked up and saw a big man with spiky blond hair and the broody-looking man called Jon Dayton walking in their direction.

That man looks very familiar, Victor thought as he watched the big man moving closer.

"Blokes," the big man simply said and nodded his head amiably at them as he walked by and entered their building. Jon Dayton ignored them, as usual.

Who was that guy?

"Shit, was that Ray Beasley!" Colin said in shock.

"Who?" Paulo asked with a scowl. He was a bit miffed that the new employee was bigger than him. A lot bigger than him, it should be said.

"He used to play for the Southern Kangaroos," Colin replied in awe. "He must have got a job here."

"Who cares?" Paulo sniffed and scratched at his arm. "He looks like a wanker with his spiky hair."

My cousin is so weird, Victor thought. *No doubt he now hates that guy, as he is so insecure with his own body image.*

"Well, I don't care," Victor said.

"I never said you did," Colin snapped, showing a little of his angry side. "I was just making an observation, all right?"

"Okay, okay, keep your shirt on," Victor replied calmly.

Colin took a steadying breath and seemed to calm down a little. *And you are weird too, Colin*, Victor thought.

"Anyway, back to business," Victor said. "Do you have any new *prospects* for me?"

Colin and Paulo now looked at each other. Reginald said nothing and just kept looking at the policemen with a worried expression.

"We don't; sorry," Paulo said.

"The missing girls have made the other whores very scared,"

Colin added. "There is talk of them hiring bodyguards, of all things."

"Bodyguards!" Victor said in shock. "How can they afford that?"

"Well, they can't," Paulo replied. "The costs for their services have gone up three-fold."

"Really?" Victor replied. "The punters won't like that."

"Well, they don't, actually, and that business has now seen a massive downturn in clientele."

Victor actually stopped smoking his precious cigarettes and turned to his work colleagues.

"Do you mean I am solely responsible for the demise of prostitution in Hobart?"

Colin and Paulo both looked at each other again.

"Well, yes," Paulo said.

And my mum said I would never amount to anything.

"So I guess our fun is over, boys," Victor said dejectedly after a moment.

I knew it was too good to last, and maybe with the bodies being discovered that was a good thing.

"Well, not exactly," Paulo said hesitantly.

"What do you mean?" Victor asked curiously.

"It's a plan me and young Paulo came up with," Colin said. "A plan you might enjoy."

"What plan?" Victor asked.

"It involves a certain tour," Paulo replied.

"What tour?"

"It's risky."

"What tour?" Victor snapped.

After Colin had told him what tour he was talking about, Victor's stunned reaction made him laugh and cough so hard that this time he *did* actually fall over.

Fourteen-year-old Fiona Milligan and her thirteen-year-old sister, Gena Milligan, walked quickly home from school in a state of teenage bliss as they looked at their mobile phones.

Whilst Fiona had the dark brown hair and blue eyes of her mother, Susan—even though her mother insisted on dying her hair black—Gena took after their deadbeat and presently incarcerated father, with the blonde hair and brown eyes. They both, however, had the forward curvature of the neck which was so common in young children nowadays.

"Get off the road, dopey," a driver said as he swerved to avoid them.

Fiona and Gena were in deep text conversations with their school friends about the coming tour, and they didn't look up to notice the pedestrians, the traffic lights . . . or the cars.

"For God's sake, are you blind!" another driver shouted.

"They are coming," Fiona squealed at her sister after reading the latest news, rather than worrying about whether she was about to get run over or not.

"Wake up, you ditzy schoolkids. I almost killed you!" yelled another angry driver.

"Are you even looking where you are going, you stupid fu—" This driver blasted the horn in the car.

"I know," Gena replied, equally excited and not caring about the traffic and her almost near-death experience. "Not only do we get to see El Froggo and the Street United Cat Kings, but the Radonculus sisters as well."

Both girls squealed again with delight and kept on with their perilous journey home, but instead of walking, they decided to leapfrog Froggo File.

"What if Mum can't afford it?" Gena suddenly said worriedly as she walked straight out onto the road with all of its busy traffic and bent down for her sister to leap over her.

"Or if she doesn't let us go, because we are not old enough?" Fiona moaned still looking at her mobile phone as she jumped over her sister.

"Oh, we never get to go anywhere!" Gena whined, ignoring the fact that her mother gave them nearly everything that they asked for and had to work her butt off to get it.

"She's just *jealous*," Fiona huffed. "She hates it that we are so y*oung* and *cool* and she is just an old fossil from pre-historic times."

Their mother was only in her mid-thirties.

"Yeah, what a *bitch*." Gena scowled as they kept leapfrogging across the road.

A car passed within two feet of the heels of Gena's feet.

"What the fuck are you doing!" the driver screamed.

"Totally," Fiona added.

A car passed just in front of Fiona, causing her hair to blow in the air.

"Are you doing that stupid Froggo shit?" another driver yelled at them.

"I hate her," Gena huffed, ignoring the driver.

"So do I," Fiona replied as they continued on leapfrogging their way home.

Neither of them really hated their mother, nor did they consider the fact that their mother loved them to death, looked after them, fed and clothed them, and if she should die suddenly they would miss her terribly for the rest of their lives.

"Speaking of old codgers." Gena suddenly frowned as they finally reached their home safely.

Both of the Milligan sisters had finally looked away from their precious mobile phones and saw their grandfather, Martin Marsh, sitting on the porch outside their family home, waiting for them.

"It's a wonder he doesn't have a *rocking chair*," Gena whined.

"Yeah, the old fart is from another *century*." Fiona smirked. He was in fact, as he was born in 1962.

"Well, well, if it isn't the spoilt Milligan sisters back from school." He groaned. "How did you manage to break your gaze away from those mobile phones to see your grandfather? You must be dying to know what inane things your friends texted in the last two minutes."

Fiona called her grandfather an old fart, which he was. The sisters did love their grandfather in their own way, as he did them, but he could be a whiny old man sometimes.

"Reality must be so hard," he continued. "Oh, quick, girls, look back at the mobile phone or gaze at the computer inside the house before you miss some *fascinating* news on what the Radonculus sisters are wearing today."

"Yeah, *whatever*, Grandpa," Gena replied, using the word grandpa to mean something else entirely.

"*Yeah, totally.* You're so *old* and *irrelevant,*" Fiona added.

"Old, am I?" Martin scoffed, then realised he was. He wiped one hand over his bald head and continued on anyway. "Well . . . well . . . hmm—oh, yeah here it goes. I used to live in a world before the Nanny State. People of my generation used to have to use their brains, not have everything labeled for them like they had an IQ of twelve. We used to lose at things and be told that to win we needed to try harder next time, or that we were just simply not good enough at what we did and needed to try something else. We didn't cry about it and shake our fist at the world, saying how unfair it all was and wonder whether we could take them to court somehow for hurting our fragile egos. We took all of this on the chin, picked ourselves up, dusted ourselves off, and continued on our way and actually became tougher in the process to help prepare us for what life would inevitably throw at us, no matter how much you hid in your safe space or whatever lame-arsed leftie foofoo rubbish they call it nowadays.

"We weren't molly-coddled and wrapped in cotton wool all the time by our parents like you kids are today, being told you are simply the best at everything you say and do, like you are some sort of superhero or something, and that it wasn't *your* fault; that it was always someone *else's* fault that things didn't happen the way you wanted it to."

Martin took a deep breath and continued.

"We used to disappear into the bushlands and play with our friends for hours, splashing through ponds and throwing rocks, falling over and getting cuts and scratches, riding our bikes, breathing in the fresh air, getting exercise. We didn't sit on our arses all day staring at the phone, making comments or liking something on Fartbook or whatever you call it about how bad the world is and thinking you have actually done something constructive in helping the problem, when in reality, all you have actually done is sweet FA. And you do all of this while ignoring the people standing around you, who are actually real and genuinely care about you."

Martin took another deep breath and continued.

"We didn't look to be offended all the time either, like you young people do today, and we could tell people honestly to their face that they were dickheads, when they were being dickheads, and not have to worry about what cultural or ethnic background they came from just in case we offended somebody who was drinking café-latte, discussing poetry whilst listening to jazz down at Salamanca Place. We used to—"

Martin suddenly realised his granddaughters had already walked inside to look at the computer.

"Typical," he muttered, and then started to wait for his daughter, Susan, to come home so he could moan at her.

"Typical," he muttered once more.

Sydney, Mainland Australia

Bland.

What an apt word that was when contemplating today's music and entertainment industry.

Bland.

The tall and incredibly handsome man with blond hair and a chiseled jaw looked at himself in the mirror and tried in vain to get that word out of his mind.

Bland.

There just didn't seem to be very many really talented people left anymore. The incredibly handsome man remembered his grandfather telling him about the old bluesmen, rockers and crooners who performed up until they were almost eighty, and the public still went and saw them perform. Today, however, stars were created and then turfed out with such amazing speed. If you didn't make immediate money, you were quickly gotten rid of. The public and the media's patience and interest were also incredibly short. The ones who had a long career in showbiz were either incredibly lucky or were one of the few who had genuine and unhindered natural talent.

But today, he had to interview the beautiful but talentless Radonculus sisters and listen to yet more crappy songs.

I don't think I can take this anymore.

But he had to keep the public happy, didn't he? That was his job, after all. He was doing the right thing, wasn't he? Brandon

Townsworth and his minions wanted the public entertained. They wanted their eyes glued to the TV, and under no circumstance were they to take an interest in global events, which seemed to be getting worse by the year.

"Two minutes, Mr Sparkles," a stagehand called out.

'Sparkles.' Who was the idiot who gave him that nickname? Brad would have liked to punch whoever it was right in the face for that. But he wasn't really a violent man.

Perhaps I could get Natalie to do it?

"One minute, Mr Sparkles."

One minute, he thought with a sigh. *One minute till the cycle starts once more.*

The incredibly handsome man looked once more at himself in the mirror and summoned his inner strength.

Time for the act to begin.

Brad 'Sparkles' Hoffington brought out the smile that had fooled so many people. He brought out the smile that made women go gaga and throw themselves at him. He brought out the smile that made him lots of money. The smile that was completely fake.

Bland, he thought as he walked out on the stage.

Whilst Remi Hiller had dark greasy hair and Frank Hiller had light brown hair and they looked nothing alike in the face, the brothers did share the exact same hairline. They both could have easily played Dracula in an old Hammer Horror Film.

"Oh, yeah, it's Froggo File," sang the man known as El Froggo.

"So how you been, Frank?" Remi asked his brother as he waited at the side of the stage for the TV chat show with Hoffington to begin after El Froggo had finished the opening number.

"You like my Froggo File."

"Not too bad, Remi," Frank Hiller replied, looking over the gathered TV audience, who were playing leapfrog up and down some steep stairs just as the singer and his music film clip told them to do. Although playing leapfrog in a much safer area may have been what they were really after.

They love this song now, Frank thought, *but very soon comes the crushing embarrassment they will feel at the fact that they did indeed play leapfrog like freaking idiots.*

"I'm surprised the Occupational Health and Safety laws have allowed them to jump around like that," Remi said.

"It's leapfrogging not jumping, mate," Frank corrected him.

"Sorry . . . *leapfrogging*," Remi replied, then winced as a member of the audience fell down the stairs in a most spectacular way.

"You know you want my Froggo File."

"Yeah, I'm surprised too," Frank replied, also wincing at what his brother had just seen. "But hey, if they are going to sue anyone if someone falls and breaks their neck, it will be on the building owner's head for having such unsafe stairs."

"But *they* are playing leapfrog," Remi replied as he watched yet another person crash down the stairs.

"Yes, and the building officials should be prepared for such an event," Frank replied.

"Prepared for it!" Remi said incredulously. "They are playing *leapfrog* on a forty-five-degree stair *incline*."

"You know how things are, mate," Frank said with his elder brother's serious face.

"It's Froggo—yeah, Froggo File."

"Yeah, I know. People don't take any responsibility for their own stupidity." Remi sighed.

"Exactly, mate, exactly." Frank nodded sagely.

Another person crashed down the stairs, falling head over heels, and then didn't move. Nobody moved to help her, or even noticed as she lay there prostrate on the stairs.

Is she dead? Frank wondered.

"Fuck you with my Froggo File."

What!

"Wait! Did he just say fuck?" Frank blurted out in disbelief as he watched the short dark-haired man named El Froggo continue to jump around and mesmerize the audience with his international mega-hit and soon-to-be either reviled or forgotten song.

"Nah, mate, you must be hearing things," Remi, who wasn't really paying any attention to the lyrics, replied. He was looking at the woman still lying unconscious on the stairs.

"Um bah lumbah, it's Froggo File."

"Um bah lumbah?" Frank asked, frowning. "Or did he just say oompa loompa?"

"No, I think it was, um bah lumbah." Remi shrugged, now paying attention to the lyrics, having forgotten all about the woman still lying on the stairs, who was now quite dead.

El Froggo kept on singing incoherently, and the electronic music kept blaring loudly, and the audience kept leapfrogging dangerously until finally, the song blessedly finished.

"Does he have any other songs?" Remi asked.

"Geez, I hope not." Frank frowned.

"Shit, here he comes," Remi whispered, "and don't frown at him whatever you do. He is a bit mental."

Don't frown at him?

"Oh, good job, Froggo," Remi now called out as El Froggo ran off the stage to join them with the rapturous applause from the audience ringing in their ears.

El Froggo's eyes now darted around his new surroundings incessantly, like he was high on some sort of drug—which he was.

"Top job, mate," Frank added as he slapped the singer on the back. "Lennon and McCartney would be *livid* with envy if they saw such *awesome* creativity."

"Huh?" El Froggo replied in confusion, now focusing those wide pupils on Frank.

"I said top job," Frank repeated.

"Huh?" El Froggo said again.

"Top job?"

"Huh?"

"He doesn't speak or understand any English, Frank," Remi said, interrupting the riveting conversation between Frank and El Froggo. "His manager said his comprehension of English or his awareness of basic surroundings . . . or anything at all, really, apart from that stupid song, is basically zero."

"Top job," Frank said once more.

"Huh?" El Froggo replied.

Frank took a closer look at El Froggo's eyes.

This guy is off his tits!

"Where is his manager?" Frank asked his brother.

"He palmed him off to me for this tour," Remi replied. "He said he needed a break from him."

"Where did he find him, then?"

"In a slum somewhere."

"What!" Frank said, shocked.

"Yeah. He was a bet, apparently, between two music moguls." Remi smiled. "One mogul proclaimed that he could turn this homeless man into an international pop star people adored and looked up to, and the other music mogul agreed with him."

"Agreed with him." Frank laughed.

"Yeah." Remi laughed back.

Was there anybody the music industry could not make into a star?

"So Froggo doesn't understand anything that I say?" Frank asked.

"Nope, not a word. Well, apart from the word Froggo, of course."

"Really!" Frank said in surprise.

"Yeah, not a word," Remi replied with a grin.

"Truly?" Frank asked.

"Truly, Brother." Remi smiled back.

Okay, here goes, but don't frown.

"You were shit, mate," Frank said to the singer, smiling for all he was worth as he shook El Froggo's hand. "In fact, my one-year-old niece has crapped out better songs than that in her nappy."

"Huh?" El Froggo replied once again, but was now smiling back at Frank.

"Well done, um . . . Froggo," Remi interrupted, trying to stifle a laugh as he indicated for El Froggo to go backstage, which he was quite happy to do, no doubt to take some more heavy drugs—which he was also quite happy to do.

"So why shouldn't I frown at him?" Frank asked after El Froggo had left.

"Ah, you know," Remi said softly. "He has a temper . . . and he has killed some people," he finished in a whisper.

"What? He has a temper," Frank said, frowning, not hearing what Remi had said at the end.

"Yeah, yep, he does. So is your new boy band any good?" Remi continued, trying to change the subject.

"Oh, they," Frank now stammered, "they are really . . . you know . . ."

"Would the answer to this question also be lying somewhere in your niece's nappy?" Remi finished for him.

Frank sighed, but a small grin was on his face.

"They are actually not too bad," Frank replied after a moment. "I might make a good earner out of these boys."

"Well, that is good. And which one is the talented one this time?" Remi asked, looking over at the five young men who were waiting patiently for their cue to sing their latest song. Their lead singer's name was Matthew—who seemed to be looking very interestedly at the three young sisters who now stood next to Remi, especially Mercedes Radonculus, who was gazing back at him—and next to him were the other band members, Ivan, Neville, Gary, and Eddy.

"I'm not sure," Frank replied, looking thoughtfully at the young men as well. "Even my music producer, Brian, doesn't know who the talented one is."

"I guess time will tell," Remi said.

"It usually—oh, here we go," Frank said.

The crowd went insane with joy as the tall and dashingly handsome host of the show walked out onto the stage. The girls in the audience were screaming, as was to be expected, but suddenly, Mercury screamed the loudest and almost destroyed Remi's hearing in the process.

"For fuck's sake, what are you doing?" Remi said in shock as he staggered and grabbed at his ear. Frank stared at her in disbelief as well and seemed to have one hand pressed against his heart. Matthew and Mercedes didn't notice and were still staring at each other.

"It's . . . it's . . . him—it's, it's . . . *Brad Sparkles Hoffington*," Mercury said breathlessly.

"I know it's fucking Sparkington or whatever his name is, but what is with the screaming?" Remi replied in disbelief.

"He is such a big spunk," Mercury replied, her chest heaving, and Remi thought she was going to be like her sister Mercedes and have her boobs break out through her dress.

Remi sometimes forgot that Mercury was just sixteen years of age and that she was in fact the same age as most of the people in the audience.

"Listen, Mercury," Remi said, trying to calm her down, "*we* are the stars—we don't scream, okay?"

"But, but, he's so handsome, hot, and gorgeous . . . and really hot," Mercury replied with a frown.

"Yes, yes, he is . . . just so, just so . . . *great*," Remi replied. "But you are the star now, so *you* don't scream, *they* scream." He finished by pointing at the audience with one hand whilst the other was again up against his ear, checking to see if there was any blood pouring out of it.

If I go deaf, I am suing her, Remi thought angrily.

"But he is so handsome, hot, and so super cool," Mercury replied again, as usual, not understanding what he was saying at all.

What am I going to do with this one? Remi wondered. *After a whole year, she still has no idea how to handle fame.*

"Sharon," he said instead to the oldest sister, who was standing next to her youngest sister, "I am glad to see you are not screaming."

She is a smart girl, Remi thought ruefully. Her condition on doing this tour was that fifty percent of their earnings be kept away from her sisters for at least a year. Her sisters whined and complained about the deal, but Remi knew that Sharon had their best interests at heart. He wondered whether Frank would have done such a thing for him. No, he wouldn't, was the answer, and Remi knew he wouldn't do any such a thing for Frank either. Still, he kind of loved his brother—not as much as money, but the love was there.

"I'm too nervous to scream, Remi," Sharon replied, her pale face looking whiter than ever.

"You'll be fine, you just—" Remi stopped talking when he noticed Mercedes and Matthew were still staring at each other. Mercedes was even adjusting her dress, a sure sign of her sexual attraction, or maybe of an ill-fitting bra, and Matthew was almost salivating as he looked back at her. Remi knew that Mercedes' sort-of boyfriend, Grantee-Grant—well, they had made a sex tape together—from the boy band Loyal Angel Memory Eclipse, was in the audience.

A plan suddenly formed in Remi's mind; he just needed to talk to his brother for a moment and get his approval for it.

"Well, that was *very* interesting, Chardonnay," Brad 'Sparkles' Hoffington said as he bestowed one of his dazzling smiles on the eldest and most nervous Radonculus sister.

It wasn't really that interesting, Brad thought, *but this girl has a bit of brains about her, unlike the other two.*

The crowd went wild, braying like sheep at even the most pointless comments that the sisters made over the last fifteen minutes, and the youngest, Mercury Radonculus, was full of pointless comments.

"We wanted to visit New Zealand." She sighed. "But our manager wouldn't let us, due to us not having enough time to get a passport."

"Oh, that is so disappointing; New Zealand is a wonderful place," Brad said, glancing at Sharon, who was still looking incredibly nervous and was drinking a glass of water to settle her stomach a little.

She really is quite something, Brad thought, but he couldn't describe why Sharon was so different from the other beautiful and famous women he had interviewed.

"But I don't understand this whole passport thing." Mercury frowned. "I mean, we are still flying over to Tasmania, and that seems to be all right."

"Oh, hahaha, you are so funny, Mercury," Brad replied kindly, offering her his most dazzling smile this time.

Mercury looked back at him, not understanding.

Oh my God, she was serious, Brad thought, dumbfounded.

Sharon looked embarrassed. Mercedes was still looking over at the side of the stage, where the boy band Street United Cat Kings were waiting to perform, and the crowd went wild, still braying like sheep.

"Any-anyway, now it is time for tonight's second guests," Brad continued, turning back to the TV camera and giving one of his best smiles. "With their new hit single 'Baby, oh yeah, I love you, baby girl', please welcome teen sensation—"

Mercury then screamed again, which scared everybody half to death.

Street United Cat Kings started singing their latest smash hit to the enraptured audience. Sharon, however, wasn't listening to the music. She was checking to make sure her hearing wasn't damaged and her hands were not bleeding from when she accidentally smashed her glass of water on the table in front of her in fright at her youngest sister's immense screaming ability. The lead singer of the boy band, Matthew, instead of performing the usual orchestrated dance routine, seemed to be looking at Mercedes and making pelvic thrust movements in her direction. Subtlety was a talent he must not have learned when growing up, but Mercedes loved every moment of it—or every thrust of it. Their respective managers, however, talked quietly at the side of the stage as to what they expected to happen.

"You sure about this?" Frank Hiller asked his brother.

"Oh, c'mon, Frank," Remi replied, "you know there is no such thing as bad publicity."

"Yes, but it is still a bit risky," Frank said worriedly.

"For whom?" Remi asked, confused.

"Me, that's whom," Frank said. "You know Grantee-Grant hates my guts."

"So?" Remi replied. "All the other ex-boy band members hate you too."

And so they should; you rip them off worse than I do.

"Yeah, true." Frank shrugged. "But Grantee-Grant has a really bad temper."

"That's what I heard." Remi smiled.

"I still don't know, Remi," Frank said.

"Well, it's too late now; here he is," Remi said.

They both turned and faced Grantee-Grant, lead singer of Frank's former boy band. He was of medium height, and had brown hair and average looks, but he had the hair that was a 'must-have' for all boy band members—thick, which, ironically, was a word well used to describe his personality.

"What do you want, *Frank*?" Grantee-Grant said petulantly. "I was quite happy sitting in the audience rather than coming over and watching from the side of the stage, *Frank*."

"Oh, sorry, Grantee-Grant," Frank said nervously. "I just, you know, saw you in the audience and thought you would like to relive old times."

"Just call me Grant, *Frank*. Grantee-Grant was my stage name, *Frank*."

"Oh . . . yeah, sure, . . . Grant."

He is still like a spoilt child, Frank thought. *Being a 'nobody' now hasn't changed him at all.*

"Hey, *look*, Matthew is singing very sexily to Mercedes," Remi Hiller suddenly said in fake surprise.

"What!" Grant said angrily as he turned to look at Matthew singing to his sort-of girlfriend—well, they did make a sex tape together—and thrusting his package towards her.

He now moved closer and got down on one knee before her and continued the crooning. It would have been more romantic if he wasn't miming, but the good intentions were there, and Mercedes looked like she loved it.

"Wow," Remi said in fake commiseration, "it must be *so* hard to be *replaced* as a boyfriend on national TV like *that*."

"I'm being what?" Grant said, turning angrily to Remi.

"Look at the way she is leaning forward so he can get a good look at that rack," Remi continued. "But maybe he has seen them before."

Half of Australia has seen them now, thanks to that sex tape, Remi thought, and she *was* indeed leaning forward so Matthew would catch an eyeful too.

"He's what? How has he seen them before?" Grant snapped, turning back towards the stage.

"Oh . . . nothing," Remi said meekly. "Just forget that I said that."

"Tell me, you little shit, or I'll smash ya one," Grant growled, turning back to Remi Hiller.

Remi considered punching the little snot in the head for that comment, but he had to continue with the plan.

"Well, I'm sure the rumours aren't true," Remi said innocently.

"What rumours?" Grant said, even more angrily.

"Oh, I'm *sure* it's nothing," Remi said offhandedly.

"What rumours?" Grant shouted this time.

"Oh, you know . . . just that"—*here goes*—"Matthew is banging your girlfriend."

"He's doing what!" Grant screamed.

"Three times a day, from what I heard," Remi continued.

"What!"

"They've been humping all over her hotel room, apparently. The neighbours have even complained about the noise and the vibrations against the walls. Some even called the police, reporting a murder in progress because she was screaming that much."

"I'm gonna kill him!" Grant screamed so loud it made some of the boy band singers turn to look at the side of the stage, even though they were performing their latest awesome and cool dance routine.

"But again, I'm sure it's not true." Remi shrugged. "I mean, who I am to know such things? And sometimes rumours are just plain lies."

"Yeah . , . yeah, I suppose so," Grant said, calming a little, and sure that his girlfriend would not two-time him like that because he was so hot and cool. He knew all too well how the media lied to make headlines.

I've been played for a fool so many times by the media, Grant thought. Grant should have realised how ironic that last thought was, as he was standing next to two blood-sucking managers who loved to play games with the media.

Remi then turned to his brother and gave him a pleading look. "It's um bah lumbah time," he said quietly.

Oh, all right, Frank thought with a sigh. *You owe me for this one, little brother.*

"But, Remi, aren't you *Mercedes'* manager?" Frank said in an incredibly fake voice, which anybody should have noticed, except for the incredibly thick ex-boy band singer previously known as Grantee-Grant. "If *anybody* should know these things it would be *you*."

"What did you say?" Grant said as his face snapped towards Frank Hiller.

He sure says 'what' a lot, Frank realised.

"Shut *up*, Frank. He doesn't need to know the truth," Remi said in what he pretended was a soft whisper but was still loud enough for Grant to overhear.

Grant's face went very pale and then turned a deep shade of red. "They *are* doing it!" Grant shouted.

"No, no . . . I'm sure the rumours of all-night hot and steamy sex sessions aren't true," Remi said.

"Fucking hell!" Grant yelled, with both his hands clutching at his luxurious hair.

"And that they laugh about you constantly, and say to everybody that will listen that you have an incredibly small dick," Remi continued.

"That son of a BITCH!" Grant screamed and ran straight onto the stage and started fighting with Matthew on live national television.

"You can't buy this sort of publicity, Frank," Remi said with a pleased smile as he watched two fit young men with big hair start rolling around on the stage floor.

Was that fighting? Remi wondered. *It looked like Grant was trying to scratch Matthew's eyes out.*

"That you can't, Brother," Frank replied, hoping Matthew would win, otherwise any street cred this band had would soon go out the window.

Is Matthew crying? Frank wondered.

The two boy band members punched on, or slapped each other, depending on your point of view, whilst the other boy band members stood mute in shock. The crowd screamed in terror that their venerated heroes were acting like everyday people in a pub. Mercedes, on the other hand, seemed really pleased about what was happening and seemed to be cheering them on. Brad took Sharon to safety at the side of the stage, forgetting completely about Mercury, and surprisingly, or not surprisingly for some, the song that Street United Cat Kings had been performing kept playing on.

Tardigrades are creatures usually 0.1mm to 0.5mm long, have sharp, dagger-like teeth in their tubular mouth and have existed for a very long time. In fact, according to fossil records, they even predate dinosaurs and have been on this planet for 530 million years. They can survive for a few minutes under 151 degrees Celsius heat or being frozen at minus 200 degrees. In an experiment conducted in 2007, tardigrades were actually taken to space in a dehydrated state and were exposed to outer space vacuum and extreme solar UV radiations and left for ten days. They were then brought back to Earth and rehydrated, and within thirty minutes they were brought back to life. The tardigrades had an amazing ability to halt all of their metabolic activities completely in a term known as cryptobiosis.

McDermott was fascinated with them, as was McLaren, and had now even engineered a new, hardier type of tardigrade species. Both of these scientists looked to this one small creature as a stepping stone on their way to achieving two results.

Cryogenics and Genocide.

Henry Abel looked down at the patient that lay twitching on one of his operating tables with half of his skull removed. He had no assistants in these operations. Richards, his security guard, would only bring in one of the subjects, then leave, and the rest was up to him.

"Just a bit more," he murmured as he continued conducting his experiments on the subject. "You'll wake up fine," he lied as he placed another microscopic sample of yet more tardigrades onto his patient's brain.

Henry Abel was yet again conducting an experiment as to how long the patient would survive with these tiny species imbedded in its brain. He had done this for years with the old type of tardigrades now residing in various places on the bodies of all of his captives.

Ever since Henry was a child, he had been obsessed by the human body. How it worked fascinated him. The heart, for example, was said to beat about 100,000 times in one day and about 35 million times in a year. During an average lifetime, the human heart will beat about 2.5 billion times. An adult is made up of 7 octillion atoms. With the 60,000 miles of blood vessels inside the average human body, you could circumnavigate Earth two and a half times. The list of fascinating facts on the human body went on and on. But the part of the human body that fascinated Henry the most was the brain.

"This time I will use the base of the brain instead of the right or left," he muttered to himself as he placed his surgical instrument deeper inside the patient's skull and brain. "I just need to move this just a little."

The brain was a very wrinkly organ. If you spread it out, it would be about the size of a pillowcase.

"Just a bit farther," he murmured to himself.

I wonder how long this one will survive with the new species of tardigrades McLaren and I have created? Henry now wondered. *They are hopefully very hungry critters.*

The patient gave a short sigh as the body shut down.

Not long. He sighed. *These tardigrades instantly killed him.*

Now that the patient was dead, he removed his surgical gear and equipment, then gave a cry of terror as the dead patient's eyes opened, his body began to move, and out of its mouth came a horrible moaning sound.

"What the hell!" Henry said in complete shock. In his panic, he picked up a nearby scalpel and stabbed it into the brain, and the body slumped once more and no longer moved. *What on earth just happened? Did the surgery right now do that, or was the ability already there, and was it the tardigrades that made it possible?*

Henry as a human was terrified at this strange event, but as a scientist, he was also very intrigued and continued on with another experiment.

Richards, the head of security, sat patiently outside Abel's laboratory in case he was needed for anything. His job was pretty boring for the most part, except when he had to kidnap the odd homeless man or woman for his boss's experiments. But he could not complain about his work, as Doctor Abel had kept him employed for the last fifteen years and had paid him very well.

Secrecy was an integral part of his job too. He knew that should he or any of the others be caught out in the abductions and incarcerations of these people, let alone the experiments, they all would be facing a lengthy term in jail; in fact, they would probably never breathe the free air again.

Another of the security guards, a stocky man named Marshall, now came rushing towards him.

"Boss, you need to see this," Marshall said urgently.

"Why, what is wrong?" Richards asked.

Marshall was not the sort of man to worry about, well, anything really, but now he looked anxious. Very anxious.

"It's the prisoners," he replied. "They are behaving stranger than usual."

Is that even possible? Richards wondered.

"How strange?" he asked.

"Violently," Marshall replied.

"Okay, mate, I'm coming," he replied.

He got up from his chair and followed Marshall, curious as to what had spooked his colleague like this. As he followed him through the various corridors, he noticed a noise that was beginning to get a lot louder. It wasn't any coherent noise; in fact, it sounded like . . .

"A jungle," Richards murmured as he reached the captives' cells.

Lloyd and Holding had been staring at the figures throwing themselves against the cell doors, waiting for Richards to join them. They were used to the occasional captive going mental and smashing their heads in on the metal bars, but now, all of them were doing it at the same time.

"What the hell is wrong with them?" Holding said worriedly as he grabbed his gun tightly. If any one of them got through their cells he was going to kill them straightaway, no matter what Henry Abel wanted.

"I don't know," Lloyd said just as worriedly. "They have all gone completely insane."

"Not all of them," the big blond-haired man named Richards said as he and Marshall finally joined them.

"What do you mean, Boss?" Holding said, relieved that his superior was here and he didn't have to make any executive decisions.

"The children," Richards replied, nodding at the smallest of their captives. "The children are silent."

The three other security guards looked at the four children, who were staring silently back at them.

"Does one of those children have completely white eyes?" Marshall said in astonishment.

"It must be the light coming off the ceiling," Richards said uncertainly.

His eyes do look all white, Richards thought, doubting his own vision.

"I don't like this," Lloyd said nervously

"Me neither," Marshall added as the captives kept throwing themselves at the cell bars and doors. Some were even biting them in the vain hope of breaking through.

Suddenly, one of the children, the one with the unusual eyes, who was a young boy of maybe six or seven years of age, raised his fist into the air, and the aggression of the captives and the cacophony of sound instantly stopped.

"Shit," Holding whispered.

"Does . . . does he control them?" Lloyd stammered, reaching for the pistol at his hip.

"It looks that way," Richards said, trying to understand just what it was he was witnessing.

His eyes did look all white, didn't they?

"He's dead," the young boy suddenly said in a voice that sounded a lot older than his actual age.

"Who is dead?" Richards replied.

"The one on the table," the boy replied with an angry sneer. The other three children were now looking angrily at the guards as well.

The one on the table?

Richards turned quickly to Marshall.

"Go check on the patient with Abel. Now," he ordered.

Marshall was quite eager to get out of the cell room and took off at a run.

"I could have got Abel," Lloyd said.

"Me too," Holding added.

Me three, Richards thought.

"How . . . how do you know that he is dead?" Richards asked the boy.

The young boy frowned at this question for a long moment as if he didn't know the answer.

Marshall now returned quickly with Abel at his side.

"What is going on?" Abel demanded. "I was in the middle of something fascinating, a discovery which could change everything as we know it."

"I'm not sure, sir," Richards said with a little flinch at his employer's anger, "but this boy here believes your patient just died."

"What?" Abel snapped.

"The boy said the one on your surgery table just died," Richards repeated.

Abel's eyes widened as he studied the young boy.

"How do you know this?" he asked the young child.

On hearing this, the young boy ignored Abel and turned to his cell companions.

"He's dead," he said angrily, and the rage of the prisoners began once more.

"Shoot him," Abel said immediately.

Did that boy's eyes just turn completely white? Abel thought in confusion.

"Sir?" Richards said in surprise. "He's just a boy."

"Taser only, and do it now," Abel commanded.

His eyes did turn white. I am sure of it.

Richards quickly took out his taser gun and shot the young boy in the chest, knocking him to the floor.

The prisoners instantly became silent and docile again as the young boy tried to control the electrical shakes Richards's gun had inflicted on him.

"Amazing," Abel murmured.

"Bloody hell," Lloyd said shakily.

"This is not right," Holding muttered.

The three other children, two boys and a tiny three-year-old girl, looked curiously at the young boy shaking on the ground.

"He's hurt, Klusta," a boy who was maybe six years old said.

"I know, Emerson," the other boy, who was maybe four years old, replied.

The three children then broke into fits of laughter; the little girl laughed the most of all.

"Thank you, Richards," Abel said with a worried frown, but Richards, who was looking at the children's joy, did not reply. *This is a madhouse*, he thought.

Hobart, Tasmania

Constable Hussein was angry. After their car was rear-ended and a young man with high surveillance technology was arrested, they were to learn that just half an hour later, the man was released, and that all of the Hobart Police were to keep clear of him at all times.

Keep clear of him? Hussein thought angrily. *He bloody well ran into us.* His neck was still sore. Perhaps he should claim worker's compensation and have a few months off.

No, he wouldn't do that; Razan loved his work.

Sometimes.

"Stop mucking around and behave." *You little shits,* Razan Hussein finished in his head.

The skateboarders glared back at him, just like most of the public did, and said nothing and wandered back down the road and away from the traffic intersection.

Little bastards could have fallen over and had their heads caved in by a passing motorist, Razan thought. *Then I would have been the one to tell their parents about their dead kid, and in this bloody it's-not-my-fault, it's-your-fault world that we live in today, I would have gotten the blame for it.*

"What's wrong, Rizo?" his partner, Eric Woods, asked, concerned. "You look more grumpy than usual."

Razan mumbled something incomprehensible.

"Is it those kids?" Eric asked.

"Nah, not them, exactly," Razan replied.

"Is it the Nanny State, which is slowly turning those kids into clueless morons?"

If an accident did happen, the police would have been blamed for not putting a 'do not skateboard in the middle of the street during peak-hour traffic' sign up somewhere.

"A little," Razan grumbled.

Eric frowned in thought. Razan had these dark moods

sometimes, and it was usually Eric who had to get him out of it.

"Is it because people nowadays are always looking for someone to blame, and we as coppers usually get it?"

"A little," Razan said again. "But . . . but I seem to get more dark looks than you."

"What do you mean?" Eric asked, confused.

"Well, you know." Razan shrugged. "You're a blond Aussie bloke, and I am, well . . . you know."

"A terrorist."

What!

"Don't fucking say that!" Razan said in shock. "And why are you laughing like that?"

"I can't help it," Eric said, trying to stop. "I just wanted to see your face when I said that."

"It's not a joke," Razan replied, still affronted.

"But it *was* a joke, Rizo," Eric told him, now sounding more serious. "That is something that has been taken from us, our sense of humour, and the ability to laugh at ourselves. I know you're not one of those evil bastards, Rizo. You are my workmate and friend, but those politically correct bastards have turned us into mindless clones. We can't say shit about anything anymore because we live in constant fear of offending somebody, and some idiots out there in the world like to spend most of their time *looking* to be offended."

That they did, Razan thought. Why someone would be constantly looking for something to complain about was confusing to him.

"But political correctness was needed," Razan said.

"Yes, it was to begin with, but it has gone way too far," Eric replied. "People only needed to change the stereotypes of the past."

"Stereotypes?" Razan said, frowning.

"Yes, Rizo, you of all people should know about this," Eric replied. "Stereotypes were the true evil of our past. Typecasting people into separate groups, as if people were all the same if they came from one ethnic group—*that* was immoral, and *that* needed to change."

"Then what went wrong?" Razan asked.

He was really surprised by this exchange. Eric usually talked about football, hot women with big bums and boobs like the Radonculus sisters, or things like that ridiculous fight Grantee-Grant and Matthew had on TV last night.

"The righteous do-gooders missed the whole point of treating people equally, Rizo. The chance for equality was staring us in the face, but they missed it."

"Missed what?" Razan asked. Eric was looking so passionate about what he was talking about; he almost looked like he was getting upset.

"A great man once said," Eric replied, " 'I have a dream that my four children will one day live in a nation where they will not be judged by the color of their skin, but by the content of their character.' "

Razan looked at Eric in shock now; there were unshed tears in his eyes.

"When I hear that speech," Eric continued, "I feel uplifted and inspired, but when I hear and see political correctness, I feel uptight and upset, almost as if something is tightening across my stomach."

Content of their character! Why did the powerful miss that? Razan wondered.

"Go on," Razan encouraged his friend.

"The righteous do-gooders fucked us over, Razan," Eric said now in frustration. "They thought that the way of improving our society was to turn us all into emotionless machines. They could only hear words and see collective groups of people; they could not see the emotions and intentions behind the words, and they did *not* see people as individuals. They failed to remove the stereotypes from society as they should have done, and all they really did was move the stereotypes around to suit their own goals—and yes, their *very own* prejudices."

"Wait. Are you saying that PC, of all the movements we have in this world, is prejudiced?" Razan said in surprise.

"Absolutely they are; they're almost as bad as the racist idiots," Eric replied honestly. "*All* men and women were meant to be treated equally in this new world of theirs, but it hasn't turned out that way at all."

"That's ironic," Razan replied softly.

Ironic! I feel like my world's been turned upside down.

"Everybody is a little prejudiced in their own way, if they were honest with themselves, Razan." Eric sighed. "But when you think you are righteous . . ."

"You think you understand the world better than everybody else," Razan replied.

Content of their character, Razan thought again. *What a simple statement it was, but it still rings so true.*

"That's right," Eric continued, "and you don't listen to other people's opinions. In fact, if they disagree with your ideas, you drown them out as much as possible."

That is true, Razan thought. He had seen those protests in person.

"The new world they have created—whoever *they* are—makes them feel good about themselves, Razan," Eric continued, "but it has made everybody else frustrated and miserable."

"They think they know all the answers," Razan murmured again. *And who were these people who had so much power and influence?*

"Too right they bloody do. They had no right to turn everybody into their own image. Who the bloody hell do they think they are?" Eric said angrily. "Debate is healthy for our society, Razan; debate allows people to discuss the problems and come to the right solution. Debate allows the public to see all the facts and to see who the smart people are and who the idiots are, for the idiots of this world cannot hide behind the truth when it's revealed, no matter how hard they try." Eric sighed again, but sadly now, his moods swinging to and fro. Talking about political correctness could do that to anybody. "But the people who rule us now have killed any form of debate. I don't know when or how it happened—maybe they control the media; I'm not sure—but we are all told what to do and what to say now, and if you don't toe the line, the righteous come down on you like a ton of bricks." He then shrugged his shoulders. "But what do I know? I am just a copper, not someone with a professional degree."

You work on the streets, Eric, Razan thought, *not away from the world sitting in an ivory tower like the career professionals do.*

"I have to say I'm a bit shocked by all of this," Razan said after a moment.

"I do have a brain, you know," Eric said, returning to his easy smiles.

"I know, mate," Razan replied kindly.

They both started walking back to their new police car.

"Oh, and by the way," Eric said suddenly, "people glare at you because you glare at them."

Bloody hell!

He knew what the glaring was; he had received comments on it for nearly all of his life.

"It's my normal face," Razan said in a pleading voice.

"Then get a facelift, tea towel head."

"Fuck off . . . Skippy the Convict Bush Kangaroo."

"Ha, you're being racist." Eric grinned.

"No, I'm just making a joke." Razan grinned back.

"Now you're getting it." Eric laughed.

They could not see the emotions and intentions behind the words.

Jeff sat at his desk deep in thought about what had happened the day before.

I was being watched, Jeff thought worriedly. He had no doubt it was to do with the chemicals he had found over a year ago. But what was he to do about it? Should he disappear and go into hiding?

It seemed pretty clear to him that his job as a detective was over.

"You're frowning again," Susan said with her own worried frown at her boss.

"I think we may be finished," Jeff replied.

"Why?"

"The man that was watching me . . ."

"Yes?" Susan prompted.

"Let's just say . . . I made some enemies in Canberra, something so significant that I can't tell anyone what it is for fear of being killed."

"And they are watching you now, after a year."

"Yes, it seems that way." Jeff sighed.

"So?" Susan said mildly.

Jeff frowned at his secretary and friend.

"What do you mean 'So?'" he asked.

"Whatever you did in Canberra happened twelve months ago, right?"

"Yes."

"And you are still alive."

"I believe so," Jeff replied drily.

"And you have kept whatever happened in Canberra a secret."

"Yes."

"And it is possible that they have been monitoring you all of this time."

"Yes," Jeff replied, frowning again.

"So?" Susan said again.

"You mean I should keep on doing what I am doing, and if I don't step on anyone's toes I should be all right?"

"Yes," she replied with a nod of her head.

Jeff sat back in his chair and processed this. If the hierarchy did want him dead, then he would have been pushing up the daisies a long time ago. Perhaps they were just watching him and checking to see if he behaved. But something still didn't sit right with this whole situation.

"So . . .?" Susan said once more with a smile.

Victor Cunnington had just masturbated again, spraying his seed all over the walls as he sat in the cubicle at his work's public toilet. He really couldn't help himself after what Colin and Paulo had suggested they do.

The Radonculus sisters, he thought over and over again. *Just imagine getting my knife into one of them.*

It was a risky plan, that was for sure. Whilst killing the prostitutes was easy, as they were not missed by the general public, abducting one of the famous sisters would direct the public gaze, not to mention the police, right on the kidnappers. *But it was worth it*, Victor thought, feeling the warmth grow again in his loins. Those women were gorgeous, and just the thought of knifing them made his cock grow hard all over again.

Victor was normally a man who spent a lot of time outside smoking cigarettes, but over the next few weeks, the depraved man would be spending a lot of time in the government toilet.

"He's disappeared again," Colin Wise said to Paulo Smythen as he sat at his workstation, wondering where Victor was.

"Yeah, but he's not nicking out to have a ciggy," Paulo Smythen replied as he swept his blond locks out of his face, then scratched at his arm. "He's gone to the dunny again."

"You don't think he is . . .?"

"Most likely," Paulo replied with his pretty smile.

He really does look like a girl, Colin thought once more, and then gave a start as he glanced at the arms Paulo was scratching and noticed a few cuts and bruises. *But what the hell is he doing to his body?*

"Either that or he must have chronic diarrhea," Colin continued.

"Chronic." Paulo smiled. "Catastrophic more like."

Colin laughed, making his whole chest rattle once more. They were joined by the new famous employee and that miserable prick Jon Dayton.

"Gentlemen," Ray Beasley said in that booming voice of his, "I was told you were the men to speak to in regards to my new portfolio, even though one of the stupid Enter buttons doesn't work on everybody's computer keyboards."

"I can't believe they still haven't fixed that keyboard problem," Jon Dayton grumbled.

"Yes, it is a bit strange," Colin replied amiably.

Paulo ignored Jon and focused his eyes on Ray Beasley. A snarl could now be seen on the corner of his mouth.

"You, Ray Beasley, the Johnny Football Hero of the public service, working on an important portfolio, what a fucking joke," Paulo snapped angrily.

"You, Paulo Smythen, growing some pubes and becoming a man, what a joke," Ray replied calmly.

"Look at your spiky hair, *Ray*. How much product do you use?" Paulo barked back.

"Look at yours, Paulo—women around the world are in a fit of jealousy right now," Ray replied, still maintaining his calm.

"I'm not a woman, cunt," Paulo spat back.

"Of course not," Ray replied calmly, "but I must admit that I was surprised when I found out your name was Paulo, not Pauline."

"Bastard." Paulo sulked.

"Child," Ray replied.

Is he going to cry? Ray wondered in amazement.

"What is wrong with you, Paulo?" Jon Dayton said shaking his head in disbelief. "You've been acting like a jerk ever since Ray started here."

Paulo ignored Jon again and looked up at Beasley with tears in his eyes before storming off, muttering again about Beasley being just a dumb football hero.

"What's up his bum?" Beasley said, still frowning at the departing teenager. "He has hated me from the get-go."

"He doesn't like the fact that you are bigger than him," Colin replied honestly.

"Really?" Jon Dayton said in a disbelieving tone, his broody face getting even darker. "He can't be that shallow, surely."

Ray preened a bit and started doing bodybuilder poses with his arms.

"He has . . . emotional issues," Colin said diplomatically, thinking again about the cuts he had seen on Paulo's arm. Not to mention that he, like Colin himself, liked to set women up for horrible deaths.

"Well, he needs to get over it," Dayton replied sharply. "We spend forty hours a week with each other on this floor; it's almost like we're living together, so we better get along."

Fuck me, Colin thought, aghast. *I live with Victor Cunnington; what a horrible bloody thought, and I'd never get to use the toilet.*

"Gentlemen, please," Beasley said with his hands now outstretched and a big dopey grin on his face, "you should not pay out on the young boy and his many strange insecurities, for, yes, I am indeed a *very* sexy and intelligent man."

Colin chuckled at this comment, then started coughing, and even Jon Dayton cracked a rare smile.

Canberra, Mainland Australia

A few of The Cabal members gathered at a small hotel in Canberra, knowing they had some serious topics to discuss, but instead being very amused at all of the news headlines on the

Holonews and Net about the so-called fight between Grantee-Grant and Matthew.

"I think this is one of the best," Phil Miller continued with a smile on his face. "Was it a fist fight, or a safe-sex demonstration?"

"That one was mine, Phil," Townsworth said with a big grin. "Those little pansies deserved what they got for rolling around on the floor scratching and slapping each other like that."

They all laughed except for ASIO Agent Brook Raller, who maintained a very serious expression.

"I particularly like this one," Gary Miller said, chuckling. "It was handbags at twenty paces on live national TV. Primary school girls from all around the world shuddered in fear."

Senator Howles laughed so loud he had a coughing fit.

"It was a pathetic attempt at violence," Senator Natalie Braiths said, amused. "I could have shown them how it was done."

That soon quietened everyone down. Nobody wanted to see a live demonstration from the scary senator.

"Where are the others?" Florian Grainger asked, who was very keen on having another attempt about setting up his countrywide water corporation.

"Henry Abel has conveyed his apologies for his absence," Natalie replied. "He says something very important has come up that needs his immediate attention."

I wonder what he is up to? Natalie wondered. *He is such a secretive man.*

"Bruce Cunnington was not invited," Brook Raller said in a short, sharp voice.

Natalie's misshapen head snapped towards the ASIO man.

"And is there any reason why you are so uppity?" she asked.

To her surprise, Raller didn't flinch at her anger.

"Yes, there is, Senator," Raller replied firmly.

Dear God, this must be really bad, Natalie thought.

"Out with it, then," she snapped, and again felt disconcerted by his lack of fear.

"It's a long story, which basically starts with Howles's ineptness in importing chemicals that could be used for various biological weapons," Raller replied.

"What!" Howles said sharply, but was still wiping the tears of laughter from his eyes at the 'handbags at twenty paces' comment.

"The policeman named Jeff Brady, or former policeman I should say, who discovered those chemicals, Senator, returned home to his native city of Hobart," Raller said, looking by turns at all members around the room. "He began a business as a private detective, and one of my spies has been keeping an eye on him ever since to make sure he . . . behaves appropriately."

"Keeps his trap shut," Phil Miller said.

"Exactly," Raller replied with a nod.

That is interesting, Natalie thought, *but why did he wince when he mentioned that Brady was being watched?*

"And what has this to do with Cunnington?" Gary Miller asked curiously.

"Well, technically, it doesn't," Raller replied. "But I received a tip-off earlier this year that his brother, Victor, was murdering a number of prostitutes by removing their skin with a knife."

"What!" Phil Miller exclaimed.

"Really!" Natalie said in surprise, and then burst out laughing. "Oh dear, how does our dear Brucie like that—or judging by his absence, I'm guessing he doesn't know?"

"Yes, he doesn't know, Natalie," Raller replied with a frown at her callousness. "The tip-off was from our very own member named 'Flowers'."

That quietened Natalie down; in fact, that shut *everyone* up for a few moments.

But Natalie did note that for Flowers to keep a close eye on this Victor Cunnington, it meant that he most likely lived in Hobart, which was pretty much the only thing she knew about their assassin.

But how did Flowers know about these murders? she wondered.

"And now, it seems," Raller continued, "that a well-known politician by the name of Bill Cooper has become aware of Victor Cunnington's 'habits' and hired our Jeff Brady to investigate."

"How did this politician Bill Cooper become aware of this?" Phil Miller asked.

"I'm not sure," Raller replied with a frown.

Not sure? Natalie thought. *This is all very strange.*

"Maybe it was politicians' gossip?" Howles queried. "We all know how secrets are not really secrets in this place."

Yes, indeed, Natalie thought, *but why doesn't Bruce know about this?*

"I have a question," Florian Grainger piped up. "Why should we care if Bruce's brother is a knife-wielding maniac?"

"Because," Mark Howles replied after recovering from Gary Miller's joke and Brook Raller's insult, "it might surprise you that whilst we do not always get along," he said with a glare at Raller, "members of The Cabal have a golden rule."

"We watch each other's back," Natalie interjected with a nod of her ugly head. "As I see it, Bruce's brother needs to be stopped, but Bill Cooper needs to be—"

"Killed," Howles finished off for her with a serious frown.

"And besides," Townsworth added in his usual charming way, "Bill Cooper is standing in the way of his royal lard-arse's ambition. I know that Tasmania is a small and irrelevant prick of a place with tree-huggers and inbreeds everywhere, but in the big scheme of things, to have one of The Cabal as a premier is not a small thing, even though Bruce is just a fat, useless flogger who couldn't get pissed in a brewery."

"So are we all agreed on this?" Senator Howles asked the gathering.

All of the members nodded their heads in agreement. Natalie was sure Henry Abel would have agreed, or not really cared if truth were told, and she knew Bruce would be very agreeable to the death of his rival.

Maybe Bruce did know about his brother, Natalie surmised, *and maybe this was his plan to get rid of Cooper. No, that sounds like something too complicated for the fat man to think up.*

"So who is to contact Flowers, then?" Natalie asked.

"I-I will," Howles said in a shaky voice and dialed a number on his phone.

Soon an apparition appeared on his Holophone. It wasn't the assassin's face, as to be expected; it was always flowers that appeared, hence the nickname.

So it's daffodils today, Natalie thought, but even though she was trying to remain calm, she could feel her heart flutter in her chest.

"Yes?" a voice answered, which sounded a lot like the brilliant Stephen Hawking's synthesised voice.

"Bill Cooper, Tasmanian politician," was all that Howles said. The Cabal members all looked incredibly nervous. No matter what power they wielded, it was always disconcerting to have the power over life and death.

"When?" Flowers replied.

"Can . . . can we . . . we coincide this event with the next Senate session in a few days, in regards to our new laws?" Howles asked.

"That's a very . . . very good idea, Mark," Natalie said in approval but had to control the frog in her throat.

Damn, I hate being this nervous, Natalie thought. *It should be other people who are nervous of me.*

"You want it messy, then?" Flowers asked.

"Yes, the messier the better," Howles replied. "Townsworth will handle the media, of course, but I want the public consumed about it as well. They must not talk about anything else when it happens."

"As soon as the money is transferred, it is a done deal," Flowers said, then immediately hung up.

The Cabal members sat for a moment in an uncomfortable silence.

"Well, we shall have to wait and see now," Townsworth said in a gruff voice, but even he sounded a bit frightened.

"I'll transfer the money," Phil Miller said quietly.

"Thank you, Phil," Howles replied.

But whilst Bill Cooper was standing in the way of Bruce Cunnington's ambition, so was his brother, Victor, and his sick perversions. That was a problem for another day.

The Tasmanian Midlands

"You look a bit unhappy," Bruce Cunnington ventured to say.

"Me?" Henry Abel replied, turning to the other man in the car.

"Y-yes," Bruce said warily.

Oh, I am fine, fat man; I just saw a dead man rise from the dead is all.
"No, I am all right," Henry replied in what he hoped was a friendly manner. He had to make the fat bastard feel at ease. After all, they were to spend the next few days together, if things went as planned. He just wished the huge man used a stronger brand of deodorant.

But the truth was, Henry felt incredibly uneasy. The body he was operating on had come back to life. Once the captives had calmed down, he went back to his surgery and had tested the body again and again and confirmed that once a certain part of the brain was stimulated, the body began to move as if it were truly alive. The heart didn't pump, the lungs didn't work, but the body moved. It defied all scientific knowledge as to how the human body worked.

It was the new species of tardigrades we created, Abel thought in pure amazement. *They somehow keep the body working. And why did the body make that weird groaning noise?*

And to add to this disturbing discovery, that little boy back at his laboratory had almost caused a riot. Richards and his team now had the boy secured and sedated, and because of these restraints, the other captives had immediately calmed down.

He couldn't have controlled them, surely? Henry wondered. *That's impossible. But so was a dead body that moved.*

Well, as soon as this venture was finished, he would return home and settle the matter once and for all. A few experiments on the boy's brain would answer all of his questions, he hoped.

But what do I do about waking the dead body?

Henry was in the business of taking life, not extending it. His obligation as McDermott in The McKay Group demanded it—in fact, the world's population demanded that death rule the planet for as long as was necessary.

"Roger Tyson is a good bloke, I think," Bruce said, interrupting his thoughts as the politician watched the road carefully as their self-driven car took them to their destination.

"Do you think he would agree to my terms?" Henry asked, trying to get his mind back to the reason he had flown down to this state.

"I think so," Bruce replied with a thoughtful frown, "but he is an opinionated, proud, and independent man; you need to realise that when you negotiate with him."

"Thank you for your advice," Henry replied with genuine gratitude.

An Independent, you say? Henry thought with a smile. *Well, I have done some secret research on this man, as it happens.*

"May I ask what you need the land for?" Bruce asked, still annoyed at having to accompany Abel.

"No. No, you may not," Henry replied firmly and cracked the knuckles on his huge hands to emphasise the point.

Bruce gave Henry a glare, but said nothing.

Roger Tyson walked out of his farmhouse as he heard a car approaching. The car was one of those fancy new ones from China, and Roger could see that the two occupants were leaning back in their seats, appearing unconcerned as to what direction they were headed.

Rich bastards, he thought.

He had been surprised when he was contacted by the famous scientist named Henry Abel, who wanted to buy some of his land. Roger had told him where he could shove his offer, and that this land had been in his family's hands for generations and wasn't for sale, so Abel had asked if he could lease parts of his land instead. He said that the crops he intended to grow would be a new food high in protein that would replace today's grains. And if he was successful, Tyson, as the first farmer to grow this produce, would make quite a lot of money in the process. But the money, he said, was not just there to make him rich; the money he would make would hopefully fund his attempts at running for parliament.

How did he know I was interested in politics? Roger wondered.

The car stopped in his driveway, and Roger was shocked that the second man in the car was none other than the politician Bruce Cunnington.

"Did *he* tell you?" Roger asked Abel as Cunnington got out of the car.

"About your political ambitions?" Abel replied amiably. "No, he didn't, but as he is a . . . friend of mine, I thought he may be able to assist you in some way."

Then who told you, Abel? Roger thought, feeling more than a little uncomfortable at this man's knowledge.

Roger then glanced at Cunnington and noticed how shocked the big man looked. It was clear that he was not the man who had told Abel of Roger's political ambitions.

Then who told you? Roger thought once more.

"Well, I won't be running for *his* party or in any State elections," Roger replied, nodding at Cunnington. "I will be running federally as an—"

"Independent," Abel finished for him, with an amused smile on his handsome face.

"I can help you, though . . . Roger," Cunnington said in a way that conveyed that he really didn't want to. "It will take some time, and you may lose at your first, and maybe even your second election attempt, but I know a few people in Canberra, and I can give you some advice on how to increase your votes."

"I can financially back you," Abel added, "so long as you—"

"Let you lease some land from me," Roger replied.

"Yes," Abel answered honestly.

Roger pondered these two men for a long moment.

He really wanted to run for the elections. The idea of being a member for Lyons and representing the everyday person in his community was a dream come true. He could possibly help the local farmers if he had some power in Canberra.

Despite his misgivings, he was about to say yes when a tractor pulled up near the barn a hundred metres away. He could hear his nephew's moaning voice even from that distance. Less than a minute later, Terry came jogging towards them. He had a disbelieving look on his face, which now had become one of anger.

"You! You fat bastard," Terry Tyson, former political reporter for Channel 12 News, growled angrily at a very surprised Bruce Cunnington. "You got me the sack, you big pile of shit."

Trying to calm his nephew down took some time. Terry would seem to be in control of his temper for a moment, and then when he got close enough to Cunnington, he would throw a wild haymaker of a punch, which went nowhere near his objective.

Considering Bruce Cunnington was such a huge man, who moved extremely slowly, this made Terry either half-blind or a really poor street fighter.

"You sack of horseshit, Cunnington," Terry grumbled as his uncle pushed him easily into the corner of the house's lounge room.

"This house belongs to me and my wife, doesn't it, Nephew?" Roger asked him, whilst gripping Terry's collar tightly with both hands.

"But he got me fired," Terry complained, "*and* he cracked my bloody ribs."

"It's our house, isn't it, Nephew?" Roger said again.

"Yes," Terry grumbled.

"And Bruce is my guest," Roger continued.

"Yes," Terry replied, now almost with a pout on his young face.

"Then you will stop throwing those girly punches of yours."

Henry Abel chuckled at this. He found Terry's attempts at violence and Bruce's angry reaction quite funny.

"It wasn't girly," Terry whined.

"Of course not," Roger replied with a small grin. "Muhammad Ali would have been proud to throw those punches."

Abel laughed out loud at this, and Bruce gave a derisive snort.

"It wasn't girly, all right."

Roger smiled now.

"I am a man you know, Uncle," Terry whined again.

His uncle shook his head and let his 'manly' nephew go. He was fond of his nephew, but sometimes he did worry about him a little.

Terry sat down on the couch, but not before glowering at Cunnington, who was sitting nervously in a chair.

"Now," Roger finally said, "can we get down to business?"

"Yes, we can," Abel said, still chuckling a little. "As I said before your nephew arrived, I am indeed looking for a small piece of farmland to test a new type of crop, which should—if we are successful, that is—replace all the current grains in Australia, as well as what is imported from overseas."

Roger's eyes lit up at the mention of replacing overseas imports with a locally grown product, which Henry was expecting.

"And why did you choose my land?" Roger asked suspiciously. "Why not look for land on the mainland?"

"Good question," Terry the ex-political reporter said, and glared suspiciously not at Abel, but at Bruce Cunnington.

"It's cheaper down here," Abel replied with what he hoped was an honest look.

It's also far away from the public gaze, Henry thought, *and I have learned that you, Roger, are in need of some funds.*

"Is it safe?" Roger queried, thinking about his earlier misgivings.

"Of course," Abel replied with a nod. "You have my word on it."

Roger looked closely at the famous scientist. Henry Abel had made such amazing scientific breakthroughs over the last decade, but it was mostly to do with the human body. Why would he suddenly be interested in the food market?

To think I almost immediately said yes to this man, Roger thought. *My foolish nephew has given me time to think.*

"I would still need it to be tested by an independent body," Roger said firmly.

Independent? Abel thought. *There is no such thing nowadays.*

"As I said before, you have my word that these grains are a healthy product, and the tests crops will only be small at first," Abel replied instead, with a touch of anger around his eyes.

"And as you can see," Abel continued as he reached into his pocket and brought out a small packet containing the grains and placed it on the table, "these are a perfectly normal produce."

To the naked eye, Abel thought smugly, *but these seeds are just the first sample of this new wheat grain. These seeds are packed full of my newly designed tardigrades.*

Roger looked at the grains, and to him, they looked just like any normal wheat grain, but he was still not budging.

"I am still holding firm," Roger said. "The initial product, even though it is just a test, still needs to be scientifically tested to ensure its safety. And this is my land you are talking about. I need to know these modified crops of yours meet all the industry standards."

For fuck's sake, it's money again. Abel frowned at him, then reached into his other pocket and brought out his Holophone. After a few moments of hitting buttons, he looked back up at Roger. "I have now financed your election costs," Abel said angrily.

"Well, thank you very much, *Henry*," Roger replied, equally angry, "but I didn't *ask* you to do that."

Henry Abel, due to the company he often kept, was used to money solving everything. He didn't realise that some people could not be bought, so he continued to glare at Roger Tyson, believing his presence alone would change the man's mind.

"Gentlemen, please," Bruce said weakly.

"Shut up," Henry Abel and Roger Tyson said together, still glaring at one another.

I hope one of them stabs the other, Bruce thought grimly. *Be good to see one of them die.*

"There will be other farmlands willing to grow this crop," Henry snapped angrily.

"Good," Roger snarled back. "I suggest you fuck off now and find them."

Henry now desperately wanted this land as a way of replacing the urge to hit this man. It was a matter of pride for him now. Terry Tyson, on the other hand, who was still sulking about Cunnington and what he had done to him by getting him fired from his job, watched as his uncle's negotiations quickly descended into what looked like it was going to be an all-out fistfight. Terry almost wanted his uncle to get into this fight after what he said about his 'girly' punching, but he knew he had to make amends to his uncle somehow.

What can I do? he thought.

He looked at the small packet of grains Abel had produced sitting there on the table, and without thinking—which his deceased father used to say he often did—he reached over, opened the package, and swallowed the contents whole.

"There you go," Terry said with a big grin on his face. "It's all perfectly fine."

He ate it, Abel thought in panic. *He swallowed them all.*

"You stupid fool, why did you do that?" Roger said worriedly. "You don't know what effect that could have on you."

Neither does Abel, Bruce thought, looking at the scientist's worried face. *This could be interesting to see what happens to the young git.*

"I see he is still alive," Abel said drily after a moment, but his mind was still reeling. *What is going to happen to him?*

"He better be," Roger said with an angry scowl. "Or I will come looking for you."

Abel sat straighter in his chair. "Listen, you piece of—"

"We better go now," Bruce Cunnington said with no real conviction. "You are both angry, so may I suggest we leave now and start re-negotiations at another time?"

Abel glared at the farmer for a long moment, still trying to quell his natural urge to start brawling. *But I need to get out of here. That boy may be in deep trouble, and I will get the blame for it.*

"You can take your money back, rich man." Roger sneered.

But on the other hand, I still really want to punch this Tyson's head in.

"Keep it," Abel snarled. "Consider it a down payment for using your land."

"Get out of my house," Roger snapped. "And get off *my* land."

Bruce Cunnington had to drag Henry Abel out of there, muttering about how proud and opinionated he was, quite surprised how easily Abel was being led away from the house.

Terry, though, watched on with a proud smile as his uncle escorted the two men off his land. He then felt his stomach begin to rumble loudly.

I'm starved, he thought.

Hobart, Tasmania

Self-driven cars were all the rage now for the rich and trendy, and whilst Bill Cooper couldn't be called trendy, he was definitely rich.

"Home," was all he said to the car computer. He felt like saying "and make it snappy" in his anger, but unlike the now-unemployed chauffeurs who had driven politicians' cars in the old days, getting angry at a computer was a complete waste of time.

So many occupations had become redundant now, due to new technology. Cooper wondered if the growing robotics would take over every manual job in the near future.

But what was he to do with his own career? No matter what he had done, no matter how many people he had brown-nosed, he was never going to get over the business donation gaffe.

Victor Cunnington, the fat bastard's even fatter brother.

"Fuck Bruce Cunnington," Cooper growled and kicked at the front of the vehicle violently. "Fuck both of them."

That was his only hope. Somehow, Brady needed to give him conclusive evidence that Bruce's brother was a psycho serial killer, and then he could bribe his way back into being named his brother's successor.

His brother, Michael, was intending on staying in his job until after the next election at least, so that gave him another four or five years to secure his position.

His Holophone rang, and after making the connection, an image of a flower appeared.

"It is you again," Bill said, frowning. "I thought you said we no longer had to make any contact."

"I'm sorry," a synthesised voice replied.

"And so you should be, fool," Bill snapped. "I do not like people who do not keep their word."

"No, I am sorry for what I am about to do," Flowers replied.

Bill Cooper felt the blood rush from his face.

"And what are you about to do?" he said nervously.

Self-driven cars, what a wonderful invention they were. All you had to do was pre-program your trip on the car computer and sit back and relax. No car accidents for the passengers, no speeding fines or inconvenient road rages, just read a book or watch a DVD or listen to some enjoyable music as you made your way home. What could go wrong?

Well, the answer to what could go wrong was in the above description.

Car computers.

Computer hacking had been going on for decades. So why didn't the manufacturer in China ever consider that these computer-run safe-haven vehicles called self-driven cars could be hacked into, to make the direction of the vehicle go haywire? Why didn't they realise just how dangerous these vehicles could be for those who had made enemies, or for those who were considered disposable?

"The Tasman Bridge has five lanes," Flowers said through the assassin's synthesised communication voice, as the assassin sat in a vehicle overlooking the bridge, which went from the eastern side of Hobart to the western side.

"Yes, so?" Cooper replied.

Flowers could hear the nervousness in his voice, but the assassin had a job to do, and the payment had already been made.

"There are no barriers between the west and eastern bound traffic," Flowers continued.

"I know," Cooper said.

Flowers could see that Cooper was trying to take control of the vehicle now, but it was too late for that. As soon as he had relinquished control of the car to the computer on his journey home, his life was over.

"There is a truck coming from the other direction," Flowers said as the assassin controlled two vehicles through the specialised equipment purchased for a job such as this.

"A-a truck."

"Yes, but do not fear, for it shall be quick," Flowers replied.

Flowers could hear Cooper violently attacking the vehicle's controls now.

The truck Flowers had stolen the night before was laden with explosives and fuel. The Cabal wanted it messy, and so it will be.

"Why are you doing this?" Cooper said frantically as he tried uselessly to get out of the car.

"It's my job," Flowers replied as he lined up Cooper's car and the non-occupied self-driven truck.

"But I thought you wanted Cunnington arrested," Cooper said, now sounding like he was crying. "You told me yourself to seek out that man Brady."

Flowers could now physically see the eastbound car and the westbound truck head towards each other. Other vehicles were veering out of their way, causing traffic chaos.

"No, I just wanted to earn some more money," Flowers replied, focusing at the job at hand. "I have bills to pay, you know."

111

Whilst Bill Cooper was a cold man who loved power, the assassin was a much colder person who really needed the money. *Boom!*

The vehicles now hit each other, and the ensuing explosion could be seen and heard for miles.

"Well, that will make the news," Flowers murmured, "and I am indeed sorry."

And it did make the news.

It made the news within fifteen minutes, and the country was riveted for the next few days by the grisly and, it must be said, very suspicious death of a locally famous politician with a brother as a Premier. But the Brandon Townsworth-owned media outlets went into overdrive in not reporting the obvious and stating that this was purely a simple traffic accident. The conspiracy theorists, in response to this obvious cover-up went nuts about this death, and the Holonet and Radio stations went into meltdown.

The new security laws that had just passed in the Senate that day went by totally unnoticed by everybody, as planned.

Sydney, Mainland Australia

"Whoa! You say the earth is flat?" Johan Franz said in fake amazement.

"Yeah, even the UN flag says so," the caller replied.

"Perhaps the UN simply wanted an arty flag that showed all of the world countries in a unique way," Johan replied.

"No way," the caller replied, getting a little miffed with Johan's negativity. "The flight paths from city to city show the planes don't fly in a straight line, but on a flat Earth map, they do."

"Maybe they have to fly within a certain distance of other airports in case they need an emergency landing, or there are certain routes they need to follow to avoid crashing into other planes," Johan replied, trying to start a debate.

"But it's flat," the caller replied in a tight voice. "It's an oblate spheroid."

"That's not flat," Johan said.

"The images from the small satellites in space cannot cover the whole planet; they put the combined images together by Photoshop," the caller growled.

"But that still doesn't mean the world is flat."

"Look, mate," the caller yelled, "even our well-known world maps do not correctly portray the size of the continents. We don't even know what our own world looks like."

So, that still doesn't mean the world is flat was going to be his next reply, but he was interrupted by someone else.

"Don't ask questions, Johan," a voice, from his radio manager in the other room, said.

Oh, all right then, the real man John France thought with a sigh. *You can't debate anybody these days; we are all turning into a country of sooks.*

"Wow, that is amazing, bro," Johan Franz replied instead. "NASA and the one percent are being totally bogus and uncool in not telling us the truth, man."

"That's right," the caller replied, much happier now.

"Okay, next caller," Johan said.

"I'm ringing to complain about your radio station," a man with a sharp voice said.

"Oh, sorry, man. Why are we upsetting you so?"

"Because, as a Christian, I find it deeply offensive that you are permitting all of this satanic talk of aliens."

"Oh, I am so sorry, Christian dude," Johan replied.

"So you should be, young man, for you will burn in hell for eternity, screaming in agony, if you do not bow down to our Lord and Saviour Jesus Christ, and for rejecting God's unconditional love, which he has so kindly offered to you."

Unconditional?

"Oh, wow, I will have to remember that," he replied.

"You better," the caller said in a harsh voice.

"And who might you be, good sir?"

"I am Reverend Paul Rainswood of the Christian Brotherhood of Tasmania," he replied.

"And why are you listening to this radio station?"

"Because I-I find your radio . . . offensive."

"Well, Christian dude, perhaps you should just—now, let me know if I am being out of line here—perhaps you should just *not* listen to our radio station."

"It is my duty to shut down Devil worshippers such as yourself."

"Oh, far out, man, that is such a heavy and righteous burden."

"It is," Rainswood snapped.

"So just to clarify this," Johan replied, "aliens, spaceships, and secret constructions on the moon are all crazy beliefs?"

"Exactly."

"But being born of a virgin, dying and coming back to life three days later, and walking on water is all perfectly normal?"

"Exactly," the man said again.

"Well, hey, thanks for clearing that up for me and my listeners, most awesome Christian dude."

"You're welcome, Sinner."

How much do I get paid for this again? John wondered. *Whatever it was, it wasn't enough.*

"Next caller, please."

"Politician Bill Cooper was assassinated tonight," a female caller said abruptly. "It was no accident that he hit that truck and the Tasman Bridge was almost knocked down."

"Whoa, how did you know that? I only heard about his death ten minutes ago," Johan said nervously. He knew who this female caller was.

"I know these things, just like Cooper knew too much."

"About what, may I ask, lady dude?"

"About the plans for world domination by Australia's very own Cabal," the caller replied. "About how they intend for us to be used as slaves for our alien reptilian overlords with probes used in our brains and anus."

"Wow, that's sounds amazing . . . and also very painful."

"It is, human slave," the caller replied, "and don't call me lady dude; it sounds like you're calling me a tranny."

Well, you certainly look like one.

"Oh . . . sorry, your lady . . . person; have a nice night then," John replied instead.

"Thank you," the caller said. "And may the evil Lord of the Reptiles be kept at bay from our minds and bottoms."

"Well . . . yeah, umm, thanks again," Johan replied.

"Next caller." *I need another job.*

"I can't believe Cooper's dead," Paulo Smythen said, smiling as he looked at the latest news showing on the TV in his work's tea room. "It's so freaking funny."

"Yeah, it is." Colin Wise laughed softly. "We are all flesh and blood, Paulo; we all will die sometime, and even famous and powerful people do. That's the only thing we have in common."

And you will die from blood loss if you keep cutting yourself like that. But at least the boy didn't require stitches when he cut himself; he only cut just deep enough to cause a light scarring.

For the moment, at least.

"And I can't believe one of the Enter buttons on the keyboards still doesn't work," Colin said, changing the subject.

"*Yeah*, when are they going to fix that?" Paulo asked, perplexed. "Surely it would be easy to fix."

Reginald Yeasmith sat there quietly, as per usual, so the two men were surprised when he spoke.

"But the four of us do have one more thing in common, don't we?" he said in his soft voice.

"There are only three of us," Paulo replied. "Victor isn't here; he is on the toilet . . . again."

"You know what I mean," Reginald replied knowingly.

"Yes, we do have things in common, Reg," Colin replied with a tight scowl on his face. "But saying that in the middle of work is not a good idea, is it?"

What is he up to? Colin wondered.

"Is it a good idea for me, Colin?" Reginald whispered nervously, brushing his comb-over hairstyle to the side of his head. "You two always get what you want by setting the women up for pain and death, fatso gets his jollies with the knife, but what do I get out of all this?"

"You get a fucking punch in the face, that's what you'll get if you don't shut up," Colin snarled, and then broke into one of his massive coughing fits.

Paulo, though, looked at Reginald in confusion. *Why was he acting like this, and speaking of this in the middle of work?*

"Well, what do you want?" Paulo asked curiously, scratching at a new cut on his other arm, whilst Colin kept coughing.

Reginald looked nervously around the tea room. Nobody was close enough to hear, and besides, Colin was coughing so loudly, nobody could hear them anyway.

"I want girls," he said softly to Paulo.

"Well, that's no problem; once we arrange for the kidnapping from the national tour, we will have three beautiful sisters all to ourselves. Victor won't mind sharing."

Reginald looked steadily at Paulo with those intense eyes of his. "No, Paulo, you don't understand," Reginald replied, now in a tight and angry voice. "I want *girls*."

Jerry McGuiness sat in his car outside the government building, tuning in his listening equipment to the floor that Victor Cunnington worked on. The spying equipment was the best in the world, but that still didn't mean you could easily track down the people you were meant to be spying on.

He felt so embarrassed. His first job had been a complete failure—not only was he caught out spying by that woman; he had run his car straight into the back of a police car.

I must be the laughing stock of Canberra, he thought miserably.

But he still had a job to do, so he went on in search of Victor Cunnington's voice.

'I'm telling you, there I was in the last quarter in the game against Hawthorn, and we were behind by just three points, and then the Full Forward Cossie Bollinger started gobbing off at me. I had to hit him, I just had to . . .'

"I know who that is." Jerry smiled, thinking of one of his favourite football players.

'They are so freaking thick; I mean, how hard is it to change a simple bloody password?'

'The idiot didn't even have his computer turned on.'

'She didn't know what a web address was.'

'This place is driving me nuts.'

'It's a cycle; it's a never-ending bloody cycle.'

"They're a happy bunch in the government," Jerry murmured.

'One of the Enter keys on the keyboard hasn't worked for days.'

'I'm sure they will fix it eventually.'

'But this could be disastrous.'

"What do they mean 'disastrous'?" Jeff said with a frown on his young face. "It's only a stupid Enter key."

'He's a good bloke, Ray is. I like him. But he's doing it tough since his wife ran out on him. He now has to raise three boys on his own, and the youngest boy, Billy, is just two years old.'

"Oh, yeah, I heard rumours about that," Jeff said softly. "She ran off to Sydney with some rich sugar daddy."

'You get a fucking punch in the face, that's what you'll get if you don't shut up.'

"Nasty fellow, that one," Jerry said in surprise and decided to stay with this conversation.

'Well, what do you want?'

'I want girls.'

'Well, that's no problem; once we arrange for the kidnapping from the national tour, we will have three beautiful sisters all to ourselves. Victor won't mind sharing.'

'No, Paulo, you don't understand. I want girls.*'*

The blood drained from Jerry's face. He now believed he had just made up for his previous failure.

The burned wreckage of a car and a truck, along with many other cars that had crashed into each other, was strewn all over the accident scene.

"What a mess," Constable Eric Woods said sadly as he surveyed the damage done to the bridge.

The whole bridge had been closed off, causing chaos with the daily traffic, and it would be closed for a few days, maybe weeks, until all safety checks were made.

"It is," Constable Razan Hussein agreed, grimacing. "We only know it was Bill Cooper's car through the computer tracking of which vehicle was where at the time of the accident."

Cooper's car had been almost obliterated, including the body inside.

"And the truck?" Woods enquired.

"Reported stolen last night," Hussein said quietly.

The two constables shared a look. All of the police in Hobart knew this death was suspicious, despite what the news and the politicians told the public, but they knew that they had to play the game as the powers that be wanted.

"What about the body of the truck driver?"

"Nothing found yet," Hussein replied.

"I don't like this," Eric said softly, looking warily at those around him. "It doesn't look like a normal accident, no matter what the news says. There are no skid marks on the road, Rizo. The two vehicles headed for each other almost in a straight line over a great distance."

"Perhaps Cooper fell asleep at the wheel," Hussein offered.

"And the truck driver too?" Eric replied skeptically. "Besides, Cooper was driving one of those flashy new self-driven cars."

"A computer malfunction then," Hussein replied.

"Yes, that is a possibility," Woods said meaningfully.

The two constables noticed that the Premier Michael Cooper had just arrived on the scene. Cooper had his arm draped around Bill Cooper's teenage son, Carl's, shoulder protectively. Off to the side of them stood the big man Bruce Cunnington, who was staring at the wreckage of Cooper's car. He didn't look that upset with the accident, but when the premier and his nephew looked in the policemen's direction, the grief was clear on their faces. But there was also something very cold about both of the Coopers' faces, something very hard about their demeanor. Their grief was not displayed in a tearful manner, but rather in anger.

"Boys," the police commissioner called out to them.

"Yes, sir?" both of the constables replied.

"We have found out from the Holophone Company that Cooper was on the blower when he died."

"And you want us to find out who he was talking to?" Hussein replied.

We are going to investigate this death properly it seems, Hussein thought incredulously. *It looks like the Premier's influence has won the day.*

"On it," Eric said keenly before the commissioner could reply, as both policemen headed straight to their vehicle.

Now, who was Cooper talking to when he died? Hussein wondered, *and why didn't he notice that the car was headed straight into the oncoming traffic?*

The private detective and his secretary sat in silence for a long time as they watched the news.

'It was a tragic accident,' the news reporter said with a solemn face, 'a one in a million chance that has left this State deprived of one of its great public servants . . .'

"Well, that didn't end well," Susan Milligan eventually said.

"No," Jeff Brady said softly as he sat at his desk, wondering what action to take next.

"So we won't get any more payments from him, obviously," Susan continued.

"No," Jeff said again, deep in thought.

Cooper was dead, and not just from some illness or freak accident; he had been murdered in cold blood. Oh, yes, the media portrayed it as a simple accident, but Jeff could see clearly that the man had been set up to die.

'The Premier has announced that there will be a State Funeral held in Bill Cooper's honour, and thousands are meant to attend . . .'

"I guess we could go back to watching people have extramarital affairs," Susan offered.

"No more of that," Jeff replied sharply.

"Then what are we to do?" Susan asked.

"I am going to look into this murder for a little bit, see if I can find some clues," Jeff finally decided. He doubted strongly that he would find any clues at all, but he had to try.

"Murder!" Susan said in shock.

"Yes, murder."

"But the media said—"

'He was a great man, a man of the people . . .'

"I know what the media said, Susan," Jeff interrupted her, "but the media has a long and ugly history of covering up the facts."

"But it looked like a simple accident; nobody in the public is questioning the official reports," Susan said, frowning.

"The public doesn't think too deeply when it comes to tragedies like this. History has also proven that time and time again," Jeff said as he stood up and gazed out the window. *Sometimes they can be so blind. Or was it a lack of caring?*

"People can't think straight when emotions are involved," he continued, "and the truth, therefore, can be easily covered up, and today, they are upset that he died—"

"The public hated him," Susan said now, interrupting him.

'Truly loved by the voters . . .'

"People tend to like the people they hated when they have just died; I don't know why they do that," Jeff replied honestly.

"But the police have said it appeared to be an accident."

"Appeared, Susan, they said it *appeared* to be an accident."

"Now you're sounding like one of those conspiracy theorists. What do they call them?" Susan said now, sounding annoyed.

"Truthers," Jeff replied, "but I say again, the public thinks only with their emotions on occasions like this. My policeman's experience says the death was suspicious."

'A truly inspirational man . . .'

"You're not a policeman anymore," Susan said.

"In my heart I am."

"Well, why should we care?"

"Because he asked us to look into Victor Cunnington being a serial killer," Jeff said pointedly, "and he didn't tell us who his informant was."

Cooper's informant could have been anyone, Jeff thought. *I need to find out the whole story so, if need be, I can find a way to get out of this mess.*

"So you are saying . . ."

"That he may have stepped on someone's toes," Jeff replied.

"But if *he* stepped on someone's toes . . ." Susan began worriedly.

"Then we may have already done so too," her boss finished off for her.

"But you don't know that," Susan said pointedly.

'This tragic accident . . .'

"No, I don't. That is why I need to do some spying to find out," Jeff replied.

"You could make this situation much worse," Susan said.

"Or I could make it better."

"You're playing with dice, Jeff."

"I am." Jeff nodded. "And you are quite welcome to leave my business today. I would not like it if you were hurt because of me."

"No, I am part of this already," Susan replied firmly.

"Thank you," Jeff said gratefully.

"Please leave this alone, Jeff," Susan suddenly pleaded. "I am *sure* we are not involved in this."

"How can you be so sure?" Jeff asked.

"I-I can't," Susan stammered uncertainly.

"Then I need to do this."

"I don't like this, Jeff," Susan said.

"Me either, Susan," Jeff replied, "but we need to find the killer before the killer finds us."

'This truly was a tragic accident . . .'

Sydney, Mainland Australia

Smash!

The walls shuddered yet again, as the neighbour in the hotel they were staying at was not behaving himself in an appropriate manner becoming of an international pop star.

"Well, that was a horrible way to die," Sharon said sadly, looking at the latest news on the death of the politician Bill Cooper.

'Oh yeah, it's Froggo File.'

"It was terrible," Brad Hoffington said, equally sadly, as he sat across from Sharon at the breakfast table.

Crash!

It now sounded like something glass-like was being smashed against the wall.

'Do the Froggo File.'

Remi Hiller, though, was only concerned about one thing with Brad and Sharon. Were they doing it or not?

'Um Bah Lumbah!'

"Are youse guys talking about the Kentucky Fried Politician on the Tasman Bridge or the Froggo File girl who broke her stupid freaking neck on the stairs during the frogman's performance and lay there dead for half an hour before anybody bloody noticed her?" Mercedes whined as she lifted her gaze away from her precious Holophone. "And speaking of the frogman, why is he trashing *yet another* hotel room?"

Crash!

"El Froggo is expressing himself," Remi replied. "You know

how these artistic people are."

'Break the TV, Froggo File.'

Smash!

Artistic or Insane? Remi wondered. Sometimes they were the same thing.

"Honestly, Mercedes," Sharon said with a frown, "they were both horrible deaths. The Froggo File can be very dangerous."

'Huh, Froggo File.'

"Shit, I think he just heard us," Remi whispered.

The five people in the undamaged hotel room froze in silence until the trashing noise of their neighbour began once more.

"Thank fuck for that," Mercedes muttered under her breath and went back to taking Holophone photos of herself for her fans.

"The people of Hobart must be so upset," Mercury said quietly after a moment, the concern clearly showing in her voice. "That death on the bridge was awful."

Smash!

"Thank you, Mercury," Sharon said softly, smiling kindly at her youngest sister, who smiled back just as warmly.

Mercedes, though, just grunted at such sentimental nonsense.

Remi pondered on Mercury's comment.

The people of Hobart must be so upset.

"You're a genius, Mercury," Remi said loudly, then cringed when he thought El Froggo might have heard him.

"What!" Sharon, Mercedes, and Mercury all said at the same time, then *they* also cringed that El Froggo might have heard *them*.

Their collective surprise, however, was not unwarranted, as this was the first time the words 'genius' and 'Mercury' had ever been mentioned in the same sentence.

"We weren't planning on visiting Tasmania for at least another month," Remi whispered to one and all, "but due to this tragedy, I think we should go now, to cheer them up."

To gain more publicity is what he really meant.

"How do you think *we* could possibly cheer them up?" Sharon asked skeptically . . . and quietly.

She still doesn't believe that people like her, Remi thought. He had seen the surveys; Sharon was by far the most popular sister, because people thought she was genuine.

"Of course you can," Remi replied softly with a careful look at the room next door. "You, Mercury, Mercedes, El Froggo and . . . Matthew," he said now with a meaningful look at Mercedes, who immediately began adjusting her boobs. "We could make a killing out of this."

"Nice choice of words," Brad said.

"Oh, you know what I mean, Bradley Bumbag." Remi grinned.

"Yes, thanks for that nickname," Brad replied with a wry smile. Sharon was smiling as well; she looked very happy today, despite how much she hated being famous.

Smash!

"I'll make all of the arrangements," Remi said, then glanced suspiciously at Sharon and Brad in turns.

Bloody hell, are they doing it or not? he wondered.

"I'll take some more photos of myself," Mercedes said keenly, which she was going to do anyway.

"I'll become depressed," Sharon said with a lovely smile directed at Brad.

Smash!

"Me too," Brad 'Sparkles' Hoffington replied with an equally big smile across the breakfast table.

They are! They are doing it, Remi thought with elation. He couldn't wait to tell the gossip mags and paparazzi . . . anonymously, of course.

"But we still don't have any passports," Mercury said too loudly.

"Um bah lumbah, passport Radonculus!"

"Shit!" everybody said together as they heard loud footsteps followed by an even louder banging on their hotel door.

'Break your room, Froggo File.'

"Shit!" everybody said again.

It was Marshall's turn to stand on guard and watch the captives in their cell. It was usually a very boring duty, but ever since that young boy had sent the other captives crazy with anger, Marshall had become a nervous wreck.

"You all right there, Marshall?" Lia Read said, causing Marshall to jump as she and Deb Fazakerley entered the prison area. Lia and Deb had come into the cell area to do their usual duties of feeding and watering the captives. The food supplies Abel had bought for them were basic items, but could last them for a few years if need be. But these people were not fed well enough to live a long and healthy life. The lack of sun itself had made them all look pale and weedy, along with the many operations they had endured.

"Yes, I am," Marshall replied, trying to 'man up' a little as he saw the two women stare at him curiously.

"Liar." Lia smiled. "I don't blame you, though. They have been behaving strangely lately. Well, more strangely than normal," she finished with a shrug.

"They seem to miss the young boy," Deb said.

"I don't think they miss him," Marshall replied thoughtfully. "I think he keeps them in order somehow."

"What do you mean?" Lia asked.

"I . . . I think the boy is their leader?" Marshall managed to say.

"He's just six years old," Deb said in disdain.

"You didn't see it, Deb," Marshall replied quickly, trying to get them to believe in his crazy theory. "You didn't see how he controlled them."

His eyes went completely white. I am sure of it.

The captives, noticing the arrival of the two women, started banging their hands and even their heads against the cell bars, wanting to be fed.

"It's time to feed them." Marshall sighed. "Just keep your distance from the cell bars."

"Now you are worrying me," Lia said. "We have never been hurt before."

"A six-year-old," Deb continued with a grimace at Marshall. "You know, for a big security guard, you sure shit yourself a lot."

"No, I am serious," Marshall said nervously. "There is something odd about the boy, and even the other three are . . ."

"Are what?" Lia asked.

Marshall didn't reply, as he had just noticed the three young children had arrived at the cell door and were staring at them intently.

"They're very . . ."

"What?" Deb asked.

"Bring us Dekker," one of the boys, named Emerson, said as his eyes turned completely white.

"They're very . . ." Marshall mumbled.

Get out of my head, Marshall thought as a massive headache began to grow. *The boy is in my head.*

"Marshall, what is wrong?" Lia said, concerned.

"What is wrong with the boy's eyes?" Deb said, not sounding as sure of herself as she had a minute ago.

"We need to . . ." Marshall stammered. "We need . . ."

To get out of here, we need to get out of here, Marshall thought now, rubbing at his temples with both hands.

"Bring us Dekker," the other boy, named Klusta, said as his eyes turned white as well.

Marshall, even though he was suffering from a blinding headache, now felt like he was losing his hearing as well.

"The other one's eyes have changed too," Lia said in terror.

"Let's go," Deb said as she turned towards the door. "I know we get paid well for what we do, but this is insane."

The other captives inside the prison cell now all stood silently as they watched two young boys try to compel the security guard.

"C'mon, Marshall," Lia said, shaking him by the shoulders. "We need to leave now."

"Bring us Dekker," the boys said together.

Marshall was moaning now and holding his head with both hands; his face had gone a dark shade of red.

"C'mon, Lia, leave him," Deb said urgently. "We need to find Richards now."

"Please don't leave us, Marshall," a small voice said, and the two women turned towards the third child, a three-year-old girl who spoke with a lisp. "Dekker needs your help to have his mind freed," she continued.

"What . . . what do you mean by mind freed?" Lia asked, her hands, still on Marshall's shoulders, now shaking badly.

"Dekker's mind is powerful, and he has needs that he wishes to express in the physical world," she said.

"What needs does he have?" Deb asked.

"He needs *you* to die, Deb," she said with a smile that was more than a little disturbing for someone so young.

The child's eyes turned completely white.

Whilst Dekker was clearly the strongest of the boys, Rainbow, as her parents liked to call her, was equally as strong as Dekker.

"Kill Deb, Marshall," she said in that small voice. "Kill her now, quickly."

All of Marshall's resistance was broken under this little girl's mental onslaught, and he immediately reached for his gun, and before either of the women could scream, he shot Deb cleanly in the head.

"Stay there, Lia, and you must be quiet," Rainbow said to the other woman.

Lia Read froze; she couldn't move any of her limbs or speak no matter how much she tried.

The two boys, though their eyes were still completely white, looked annoyed that the little girl had stopped their fun.

"Now you too," Rainbow continued to the security guard, who still had his gun in his hand. "You must join Deb now, Marshall, as she misses you terribly."

Marshall placed the gun in his mouth and immediately blew his head off.

"Now you are *our* prisoner," Rainbow said to Lia as Marshall's headless body fell to the floor. "You are to give me Marshall's gun and open the cell doors, but are to remain here to look after us. We do need looking after, Lia, for we do need your loving care," she finished with a cute smile that only a three-year-old could give.

Lia did as she was commanded, but tears were streaming down her face as she did so.

The captives still stood in silence, looking at the two bodies lying on the floor in confusion, but the three children, whose eyes had now returned to their normal colour, started arguing.

"Rainbow!" Emerson moaned. "We were meant to try and get Dekker *back*. He is still in the other room with Richards."

"We almost had him, Rainbow," Klusta added. "He was beginning to give in. Dekker is still asleep."

Rainbow giggled. "Who cares? We will get him later, after we have some fun," she said, shrugging her tiny shoulders. "Dekker is a big poo-poo head."

The two boys chuckled at that, for seven-year-old Dekker was indeed a big poo-poo head.

Canberra, Mainland Australia

"So that went well," Senator Natalie Braiths said with a pleased smile at the gathered members of The Cabal in yet another small house in the Canberra suburbs. "Flowers may have overdone it a little with the explosions, but the media was focused on the event, so part two of our new laws went through the senate completely unnoticed."

Senator Howles nodded proudly at this achievement, and his advisor Aiden Wilkinson, on seeing this, nodded as well. Phil and Gary Miller shrugged as if to say they didn't care, which they didn't really, as money was their one and only priority. Florian Grainger was looking out the window again, no doubt wondering how much money could be made from the rain falling from the free sky, and Raller was frowning yet again. *What is wrong with the man now?* Natalie thought.

"Overdone it a little," media mogul Brandon Townsworth barked. "The bastard almost brought down the Tasman Bridge."

"Yes, yes," Natalie said testily, "but it drew the public's eye, which was what we wanted."

"You mean my media's eye." Townsworth glared. "I am the most important member here, Braiths."

"Of course." Natalie nodded.

What I would give to just punch you in the head, Brandon. Just the once, Natalie mused. *It wouldn't hurt you that much, just break your nose a little, perhaps.*

"But looking at our gathering, I am getting a case of déjà vu once more," Natalie continued. "It seems that Henry Abel and Bruce Cunnington are not here, and our very own ASIO agent Brook Raller looks upset again. Did the death of Bill Cooper upset you so much, Brook? Did you hold a little man-crush on our Tasmanian politician?"

"Not in the least, Natalie," Raller replied, "though it did upset the Tasmanian public, even though they have always hated the man."

"Well, there you go, Brandon," Natalie said, glancing at the media mogul. "When you die, people will indeed become upset."

"Get fucked," was Brandon's only response.

Natalie chuckled at his response. *Perhaps two punches in the head would suffice.*

"I think it was the nature of the death, rather than the man himself," Gary Miller said mildly.

His father, Phil Miller, nodded his head in agreement.

"So why do you look so depressed?" Natalie asked the ASIO Chief.

"I am not depressed either, Senator," Raller said wryly. "I am, in fact, curious as to how you will all take the next bit of news I have to tell you."

What now? Natalie thought, intrigued.

"Oh, and what is that?" Phil Miller asked curiously.

"Is it to do with the weather?" Florian Grainger added keenly.

"Enough with the bloody weather, Florian," Natalie snapped, irritated at his one-track mind. "Your idea of a countrywide water corporation is being seriously considered, so just relax."

"Truly?" Florian said, as if he had seen the face of God Almighty himself.

"Yes, truly," Natalie snapped again.

Florian was ecstatic. Once upon a time capitalism was aimed at the average man so he could reach for the sky, but now, with corporate profits being made the main agenda for the economy by the politicians, the big businesses ruled the roost and ate through the country like an insatiable and unstoppable monster.

"Yes, it is true, Florian," Howles said firmly. "Now, Brook," he said, turning to the ASIO agent, "what is today's problem?"

"Well, as you know, Bruce's brother, Victor, is a knife-wielding psychotic maniac," he replied.

"Yes," Natalie said curiously, and then had to suppress a laugh at what she thought Bruce's reaction would be if he heard the news.

Bruce is going to be so devastated when he finds out, she thought joyfully.

"Well, it seems he and three others who share his . . . *passion*,"

Brook continued, "are planning on kidnapping and killing one or all of the Radonculus sisters when they tour Tasmania next."

All of the other Cabal members were stunned into silence, except for the strong-looking female senator, whose face looked like it was going to explode.

"That is *brilliant*," Natalie said, bursting into laughter, though some people would say it sounded more like a growl. "How the public would cry at this, and poor old Bruce would have a heart attack if he knew."

She continued to laugh loudly for a few more moments with tears running down her cheeks, whilst everybody stared strangely at her. Nobody was brave enough to interrupt her laughter.

"So I am guessing we will not be intervening with this madman's demented perversion," Phil Miller said after Natalie had finally stopped laughing.

"No," Senator Howles said thoughtfully. "In fact, we should see that this act is carried out."

"When?" Natalie asked with a knowing smile on her ugly face.

"When the third part of our new laws goes through the Senate, of course, Natalie," Howles replied with a small smile. "This is all perfect, don't you think?"

"It is," Natalie almost purred.

"Yes, I agree," Raller replied, "but there is something else. One of the kidnappers wants some girls there," Raller continued. "Very young girls by the sounds of it."

"Oh no," Phil Miller said, aghast. "Not little girls, surely—have we stooped so low?"

"The public would go insane at this tragedy," Gary Miller said sadly.

"So I bet you could pass all of your new laws through in one go when this happens," Florian said thoughtfully. No doubt he thought the sooner the five laws were passed, the sooner they could start on his water corporation proposal.

"No, it still must be one at a time to avoid suspicion," Howles replied firmly. "The laws make no sense on their own, but together, they are political dynamite."

"Kids die or are kidnapped all the time," Townsworth said callously with a wave of his hand. "Who cares about two more if our national security is at stake?"

"I can arrange for the young girls to be there," Natalie said, wiping at the tears of laughter in her eyes.

"We must think of the bigger picture with our new laws." Senator Howles nodded sagely. "And we must protect our people as a whole, not look after the individual's interests alone."

His advisor, Aiden Wilkinson, nodded as well. Nobody was really sure who advised whom in their relationship. Natalie was sure Aiden was just a 'yes-man' who satisfied the senator's ego by agreeing with everything he did and said, but there was something in young Aiden's eyes that suggested he was a man who longed to call the shots, not just say 'yes' to everything he was told.

Thunder roared overhead, causing the house to shake; this was followed by a massive hailstorm that lashed against the window.

"Bloody weather," Gary Miller muttered.

"To think there is a drought in Sydney," his father, Phil Miller, said and grimaced.

Florian again smiled at the rain outside.

"So your decision?" Senator Howles asked.

All of The Cabal members then looked at each other for a long moment, weighing their final decision.

"Are there any objections?" Senator Howles continued into the silence.

Nobody replied. Some looked upset at what they were about to condone, but others thought they were doing the right thing for the country.

"So be it," Howles said. "The Radonculus sisters are to be the diversion we need to get part three of our laws through the Senate."

Axel Rigozzi had been up all night at Parliament House with his colleague, trying to fix the nationwide problem of the Enter key on the computer keyboards not working properly.

"I'm sure it will be all right now," Axel said confidently as he entered the final upgrades.

"Are you sure?" Fred replied worriedly. "These computers are old; instead of being replaced, these old clunkers have been simply repaired and upgraded for decades now."

"Yeah, mate," Axel replied. "The upgrades always fix the problem. She'll be right, mate."

"They don't always fix the problem," Fred replied with a shake of his head. "We just say that to save our bacon; sometimes our fixes actually make things worse, ergo the keyboard problem."

"Ergo or Erstop, I'm sure we have fixed this problem," Axel replied with a small smile.

"That's not funny," Fred said.

"Sorry." Axel smiled all the more.

"Are you sure you fixed it?" Fred asked again.

"Of course," Axel said with a bigger grin. "Now let's go and have a beer; it's my shout."

"Oh, all right then." Fred sighed.

I'm sure the upgrades will be all right, Fred thought. *Axel is right, the government departments always muddle through somehow.*

And besides, he really needed a drink right now.

The Tasmanian Midlands

"Terry, are you all right?" Roger Tyson asked his nephew as the young man's stomach rumbled incredibly loudly once more.

"Yeah, I just need to lie in for a while," Terry replied with a yawn from his bed. "Another few hours' sleep won't hurt."

"You've been asleep for sixteen hours."

"What?"

"You went to bed at two o'clock yesterday afternoon, and it is now six in the morning."

"And you woke me this early in the morning? Bloody hell, Uncle, this is inhumane treatment, I must say."

Roger walked over to him and lifted Terry's head from his pillow. "The doctor said he couldn't find anything wrong with you," he said, studying his nephew's face.

"No, he said I was in perfect health," Terry replied with a huge yawn. "Fit as a fiddle, he said."

"Really?" Roger asked, concerned.

"Yes, really," Terry replied, a little touched by his uncle's concern.

"Then get the fuck out of bed," his uncle growled, then threw off Terry's doona cover and pushed him out of his bed.

"But I need to rest," Terry moaned from the floor.

"No, you need to get your arse into gear and do some bloody work," Roger snapped.

"But—"

"No buts, Terry," his uncle replied firmly. "Now get on that tractor and start working; there are crops to plant."

"Abel's crops?" Terry replied, trying to get a rise out of his uncle.

"No, not that bastard's crop," Roger replied angrily. "Anyway, you ate all of his crop seeds and—"

Terry had fallen asleep again.

"Nephew!" Roger shouted.

"Wh-what?" Terry replied, trying to open his eyes.

"The tractor!"

"What tractor?"

His uncle raised his fist as if to hit him.

"Okay, all right then, hold your horses," Terry said as he got up off the floor and then started staring longingly at his bed.

I really can't be stuffed doing anything, Terry thought.

"Terry . . ."

I mean, what is the point; other people can do my work, can't they?

"Terry . . ."

Roger gave up on talking his nephew into working and threw some of Terry's own clothes at him instead, which included his boots.

Terry then fell down on the floor in a heap again, rubbing his head and complaining, and it took him another ten minutes to get clothed and ready for work. His stomach rumbled like crazy all the way to the tractor.

Hobart, Tasmania

Jeff Brady sat on his couch, deep in thought about Cooper's death, whilst he watched tonight's Footy Show on TV. Every avenue he had tried today, every contact he had within the police force, had led to a dead end. The Holophone records showed that the phone call Cooper was on before he was killed was with an untraceable number, and no prints were found on the stolen truck.

Professionals, Jeff thought. To have an untraceable number today means that whoever Cooper was talking to was very well protected. In fact, it turned out the stolen truck was indeed driverless. This meant it could have been controlled by outside means, which confirmed it was a set up, but the media glossed over this fact and still stated it was an accident.

"This is definitely a cover-up," Jeff muttered. "This accident stinks to high heaven."

He patted the pistol he would carry with him everywhere from now on. If Cooper's killer was going to tie up loose ends and kill him, then the assassin, whoever he was, was not going to take him down easily.

'Welcome to the Footy Show,' the holographic presenter announced.

"Perhaps I should stay out of it from now on and hope for the best," Jeff muttered once more. "Susan definitely seemed pleased that my leads went nowhere."

'And on tonight's Footy Show, please welcome, from the Carlton Football Club, Captain Gabster Clark.' The TV audience applauded in a controlled and polite manner.

'Welcome, Gabster,' the main presenter said.

The Carlton Captain walked nervously onto the set and sat across the table from the five main presenters, who were all holographic images and spoke with an electronic voice.

Appearing on the Footy Show today was not something footballers wanted to do anymore, but as the captain of a football club, you did have to meet certain contractual obligations.

The TV Channel executives had decided years ago that the real presenters—who were all ex-footballers—were too sexist for today's society, so they were replaced by computer images and voiced over by professional actors, who all had the very highest PC credentials.

Five male faces were initially chosen for the Holograms, but some members of the public complained about the TV station's shocking sexism in choosing only men, so from that day on, two female images and three men were used instead. Then, yet another change was recently made, as one of the three male images was replaced because of complaints that the LGBT community was not properly represented on the panel. Tonight, there were two male holographs, two female, and one who looked like a male but seemed to have a lot of makeup on and a voice that went from being male to female at any given moment. Two actors, obviously a male and female, were employed for this one position, and they had to work very hard to synchronize the sentences.

It wasn't any members of the LGBT community who actually complained about not being represented on this show; it was the people who enjoyed complaining that had complained about the LGBT community not being represented on the show. In fact, according to a recent survey, members of the LGBT community really couldn't give a shit whether they were represented on the show or not. But in another more telling recent survey, it was revealed that people who complained a lot seemed to bully everybody into getting their own way more often than not.

'And, Gabster,' one of the male holographic presenters said, 'are you looking forward to this weekend's big game against your old arch rival, Collingwood?'

"Yes . . . yes," Clark stammered. *"We always like to beat the old black and whites."*

The Collingwood football jersey was vertical black-and-white stripes, but that was not how you described the uniform nowadays.

The presenters' holographic images all zoomed in angrily on the Carlton Captain as the audience inhaled in righteous shock.

'What did you say?' the transsexual holographic image said angrily in a female voice.

"I mean . . . I mean, the-the . . . Opposite Colour Spectrum Team," Clark said, sounding terrified, which, in fact, he was.

The Carlton Captain could see it all now, his captaincy and even his career now hung in the balance; relentless vilification by the media and all-knowing TV personalities was only a heartbeat away. A large fine, suspension from playing football, counseling, the endless cultural sensitivity courses he had to take to say how truly sorry he was, donations to be made to politically correct organisations, the media interviewing his parents, who would tearfully apologise for his outrageous comment as they told all of Australia what a good boy their son truly was, and all the while this was going on, he and most of the public would still not really understand what exactly he had done wrong.

'Just as well,' the transsexual holographic image said, now in a male voice, as it zoomed back to its normal position.

The Carlton Captain's face looked like he was about to pass out from relief.

The cameras panned around to the Footy Show audience, taking in their relieved faces whilst they sat at their tables in their tuxedos and expensive dresses, drinking champagne.

"Baa-baa, Rainbow sheep," Jeff said in disgust as he switched the television off. "The world has truly gone mad."

The front doorbell of his house then rang, and upon opening the door, Jeff was surprised to see two policemen standing there.

"Jeff Brady," a harsh-looking policeman said.

"Yes," Jeff replied cautiously.

"I am Constable Hussein, and this here is Constable Woods," the policeman replied, gesturing to his companion. "We need to talk to you about Bill Cooper's death."

Above Hobart right at the very moment two policemen and an ex-policeman sat in serious discussion about Bill Cooper's murder, an airplane was arriving from Sydney with lots of special guests, who were the toast of Australia and admired by one and all and were to bring much-needed happiness to the upset public of Hobart.

"Ya, ya, ya, Froggo File."

"For fuck's sake, will you tie him down?" Remi screamed, as he had an international pop star in a headlock.

First he trashes our hotel rooms, now this.

"I want to fly Froggo File," El Froggo yelled as half of the flight attendants tried to tie him to his seat.

El Froggo, whilst having been quiet for most of the journey, had spent the last ten minutes trying to unlatch one of the airplane doors.

"Just shoot the prick in the head!" Mercedes screamed from the back of the plane. "I'm too young, sexy, and hot to die by being sucked out of an airlock."

"Give me a gun and I will," Remi screamed back.

"You cannot stop the Froggo File," El Froggo cried out.

"Well, I can bloody well try," Remi growled in reply.

No wonder his manager needed a break from him.

"Matthew, do something," Mercedes then screamed at the boy band singer sitting on the other side of the plane.

"No. I have had enough of rolling around on the floor fighting." Matthew sulked and then muttered something about handbags. Brad and Sharon were looking on in horror, but young Mercury had her head back against the seat, deep in sleep.

"Um bah lumbah, Froggo File!" El Froggo yelled as he squirmed under Remi's tight headlock.

"I have some drugs," one of the flight attendants said.

"For me or for him?" Remi grunted as he continued to grapple with the pop star.

"Drugs!" El Froggo said as he stopped squirming.

"No, just some sedatives to calm him down a little," the flight attendant replied.

El Froggo started squirming again.

"Whatever it is, double it," Remi shouted.

"Really?" the flight attendant asked.

"Yes, fucking really," Remi growled.

Whilst international singing sensation El Froggo was injected with tranquillizers strong enough to sedate a horse, four twisted men sat at Victor Cunnington's kitchen table in deep discussion as to how they were to kidnap and kill the Radonculus sisters.

"So you like young girls," Victor Cunnington said in disgust to Reginald Yeasmith.

"Don't go all judgmental on me, Victor," Reginald replied softly.

"You like to cut girls into pieces, remember? Besides, Mercury Radonculus is only sixteen."

"Yes, I know that," Victor said primly, "but my other victims were all adults."

"You asked them for ID then, before you stabbed them?"

"They looked older," Victor growled.

"That was the drugs they were on."

"No, it bloody wasn't; they were of legal age."

"Does that make it better, then?" Reginald asked.

"Of course," Victor replied. "Adults are fair game in the jungle that we live in."

What is wrong with him? Victor wondered. *Why is this loser all of a sudden getting more aggressive?*

Reginald rolled his eyes as Victor lit up a cigarette.

"Look, whatever you guys do to the female victims is none of my business," Colin Wise interrupted, "but getting them to you is."

"And mine," Paulo Smythen added, clenching his fists.

"Then what genius plan have you come up with?" Victor asked, still looking at Reginald in disgust.

"Well, it's really not a genius plan as such," Paulo said.

"Oh, great, so we are all going to get caught and thrown into jail then; you'd be very popular there, Paulo, or would they put you in the women's prison instead?" Victor snapped, then took a long drag on his cigarette to calm himself down.

"Fuck you, fatarse," Paulo spat back.

"Oh, at last my cousin shows some balls to avoid confusion over that pretty face." Victor smiled viciously. "Perhaps you need to be there when I slice one of the sisters up instead of cutting up your own body instead."

"Perhaps I will," Paulo snapped back, scratching at his latest scar.

"That is good to see," Victor replied with a look of almost pride. "We are very similar, you and I, Paulo—well, apart from about fifty kilos."

Paulo grimaced at the comparison. "Sixty," he muttered under his breath.

"Sometimes a simple plan is a good plan," Colin replied, getting back to the subject at hand. "We only need to lure one of the sisters into our trap."

"Which one?" Victor said keenly, starting to get a boner underneath the table.

"It will be the luck of the draw." Colin smiled.

"But you will need to get a ticket to the concert, as they are all sold out," Paulo said, still in his angry voice.

"Which, of course, requires someone who circulates in very high places," Reginald replied with a pointed look at Victor.

"My brother." Victor sighed. "I suppose I could get a ticket. He has been in a good mood ever since Cooper blew up."

"That was funny—" Paulo started to say.

"No, it wasn't fucking funny, Cousin," Victor growled. "He was an arrogant turd who was more interested in himself than us, but he left a young son behind, and for me, that means something and is not funny."

Reginald was now looking at Victor in complete disbelief.

Paulo, though, looked like he was about to attack Victor for a moment, but his cousin stared him down.

He is going to be very hard to control in a few years, Victor thought.

"Like the prostitutes meant something?" Reginald ventured to say.

"Fuck off," Victor snapped as he took another drag on his cigarette. "Nobody misses those bitches."

Reginald rolled his eyes again.

"Well, at least Cooper's death opens the pathway for your brother to be the next premier," Colin said.

"Yes, it does allow Bruce to fulfill his goal." Victor frowned. "Which is bad news in some respect."

Bruce has always wanted to be premier, Victor thought, *ever since he won his first election, he has always looked upon the Coopers with envy.*

"What do you mean?" Paulo said, frowning.

"The public's eye, or I should say the media's eye, would be focused on Bruce," Victor replied.

"And some of that may rub off on you," Colin added thoughtfully.

"And then maybe us," Reginald said softly.

"Guilt by association," Paulo said.

"Please don't say guilt," Colin replied.

"But Michael Cooper looks happy in his job as the premier," Victor replied to all of them, "so my brother may have to wait for a few more years yet."

Victor's mobile phone then rang. "Oh, speak of the devil," he murmured.

Victor's three companions sat back in their seats as the sadistic fat man began talking to his brother.

"Bruce, my big brother, how are you?" Victor said pleasantly.

"Yes, I know how great it is that Cooper is dead. Yes, he was an arsehole, but if you could stop laughing for a moment, I need to ask a favour from you . . . No, it's only a small favour this time; I need a ticket to this big concert they are planning this weekend . . . What? Yes, I have always loved the latest . . . craze,
Froggo thing . . . No, I would not break the back of whoever I was leapfrogging."

His other three companions were sniggering now.

"Look, Bruce, are you going to give me a fucking ticket or not?"

"A simple plan?" Jerry McGuiness murmured as he listened in on the four men's conversation as to how they were going to kidnap and kill one of the sisters.

It was very simple plan, but also one in which so many things could go wrong. Get backstage access for three of them only, and somehow get one of the sisters on their own.

But this whole scenario was all too complicated for Jerry. He didn't understand why these people were allowed to go on with what they were planning and why his boss, Raller, had instructed him to *watch* Victor Cunnington and his friends only, not to arrest them, or better yet, go in that house and kill them all.

He knew one thing for certain, though: he wasn't going to let them hurt Mercury Radonculus, no matter what his boss wanted. She was the youngest sister, only sixteen years of age and absolutely adorable, the way she faked at playing dumb all the time was so endearing to Jerry.

"You're not getting your hands on *her*, Fatboy," he said determinedly.

"So," Constable Hussein said as he glared across the table—or simply looked, depending on your point of view—at the private detective Jeff Brady.

"So indeed," Jeff replied nervously.

"Why is it that all of our investigations into Cooper's accident, led us into the same areas you were seen?" Hussein asked.

"Everywhere we went," Constable Woods added, "the people we talked to said that you were there just before us."

Jeff sighed. He should have known that his investigations would have been noticed, but he had been sure that the Hobart Police Department would have been told to stay away from the case.

"My last case involved Bill Cooper," Jeff said truthfully. If these two men were assassins, he would be dead by now, and he really had no justifiable excuse as to why he was asking so many questions about Cooper's last moments.

"Your last case?" Woods said curiously.

"And what would that case involve?" Hussein asked pointedly.

Jeff took a deep breath and answered the question. "He believed that Bruce Cunnington's own brother, Victor, was directly involved in the murder of a number of prostitutes in the last year or so."

Constable Hussein had a hard face, but it seemed the hardness of his face could go to another level completely.

Eric Woods was looking at his partner in concern.

"Now let me get this straight," Hussein replied through gritted teeth—even his hands were now clenched into fists—"you were hired by Cooper himself to investigate whether Victor Cunnington was cutting those poor girls into pieces?"

"Yes, that's right."

"And you think Cooper was taken out because of this?" Woods asked.

"Yes," Jeff replied. "The *accident* was no accident; you of all people must know this."

Hussein now shrugged his shoulders in a non-committal way, but Woods went as far as nodding his head in agreement.

"The killer could have killed me instead of Cooper to stop me from snooping," Brady continued, "but the easiest way to stop this investigation completely was to simply end Cooper's life."

Despite the direness of the situation, he was enjoying the discussion he was having with these two policemen, as it reminded him of when he was part of the police force.

"How did Cooper know of Victor's perversions?" Woods asked.

"He wouldn't tell me," Brady replied.

"So you have no evidence on these murders?" Hussein asked. "No evidence at all to suggest it was Victor Cunnington?"

"None, I'm afraid," Jeff said dejectedly, "apart from him having a few odd friends, I have no evidence he was involved in any way."

"Then we are back to square one," Woods said dejectedly.

"No, we are not," Hussein said determinedly. "We have a suspect now."

"But aren't we meant to be investigating Cooper's death?" Eric Woods asked.

"We are," Hussein agreed, "but we will be keeping an eye on Victor Cunnington at the same time, as they may be connected somehow."

"That's what I wondered," Brady added.

"Do we tell the commissioner?" Woods asked.

"No, mate. Victor is a high-ranking politician's brother," Hussein replied. "We will keep this info to ourselves for the moment. Won't we, Jeff?" Hussein finished with a hard glare at Brady.

"My involvement in this case is over, Constable," Jeff replied sadly. "I guess it's back to just watching very large people having affairs."

Woods and Hussein were surprised by this comment and how easily Brady was stepping aside from the case, and then they were even more surprised when Jeff started gagging.

"Do it, Fi." Gena giggled at her older sister, Fiona, as she sat in her bedroom. "Dazza will love you for it."

"I don't know," Fiona replied uncertainly, holding her mobile phone in her hand, ready to take a picture.

"Do it."

"I'm not sure."

"But he asked for a photo of you," Gena replied. "He would think you were a chicken if you didn't do it."

"But he asked for a topless photo," Fiona protested.

"Yes, so?" Gena replied. "Well, just show your bra at least."

"If your mother knew what you were doing, Fiona, she would kill you," a voice said from beyond the bedroom door.

"Granddad!" both girls squealed.

"You shouldn't be listening in to us, you old bastard," Gena said.

"I wasn't," Martin Marsh replied, still from beyond the door. "I was just going to have a piss, which at my age happens twenty times a day, and I overheard you girls discussing whether or not my own granddaughter Fiona should send some dirty young pervert a picture of your gazungas."

"Granddad, ewwww!" Gena whined.

"Don't ewwww me, young lady," their grandfather replied. "I wasn't the one who wanted to prostitute myself over the Internet."

"It was just a *mobile phone* picture, that's all," Fiona replied with a roll of her eyes.

"Yes, for the moment," Martin replied, "but who knows where this *Dazza* would send it next. On to his mates, most likely, as he will no doubt want to brag about how cool he was to get you to send him a naked photo. Besides, I am too old to go over there and beat the crap out of him to defend your honour."

"Granddad," Fiona replied, feeling more than a little embarrassed at having this conversation with her grandfather of all people. "Lots of girls do things like this; the Internet is full of girls taking naked, sexy selfies."

Even through the door, they could hear their grandfather sigh.

"I may be old, Fi, but I do remember what it was like to be a young boy, and let me tell you this," he said, "boys will like you if you do things like that—yes, they will all think you are pretty hot and sexy and all that, but please, Fi, don't delude yourself into thinking that they will respect you for it."

Fiona looked at Gena for a moment, then quickly looked away.

"Now, it is up to you whether you want to be liked by this teenage knob and his mates," their grandfather continued, "or whether you want to be respected by them. It's your choice, Fi, but I hope you have the common sense to make the right one."

"Yeah, *whatever*, Granddad." Fiona sighed.

"Yeah, on your way, *Pops*," Gena added.

"I am on my way, believe me," Martin said as he continued to walk on. "Oh, dear, it feels like I have to drop the kids off at the pool this time."

"Ewwww!" Fiona and Gena said at the same time.

"He is *such* an old fart," Fiona huffed after he had gone.

"He's *so* embarrassing," Gena replied.

Neither girl, though, said any more about Dazza's request, nor did they admit to each other that their grandfather was right. They were teenagers, and as we all have experienced, once you became a teenager, you instantly knew everything.

"I know," Fiona suddenly said keenly, as a way to change the subject, "let's ring the Franz radio show and see if we can win some free tickets to the concert."

"Sweet!" Gena said, grinning from ear to ear.

Sydney, Mainland Australia

"The McKay Group? No way," Johan Franz said to the caller. "I have to say I have heard very little about them. They are so bogus with their secrecy."

"Yes, and they have been around for decades," the caller replied. "They make the Illuminati look like a Child Care Centre."

"Awesome, dude, and what are their plans?" Johan asked.

"To create a disease that will wipe out most of the human population."

"Wow, thanks for the warning, dude."

"You're welcome, but there is nothing we can do about it. We're totally doomed."

"Whoa, what a bummer, man. Next caller, please."

"I have called to tell you that the end of the world is coming."

"Oh, really! No way, not the apocalypse, man. That is totally oppressive and uncool," Johan replied.

"Yes, I am here to give you fair warning."

"Man, that's totally far out for you to do that."

"I know it is," the caller replied proudly.

"So when will this happen?"

"It will happen in the time of huge wars, disease, famine, overpopulation, and dwindling resources," the caller said confidently.

I think you have just described every prophecy for the last three thousand years, Johan thought. The two things that worried him about prophecies was firstly, statistically speaking, someone had to get one right someday, and then that person would be falsely seen as a prophet of some sort, when all they were was just plain lucky, and secondly, that some people liked to change people's and even countries' destinies in order to fulfill an old prophecy that totally rendered invalid the idea of the foretelling being a prophecy in the first place.

"So when is this bad-arse trippy day happening?" Johan asked.

"It starts tomorrow."

"Wow . . . what . . . hey, that's only four hours away."

"Yes, it is."

"And how do you know this will happen?"

"It is foretold in the Book of Cyril that when the face of Mars comes crashing down into the desert, the dead shall rise and devour the living, and giant spiders will then soon wage war on the remaining human survivors."

Giant spiders! Well, that is a new one.

"Well, yeah, far out . . . man . . . that is going to be a totally sick day for mankind.

"*Man*kind!" the caller said in shock.

Shit!

"I mean humankind, or, or personkind—yes, that's what I meant, for all you lady listeners out there."

For all the complainers, that's who I really mean, he thought in terror. Sprouting conspiracy theories was one thing, but being politically incorrect was a whole new level.

"Next caller, please," he said breathlessly.

Johan's ears were now blown away by the terrifying noise known as 'teenage girls screaming'.

'Sell some tickets to the Radonculus concert,' Natalie Braiths had told him recently over the Holophone, 'but only sell them to teenage girls.'

'Why?' Johan had risked asking.

'Because, Johan, if you don't sell them to some air-headed young girls, I am going to come over to your place of work and beat your head to a pulp,' Natalie had growled, looming almost out of the Holophone, as if she was going to do that right at this moment.

'Yes, Senator,' Johan replied meekly.

'Good boy,' Natalie said, now purring like a kitten. 'You know, I could still come and visit you . . . for other reasons.'

'I've got to go,' Johan said quickly and hung up the phone.

"Wow, you girls certainly do have very loud voices," Johan said to the callers.

More screams was the only reply.

"I'm guessing you want some free tickets to see the Radonculus sisters and El Froggo."

More screams continued.

Johan moved his headphones away from his ears in preparation for what was about to happen next.

"Well, congratulations! Not only have you won four free tickets, but you get VIP all-access to the backstage, where you can actually meet all of the stars."

Johan waited patiently until the cacophony of screaming stopped.

"And your names?" he asked.

"Gena and Fiona Milligan," one of the callers squealed.

"Well, I hope you have a wonderful time," Johan replied kindly.

Later that night, Henry Abel was still an angry man as he approached his secret facility, which was situated underneath the main CBD of Sydney.

I should have just punched him one, he thought as he remembered the defiance shown by that bloody farmer. *I should not have let Cunnington drag me out of there like a coward, and just biffed the bloke in the head. Who cares what the consequences would have been? I should have punched the smug prick's lights out.*

But he'd had no choice but to leave, as that stupid young nephew of Roger's had just eaten all of his specialised crop seeds. Because of this act of stupidity, Henry now had to hire Flowers to kill both the nephew and uncle.

And what has happened to the boy now? Abel wondered. *The apathy would be growing in him, as expected, but what would those latest genetically altered tardigrades be doing to his body right now?*

Henry Abel's idea as a Cabal member was to grow a grain of wheat with a specialised chemical that dulled the brain of the consumer, making them more docile and malleable than they were even today. This product had been developed and tested many times and was proven to work very effectively.

But Henry Abel, a.k.a. McDermott as a member of The McKay Group, had been testing tardigrades for years and had designed his very own offshoot of the tardigrade species, which could reside dormant in foods such as wheat for months, and have a voracious appetite when awoken. The tardigrades, upon entering the human stomach, would be indigestible, but after a few days, would quickly begin to feed, causing massive damage to the inner human body. Or so he hoped.

That boy has hundreds of them in his stomach right now, Henry thought curiously as he opened the door to the office he rented and then began his long descent down the secret stairwell inside. *I need to know what happens to that boy before he is killed.*

"He'll probably die painfully, but be too lazy to go to the hospital," Henry muttered. "Or maybe that prick of an uncle of his will drag him there to save him."

That is why Terry Tyson needed to be killed. If the doctors tested his blood and found those creatures, however unlikely that was, Henry was done for.

"Well, I just need to get Flowers involved to do what he does best," Henry said to himself as he opened the last door to his hideout. "And then I need to—"

Henry stopped in mid-sentence as he saw a dozen of his mutilated patients walking aimlessly around the entrance hallway.

"What the hell is going on!" he murmured as he quickly walked to his laboratory and saw more of the brain-damaged idiots wandering around, touching everything they could see.

"Get away from my equipment!" Henry shouted as he tried to shoo the filth away from his laboratory. "Richards!" he yelled. "Holding, Lloyd, Marshall, get in here now!"

"They don't work for you anymore," a young voice said.

Henry turned around and saw one of the young children, a girl about three years old, smiling at him.

"What do you mean, they don't work for me?" Henry said nervously. This little girl was far too articulate for one so young.

"They work for me now," a boy with a nasty scowl said as he arrived by the girl's side. It was the seven-year-old boy named

Dekker, the one who was meant to be sedated, waiting on Abel's experiments.

Henry was now starting to feel more than a little nervous; in fact, if his ego would have allowed him, he would have gladly admitted that he was frightened by this boy.

"Richards, where the bloody hell are you?" Henry yelled.

"Yes, let's get Richards, Dekker," little Rainbow said to the young boy. "And Lia too, yes, I want to see Lia."

Lia, Henry thought, *what is Lia doing here so late? And why has Richards allowed this to happen?*

The boy Dekker nodded in agreement, and to Henry's horror, his eyes turned completely white as he left the room yelling for Richards and Lia.

"Dear God in Heaven," Henry said in a trembling voice, "what are you?"

"I don't know, Human," Rainbow replied curiously. "What are you?"

Human, Henry thought, trying to control his breathing, *McShane speaks the same way about our race.*

Richards arrived quickly and had his weapons on his hip as per usual. Henry breathed a sigh of relief when he saw him, but was shocked when Lia Read arrived carrying two newborn babies in her arms.

"Richards, thank God you are here," he said, but Richards's attention was solely fixed on the young boy who had returned by his side.

"Yes, Master Dekker," Richards said to the young boy.

Master!

Henry could see the look of tension clearly on his security guard's face. Lia looked like she was about to cry, but she still held the babies steadily in her arms.

"Richards, look at me," Henry yelled. But Richards didn't acknowledge him at all; his mind was completely focused on the young boy.

"Henry likes to experiment on us," Dekker said, his eyes still white. "It is time we experimented on him."

"What!" Henry said in horror.

What the hell is happening?

"Experiments," Dekker said again.

"You can't do this," Henry said to Richards.

"Yes, he can, Henry, and he will in a moment," the little girl said, which caused the young boy to frown at her. "Then we will get Lloyds and Holding to kill all of the other captives," the girl continued. "We need all the food for ourselves, Dekker."

"Even our parents?" Dekker asked.

"Yes, even them." Rainbow nodded.

Dekker considered the deaths of his parents for a moment, then shrugged his shoulders, as if to say he didn't really care, which he didn't.

"Now where were we again?" Dekker now grinned viciously.

"The taser, you can do it now, Dekker," Rainbow replied, and then muttered the words 'you big poo-poo head' under her breath.

"Taser him, Richards, now!" Dekker said with white eyes and a snap to his voice like a whiplash.

"No, Richards!" Henry screamed.

But Richards immediately brought out his taser gun and shot Henry in the chest. Henry Abel, renowned scientist and member of not only The Cabal but The McKay Group itself, hit the ground, shaking uncontrollably but still aware enough to notice he was now being lifted onto the surgery table.

"Get the knives," Dekker snapped.

"Scalpels," Rainbow corrected him, "and we need some stools so we can see." Clearly, these two were battling as to who would be the Alpha in their little group.

Thus began ten minutes, or to Henry what must have felt like a lifetime, of intense pain and gut-wrenching screams. This continued until, blessedly, his strong heart gave out.

"Well, that is interesting," McShane murmured as she looked down through the Holoscreen upon two young children and a grown man cutting scalpels deep into McDermott's skull whilst a young woman carrying what looked like two newborn babies cried in the corner of the room.

"It is interesting," her lover and bodyguard, Gabriel Ferreno, said beside her with a playful smile. "The pain he is going through would be . . . intense."

"Settle down, Gabriel, now is not the time," McShane said sternly, noticing her lover's interest in the torture of McDermott. McShane had been spying on McDermott and McLaren for years. Both of the Australian men had made significant inroads into how the human body works, especially the brain, and McShane had plagiarized all of their work and, through her own brilliance, expanded on it.

"Poor McDermott," McShane said as she watched him writhe in agony. "Not only does he have poor security when it comes to being spied upon, but he seems to be crying like a baby from where they are playing with him."

"They are cutting deep into his head, with no anesthetic, my love," Gabriel purred.

"Yes, they are," she replied, giggling for a moment, "but how do those children control the adults like that?" she finished thoughtfully.

"You need to study the children some more, my love, and work out how they were born like that, or if indeed it is just a learned skill that we don't know about."

"Yes, I will," McShane said and settled back in her chair. "I will also have to study about those tardigrades that seemed to bring that patient back to life."

"But we are in the business of culling humans, not reviving them," Gabriel replied, confused.

"That we are, and so we shall always be." McShane smiled contentedly. "But for now, let us simply sit back and enjoy the show."

Poor McDermott, or should that be Henry Abel? she thought. *Who will McLaren have to play with now?*

The Tasmanian Midlands

Terry had been sitting on the tractor staring aimlessly into the distance for hours. He had also been yawning constantly.

I'm so tired, he thought.

It was the dead of night and pitch-black, and Terry didn't know or care where he was. His mobile phone had been ringing almost non-stop—no doubt it was his uncle wanting to know where he was and why he hadn't returned home, or why he hadn't returned his tractor more like—but Terry couldn't be bothered answering it. *He'll just have to wait.*

"I need to get moving," Terry muttered to himself. But instead of starting up the tractor and driving home, he slid off the tractor and landed face-first in the dirt.

That should have hurt, he thought as he lay on the ground, *but I'm too tired to feel anything.*

Terry should have then wiped the dirt off his face after he slowly stood up, to see more clearly where he was headed, but he couldn't be bothered even doing that, so he decided for no real logical reason to walk aimlessly to the south in pitch darkness.

"Life sucks," Terry moaned, thinking about what a great life he had led as a TV reporter. "I mean, it was hard work and all," he said, then yawned once more, "but it was much more exciting than this."

But thinking about those past interviews that he had done with politicians, he wondered what the point was. He wondered what the point of anything was.

"They don't change anything," he said to himself. "The politicians are just part of a system that trashes everything around them in search of profits." He broke out into another huge yawn, and then coughed when a passing insect went straight into his mouth.

"Insects are protein, I guess," he said as he tried to get some saliva back into his mouth. "Insects suck too . . . just like politicians suck . . . and everything else."

He yawned some more and kept walking south as he chewed on what was left of the insect.

"I mean, capitalism is good from the perspective of someone working . . ."

He yawned again, and another insect went into his mouth. "Someone working . . ."

He yawned once more and started chewing the new protein. "Someone working hard, and making heaps of money as a reward for their efforts, is fantastic and good luck . . .to them, but today . . ."

Another yawn and yet more chewing.

"Today, it's all in favour of the big corporations . . ."

A yawn and yet another insect found its home in his mouth.

"Hmm, that one is actually quite tasty . . . hmmm, yeah, where was I? Right . . ., corporations which the politicians love and serve more than us."

A slight yawn.

"Because they believe in this trickle-down economics malarkey, which is a bunch of—"

Another yawn, quite large this time.

"A bunch of—"

More chewing.

" . . . horseshit."

A yawn.

"What did people expect to happen to our world when businesses are put before people? They don't even pay their fair share of taxes."

Yawn.

"Isn't that a massive and blindingly obvious hint to the public . . . to the public . . . that something . . . is seriously wrong with the system?"

He swallowed the last bit of the insects.

"Don't the public care that these . . . fuckers don't pay their fare share?"

He felt like lying down and sleeping, but he kept on walking aimlessly to the south.

"I mean, what is wrong with people? We get taxed . . . but they don't."

Huge yawn.

"Are they too lazy to care?"

Another yawn.

"I know I am."

A small yawn.

"Corporations across the globe are in each other's pockets."

A yawn, and another insect entered his mouth this time.

"Was that a fly or a mosquito?"

He didn't care and chewed on it anyway.

"They are international corporations now, not just countrywide, and they fuck us over big time."

By now, he was thinking that he needed a drink, but that it was too much of an effort to find water, so he kept on walking south.

"Bandits, they are—"

Yawn.

"They don't care about the future."

Yawn.

"They just suck everything dry."

Another extra huge yawn.

"And leave the mess"—yawn—"for the future generations to fix."

A medium-sized yawn.

"They suck."

A smaller yawn.

"We suck."

Yawn.

"We knew what was going to happen with the lust for profits—future generations will despise us."

A big yawn.

"We knew what the consequence of our indifference was; we knew the price."

A really big yawn.

"But we did nothing about it."

Yawn.

"I should protest."

Yawn.

"If I could be bothered . . ."

Just then the rain started belting down, and Terry looked tiredly towards the night sky and opened his mouth wider.

"A bit of water, some luck at last."

A medium-sized yawn.

"But rain still su-uucckkss!"

Whilst Terry was looking towards the sky letting the rain quench his thirst, he fell into a small hole in the ground, which might have been part of a disused mine many years ago, or maybe was one of those many sinkholes that kept appearing out of nowhere nowadays.

He broke many bones in his body and sustained life-threatening internal injuries as he fell twenty metres into a dark and dingy hole in the ground, but somehow, he managed to survive, and somehow, his body was reacting to this life-and-death situation. As his body started to enter a state of deep coma caused by the hundreds of Tardigrades who had migrated all over his body the last few days, he managed to get one final sentence out.

"Well, this certainly sucks."

Hobart, Tasmania

Early the next morning, two adults and two very excited teenagers prepared to head to the city of Launceston to see three of the most famous acts in the entertainment industry today.

"I'm telling you," Martin Marsh said as he leant against the front door watching his family leave, "PC means professional complainers, not political correctness."

"I actually agree with you, Mr Marsh," Jeff Brady said with a small smile. Susan's father reminded Jeff of his own dad. *It must be a generation thing*, he thought.

"I know, Dad," Susan replied, "but you do complain a lot yourself, you know."

Susan then heard her daughters grunt in agreement.

"Yeah, but his generation didn't complain about the environmental damage, though, did they?" Gena muttered.

"Knew about it for decades and did nothing," Fiona added.

"That we did, to my own shame," Martin replied.

Susan Milligan sighed as she kissed her father on the cheek. "Just be good whilst we are away," she said.

"I will," Martin grumbled, then focused his old eyes on his granddaughters. "Now, Fiona and Gena, I don't want to see too many selfies of you when you are at this concert."

"Granddad, that's *impossible*," Fiona whined. "How are we to tell our friends what we are doing?"

"That's the thing, Fi," their grandfather replied, "you won't be doing *anything* if you're just taking photos all the time; all you will be doing is living your life on a computer, and that isn't real living."

"Yeah, *whatever*, Granddad," Gena moaned, looking at her mobile phone.

"No, listen to your old granddad for once," Martin replied firmly. "I want you to look around yourself at the concert, hear the music, listen to the crowd, and feel and smell the atmosphere of that place. Not just stand there like zombies with your mobile phone in the air. If you are there just to take photos, you are just there to impress your friends, and everybody knows it. You're not fooling anybody, girls, believe me."

Gena rolled her eyes at this.

"That isn't life, girls; that's fakeness," their grandfather continued. "I want you, when you are old like me, to remember the feel of the place, not how many duck-faces you can make in one day."

Gena and Fiona were now already in the car, already taking lots of photos of themselves to document the exciting day—and download it on Facebook to show their friends.

Their grandfather sighed. "Well, don't come complaining to me about your neck problems from looking down all the time, you hear me."

They still weren't listening.

"See ya, Mr Marsh," Jeff Brady said with a smile. He really did like the old fella.

"Bye, Dad," Susan called out, and very soon they were driving up the highway to Launceston.

Victor Cunnington watched as his three work colleagues all hopped into the red van they had rented, about to start their journey to Launceston.

"Are you sure this is going to work?" Victor said worriedly.

He would be driving in his own van. If they were successful, one of the gorgeous Radonculus sisters would soon be tied up in the back.

If they were unsuccessful, Victor intended to bail on the plan and leave his so-called friends behind. His brother, Bruce, would help with any legal trouble he may find himself in or any cover-up after that, of that he was sure.

"Yeah, it will work," Colin Wise said. "There are always charity volunteers asking for donations at these events."

"There will be thousands of people in front of the stage," Paulo added in a hard voice, "but at the back of the arena are only a few people."

My word, Victor thought in surprise, *has my cousin just changed his nature, or was the new man always waiting to come out from hiding?*

"We will be careful, Victor," Colin continued. "Only if we have a clear chance will we make our move. If not, then it's just your bad luck."

Colin's brother was a manager at one of these major charity institutions and was amazed that Colin had volunteered for this weekend.

'Really, Colin?' his brother said. 'You are going to do something charitable?'

'I do have my moments,' Colin replied, then began to cough up half his lungs.

'Yeah, well, make sure you don't die on your way up there,' his brother said in distaste, and then frowned, looking more than a little concerned. 'You don't have cancer, do you, Colin? Is that why you are doing this? Is that why you cough so much?'

'No, I don't, mate,' Colin had said, a little surprised at his brother's concern, as he had always hated him. 'I won't be dying, either.' Colin smiled.

He did actually have lung cancer in truth, and the doctor said he had only one year, at best, to live. That was part of the reason he liked setting people up to die. If Colin had to die early, then why didn't other people as well? Victor's reason for the killings was sadism, Paulo hated himself and everybody else, but Colin's reason was pure spite.

"The volunteers have access everywhere," Paulo Smythen added thoughtfully. "If we are quick about it, we should be in and out of there before you know it."

"I have the drugs to knock them out," Reginald Yeasmith said in his soft voice.

Well, there is a surprise, Victor thought.

"The bathrooms are at the back of the stars' pavilion," Colin said, "so if they go for a slash—"

"Then so will I," Victor said with an evil smile, touching his lucky knife he had in his jacket pocket.

"Just remember," Reginald said quietly. "You know what I want."

"Yes, young girls," Victor snapped in disgust.

"Exactly," Reginald said in his usual soft voice, but there was something hard about his face today. His blank eyes had a look of determination about them.

"Well . . . well, you better get going," Victor said, a bit disconcerted about Reginald's new demeanor. "Remember where I will be parked."

"Yes, you will be safely off the grounds." Paulo smirked. "So brave of you, Cousin."

Victor was about to snap at Paulo, then realised he was being a coward waiting for these men to do the kidnapping. He had often wondered why these men did the 'scouting' for him before, and now they were taking an extra huge risk.

"You have me there, Paulo," Victor conceded to his cousin with a nod of his fat head. "Just be careful, all right? I don't want any of you getting into trouble."

They smirked at this comment, except for Reginald; they knew that Victor was only worried about himself ending up in prison, and he really didn't care about any of them.

"I will," Paulo said, thinking about the knife he carried in his own jacket pocket and wishing he was able to walk around with his longsword he liked to practice with. "With luck, I want to do some cutting this time."

Well, it seems Paulo does take after me, Victor decided. *He's definitely changed in nature, that is for sure. I believe he really wants to do the killing this time.*

"It will be a laugh," Colin said, then started another coughing fit. He was carrying a pistol in his jacket pocket. He wasn't planning on getting out of there alive if he was caught.

"Yes, it will be," Victor replied. *I believe Colin just thinks setting someone up to die is fun.*

Reginald just stared at Victor with those dead eyes. "If we go down for this, so will you," was all he said.

And Reginald is changing as well, Victor thought angrily, *and is looking to be my next victim, after one of the Radonculus sisters, of course.*

Reginald frowned, as if knowing what Victor was thinking.
Yes, you are definitely next, Victor thought, giving Reginald what he hoped was a kind smile.

Constable Hussein and Constable Woods sat in their plain clothes in an unmarked police car and watched the very large man named Victor Cunnington say goodbye to three friends and then struggle to get into his own grey vehicle.
"Victor has his own grey van," Woods said quietly.
"And so do his friends," Hussein replied.
"But a red one," Woods said.
"Yeah, so?" Hussein frowned.
"A little suspicious, don't you think, Rizo?"
"Why?"
"Because it's red, and red is an aggressive colour."
"Are you dicking with me, Eric?"
"Yes." Woods grinned.
"Thank God for that." Hussein sighed. "I thought you had suddenly gone all hippy on me."
"Well, we better follow the fat man, I guess," Woods said after a moment.
"But what if they are all going to the same place?" Hussein said thoughtfully.
"Well, that is why they give policemen guns," Woods replied as they drove slowly after Victor Cunnington's van.

Jerry McGuiness sat in his car and warily watched the two policemen who had previously arrested him for destroying their car watch Victor Cunnington and his crew drive off to the north.
"This is getting weird," Jerry said to himself.
His orders were to keep Victor Cunnington and his 'associates' under surveillance. But now it seemed that the two policemen were watching Cunnington as well.
"It's a wonder Jeff Brady isn't here as well," he muttered to himself, and then looked nervously over his shoulder just to make sure. But Jeff Brady was a second priority now. Only Cunnington and the Radonculus sisters mattered today.
The spy from Canberra slowly drove northwards, following two

plain-clothed policemen, who were also following a brother of a powerful politician, who was also a knife-wielding psychopath, in their unmarked police car.

Canberra, Mainland Australia

"Senator," young Aiden Wilkinson said as he poked his head nervously around Senator Braiths's door.
"What do you want, boy?" Natalie Braiths barked in reply.
Today was a busy day with the final preparations to be made on part three of their new laws. Also, she really hated working on the weekends.
"Senator Howles wishes to see you," Wilkinson said quietly.
"Well, he can wait," Natalie snapped. "And isn't he meant to be busy like me, preparing for today's senate meeting?"
"He is, Senator," Wilkinson replied, "but there is some concerning news in regards to Henry Abel."
"What news?" Natalie asked curiously. "Isn't he meant to be up to some science business in Tasmania?"
"That's the thing, Senator," Wilkinson said sadly. "He won't be doing anything anymore."
"What?" Natalie said, confused.
"Please, Senator," Wilkinson said softly. "You really need to see this."
And to Natalie's surprise, the young man walked out into the corridor, as if expecting her to automatically follow like some sort of lost puppy dog.
If this is a frivolous request then I am really going to beat Aiden up, whether he gives me permission or not.
Aiden Wilkinson led her straight to Senator Howles's office, and to her surprise, the senator had a frightened look on his face.
"What's wrong?" Natalie asked, trying to gather her courage.
"I'm not sure whether we have a rival group or this was just an isolated act by a depraved mind," he replied.
Aiden Wilkinson flinched at the senator's comment.
"What do you mean?" Natalie was frightened now.
Howles turned on the TV and showed the latest news.
Renowned scientist Henry Abel was found murdered this morning, hanging

from a . . .'

Natalie stopped listening to the news reporter and looked at the image on the screen.

It was Henry Abel, hanging spread-eagle from a dingy underpass of a main highway. Someone had tied his half-naked body by rope to the supporting beams of the highway, but that was not the worst of it. His face was covered in blood, and there were cuts all over his head, which appeared to be very deep, almost surgical in appearance. Beneath him were dozens and dozens of equally deformed bodies, lying haphazardly on the ground.

Who could have done this? she thought in amazement.

Hundreds of people were standing in the distance with their mobile phones in the air, taking photos. A small part of Natalie's mind wondered why they had not bothered taking his body down, or at least covered it up somehow, but another part of her mind, the dominant part, could see an opportunity.

"Mark," Natalie said in a shaky voice.

"Yes?" the senator replied.

Take a deep breath and focus. People die all the time, even friends and colleagues, Natalie thought. *Not that Henry was truly a friend.*

"I think we can get parts three *and* four of our new laws passed through the senate today," she said.

Senator Howles smiled in reply.

"I will ring Townsworth to control the media, but judging by the media frenzy and lack of respect for Henry's body, I think he has already got things under control," Howles replied. "I think with this murder and what's going to happen in Tasmania, we should have no problem avoiding public scrutiny."

"It could be a constructive day, then," Natalie said, feeling much better about Henry's death.

"That it could, Natalie," Howles replied, feeling a lot better himself. "That it could."

Launceston, Tasmania

"I can't believe I am going to this concert," Jeff said as they finally arrived at the event. The gathered crowd was huge, and getting a parking spot would usually be a very difficult assignment, but as the girls had won VIP access, they just cruised past all the checkpoints and were headed to a very spacious parking lot at the back of the arena.

Two young girls were talking excitedly in the back of the car about what they were going to say if they met their heroes.

"Well, the girls won four tickets," Susan replied. "My idiot husband is still in jail, and my father didn't want to go, obviously, so you're it, I'm afraid."

"Yeah, I know, but the Radonculus sisters . . ."

Small squeals could now be heard from the back of the car.

"And that boy band . . ."

Louder squeals.

"And that El Froggo idiot."

Huge screams could now be heard from the back of the car, almost causing Jeff to rear-end the red van in front of them.

"Jesus Christ!" he shouted.

"Girls," Susan said calmly, looking back at her daughters, "this isn't a self-driven car, so if you could stop terrifying Jeff into making us crash and all dying, that would be very much appreciated."

"Sorry, Mum," Fiona replied. "Sorry, Mr Brady."

Gena gave an apologetic wince.

"That's all right, girls," Jeff replied, regaining his calm.

"Damn. That fucking prick behind us almost smashed into us," Paulo snarled, looking through the rearview window with a grimace on his pretty face. The tension was starting to build in Paulo's mind. Making plans was one thing; acting on those plans was another thing entirely.

"Yeah, I know, it was a close one," Colin said with a shake of his head as he drove the car into the VIP parking lot. "It looks as if they are following us into the backstage area too; maybe they are charity volunteers as well."

"Or they are the caterers," Paulo said, trying to control his breathing.

"Or the roadies." Colin smiled, and then broke into another coughing fit, swerving the car a bit to the right.

Paulo flinched, and once more wished that he was the one

driving the van as Colin almost ran off the road into one of the security fences at the back of the concert. *Colin is fucking going to kill us before we have a chance to kill somebody.*

Reginald didn't say anything as he gazed out of the van's back window; all that he noticed was that the car behind them had two young girls in the backseat.

Mercedes Radonculus was keenly reading all the tweets on her Holo-twitter account—some of the questions could be ridiculous, such as politics and the environment, but other questions were insightful and full of meaning, such as which football team she supported, what brand of clothes she liked to wear, and who she thought was the hottest male TV or movie star today. But most of all, she liked seeing questions about how hot and sexy she was.

'Goddamn, girl, your arse is just so fine,' Crabman from Huonville tweeted.

'Oh, what a lovely thing to say,' Mercedes typed in reply via her Holophone.

'Sweet Jesus, you have the best legs I have ever seen,' Robbo from Geeveston tweeted.

'Oh, what a lovely thing to say,' Mercedes typed again in reply.

'I'd really like to **** your **** and give you a **** **** down your **** in a car with a ****** whilst watching the footy,' a heavily censored Grogan from Ranelagh tweeted.

'Oh, what a lovely thing to say,' Mercedes typed in reply.

'Hey, Mercedes, the news about Chardonnay and Brad is just so sweet, as they both are so intelligent and nice and really worth watching, as opposed to the other talentless fame whores out there. You know who I mean, don't you, Mercedes? Hmmm, talentless, dumb, and pretty. Who can that be I wonder, hmmm?' Kirstin from North Hobart tweeted.

"What news?" Mercedes typed in reply.

'OMG, LOL, they are dating each other, you DMF. Perhaps if you could stop making sex tapes for five minutes, you might actually see the world around you,' Kirstin replied.

"What!" she said in shock, looking at her elder sister. "Bloody hell, since when have you been banging Brad Hoffington, and how did the public find out before me?"

Sex tapes? I've only made one sex tape. And what does DMF mean?
The stars were already settled in the massive tent at the back of the stage, waiting for all of the paying public to arrive.

Sharon glared at her manager, Remi Hiller, who looked back at her as innocently as he could, which was a lot, as he was a professional liar after all.

"Apparently, they received an anonymous tip-off," she said sarcastically.

"Don't look at me, Sharon," Remi lied. "I didn't tell any of them, honest."

This is brilliant, Remi thought happily. The entertainment shows were having a field day with this revelation.

Sharon sniffed and looked away angrily, knowing all too well that Remi had told the gossip shows.

Mercedes sniffed and looked away angrily as well, as she believed she was the hottest sister and was used to being the centre of attention. *And what does DMF mean?* she wondered again.

"Well, I think it is wonderful," Mercury said kindly. "You make a lovely couple."

"Thank you, Mercury," Sharon said, feeling a little better.

"Where is the new boyfriend *anyway?*" Mercedes said more than a little jealously.

"He is with Frank, trying to figure out the logistics of the show," Sharon replied.

"What do you mean?" Mercury asked curiously. "Who goes on first and all that? I thought we just do what we always did with the other shows."

"No, I think the logistics involve mostly how we go about controlling El Froggo," her eldest sister replied.

Mercedes groaned, and so did Remi.

"Hang on," Sharon said to Remi, "aren't you meant to be managing El Froggo?"

"I needed a break," Remi replied.

"Don't we all?" Mercedes muttered.

"Well, the tranquilizers did go well," Remi said. "He was very quiet from the plane to the hotel."

"He was comatose," Sharon said with a shake of her head.

"Yeah, so?" Remi shrugged.

"So are you suggesting after he sings his song we jump on him and ram a needle in his bum?" Mercedes said, and then frowned back at her Holophone as she re-read the last tweet from Kirstin.

"Well, I was thinking *before* he went on, but yeah, that's about the gist of it," Remi replied. "But I think we may have found a way to calm him down."

"How?" Sharon asked curiously.

"We found his drugs." Remi grinned. "And the hallucinogenic drug that he loves so much has now found the toilet."

"You didn't," Sharon said, shocked.

"Oh yes." Remi laughed. "Frank flushed the drugs, Froggo File."

"That bitch!" Mercedes cried out, after finally working out what DMF stood for. She then vigorously began a tweeting war with Kirstin from North Hobart.

"What do we do?" Constable Eric Woods asked his partner.

"I have no idea." Hussein sighed.

Eric and Razan were sitting in their unmarked police car, watching Victor Cunnington in the distance, who was also just sitting in his own grey van.

"The others kept going?" Eric said.

Victor's grey van had stayed on the heels of his friends' red van for nearly the entire trip, then, all of a sudden, Victor pulled over to the side of the road, and the red van continued on.

"You don't think they do the kidnapping, do you?" Hussein asked. "You don't think that Cunnington works alone?"

"Well, they *were* driving a red van." Eric grinned.

"Enough of that," Hussein growled.

"I think we have no choice but to stay here," Eric then said seriously. "If those three odd men do have some involvement in this case, then they will return to their master so to speak."

"And then we can nab them." Hussein smiled.

"Indeed," Eric said, smiling as well.

The two policemen sat in their car and patiently waited for something to happen.

"I wonder where they are going, though," Eric said after a moment.

"They might be abducting someone from the concert," Hussein said with a grimace. "I wonder who the poor person is."

"Boss," Jerry McGuiness said to his spymaster.
He's going to kill me.
"Yes?" Brook Raller replied.
"It's getting a bit tricky now," Jerry said.
More than a little tricky, you idiot, he thought to himself.
"What do you mean?"
"I'm sitting here watching Victor's van parked on the side of the road a few miles away from the concert."
He was parked a longer way away from Victor than he should, but he really had no choice.
"He didn't go?" Raller asked, concerned.
"No, he didn't, but his three friends kept on going in that red van of theirs."
"Shit," Raller muttered. "Well . . . well, it looks like his friends are doing the kidnapping."
"I agree," Jerry replied, and now came the part of the story he was dreading. "But . . . but Victor is being watched by two policemen as well."
"What? They are watching him now?" Raller said, surprised.
"Yes, now, and to make matters worse, it's the two policemen who arrested me for rear-ending their car."
Jerry now prepared for the worst and cringed a little.
"What the fuck have you done?" Raller shouted down the radio.
"I-I'm not sure, Boss," Jerry said, wincing. "They started following Victor in Hobart."
"What!"
"Yeah, I know. I was shocked too," Jerry replied lamely.
"He must be a suspect," Raller growled. "Somehow, the Hobart Police know how fucked up he is."
"What do I do?" Jerry asked.
Raller was silent for a long moment.
"You find those men in the red van," Raller eventually said, "and let them attempt to kidnap the sisters . . ."
"Really, you're kidding!" Jerry said out loud. He was really hoping that he would be able to be a hero and save Mercury . . .

and the other sisters, of course.

"Yes, *really,* and I am not *kidding*," Raller said sarcastically.

"Before they actually kidnap the girls, though, you can come in like a hero and stop them by any force you deem necessary. Is that okay with you, McGuiness?"

"Really!" Jerry said, now with a big grin on his face.

I am going to save someone, he thought deliriously.

"Yes, really," Raller snapped, "and fucking focus this time, McGuiness. Don't go smashing into any stationary cars."

"Yes, Boss."

"And stop thinking with your dick."

What the hell!

"I-I don't know what you mean, sir," Jerry lied.

"Don't lie to me, Jerry," Raller growled. "I know what young men think about all of the time, for I was once one of them, and with Mercedes Radonculus, well, I don't blame you one bit. But I want you to use your real brain, do you hear me?"

"Yes, sir," Jerry replied.

Ha! Mercedes. Well, at least you got that wrong. She's hot outside but seems a very vain person inside.

"And what about Victor Cunnington?" Jerry asked.

"You leave Victor to me," Raller said. "I think I have a way of sending him packing."

I wonder what that is? Jerry thought.

"Yes, Boss, I'll leave that to you," he said out loud.

"Oh, how gracious of you. Now get going!" Raller snapped.

"Yes, Boss," Jerry replied again.

I am coming, family Radonculus, he thought. *Don't worry, I am coming to save you.*

And he did get going and joined the slow-moving traffic driving towards the concert, but not before having to duck his head twice as he firstly passed the two policemen and then the fat man as they all sat patiently in their vehicles.

Jeff Brady couldn't help but grin whilst observing Susan's daughters and the delighted look on their young faces. Sure, he was a touch embarrassed at being at a concert aimed purely at the young, but there was no doubt there was something quite heartwarming at seeing genuine smiles from the two young teenagers.

"What are you smiling at?" Susan asked.

"I just remember a time when I was happy," Jeff replied, still looking at Gena and Fiona's excited faces.

"When you didn't have a job or mortgage to worry about and life seemed full of opportunities and promise?" Susan said.

"That's the one," Jeff said, still smiling, albeit a bit more sadly now. "I'm not sure what went awry."

"There is something wrong with our society," Susan suddenly said, looking at her daughters giggling in front of her. "Only one in ten people are happy in their job. That's a lot of miserable people, Jeff. And nobody really protests anymore, apart from the rent-a-crowd protesters; nobody really stands up for their rights."

There is something weird going on in our world, Jeff,' his father had told him. 'Back in 1983, twenty five thousand people in Hobart protested about a dam being constructed on the Franklin River. In 2003, we had fifteen thousand people protesting about the Iraqi War. Nowadays, people think protesting is simply liking and sharing something on Facebook or changing your profile picture for a day. They don't really know how useless of a gesture that truly is.'

'But it makes them feel good,' Jeff had said.

'Oh yes, they feel good all right, for a day or two, but it doesn't change anything at all, and the problem is still there when everybody has forgotten about it and moved on to the next promoted cause,' his dad said, shaking his head.

'People don't really believe they can truly change anything anymore, Dad,' Jeff replied sadly. 'And they don't want to be associated with the rent-a-crowd protestors who appear at every small rally.'

'That's right, Son, and I don't blame them for that,' his dad had replied seriously. 'But believe me, Jeff, somewhere out there are people who have all the power in the world, and they are laughing now very loudly at our self-centredness and apathy.'

"Is this your way of saying that you're resigning?" Jeff now said worriedly, glancing at Susan.

"Oh, I like my job with you," Susan said, patting Jeff on his arm. "But some jobs I have done . . ."

Jeff looked closely at his friend and noticed she looked a little sad.

"What do you mean?" Jeff asked. "You weren't involved in any of your husband's . . . exploits, were you?"

That man was still in jail, and Susan had never told him the entire reason. Jeff had thought about doing some snooping to find out the truth, but it felt like a betrayal of Susan's trust, so he didn't follow through on it.

Susan didn't respond to his question and had a distant look in her blue eyes.

"Susan . . .?" Jeff asked again.

Suddenly, Fiona and Gena started screaming as the boy band Street United Cat Kings took to the stage.

Oh, here they are, Jeff thought with a sigh, *and here I was enjoying a pleasant stroll, thinking today might be at the very least bearable.*

The singers all rushed towards their microphones, all looking fresh, happy, and young.

'Fuck you, fuck you all, you bunch of stupid pricks!' the lead singer, Matthew, screamed back at them from the stage.

What the hell!

"Did he just say what I thought he said?" Susan said in shock.

The girls didn't notice; they just kept screaming incoherently.

"I think he did," Jeff said in disbelief.

"Well, we are going backstage right now," Susan said firmly as she grabbed her two daughters by the collar. "I'm not letting them listen to such filth—and I thought boy bands were meant to be lame anyway?"

"But, *Mum*," Gena whined. But their mother was not having them listen to such bad language, and that was that.

"All right, but . . . hey, Susan?" Jeff asked as he trailed along behind her. "Isn't that El Froggo idiot meant to go on the stage first?"

"Isn't that El Froggo idiot meant to go on stage first?" Mercedes said angrily as she stood by the side of the stage. She was still in a huff about the online trolling fight she'd had with Kirstin from North Hobart.

Sharon looked at her sister and shook her head in wonder; didn't she notice that Matthew had just abused all of the audience? Mercury hadn't noticed either and was watching the band and humming along to the first song.

"Yeah, that is weird," Remi replied, looking around for his brother, Frank, whilst also glancing warily at Mercedes. He didn't hear the abuse either.

Honestly, does anyone pay attention to what the singers say today? Sharon thought, now listening closely to the lyrics being sung.

'Oh yeah, baby, baby. I want you, baby, baby, you're my baby baby baby. Give it to me, girl, oh yeah give it to me all night long, baby—yeah!' Hmmm, maybe they shouldn't bother, Sharon thought.

"You all right, Mercedes?" Remi eventually asked. He was their manager after all, and the well-being of his clients meant the well-being of his bank balance.

"Fine!" Mercedes snapped.

"Well, that is good then," Remi said, trying to sound like he cared, and failing judging by the angry look still on Mercedes' face.

Remi had let the online tweet bitch-fest between her and Kirstin go on for twenty minutes or so, and there was no doubt whatever was said would be re-tweeted around the world in the next thirty minutes.

No such thing as bad publicity, Remi thought, but in hindsight, he had let the fight go on for too long, as the language Mercedes used in response to Kirstin's trolling was quite colourful, but her spelling was absolutely atrocious.

Frank and Brad now came walking briskly towards them, physically dragging El Froggo between them. The international pop star looked different somehow.

"We have a problem," Brad said urgently.

"What do you mean?" Remi replied, looking worriedly at El Froggo, who seemed to be very normal today—a little too normal you might say, timid even.

"What's up, Brad?" Sharon asked.

"This, this is what's up," Brad said and slapped the back of El Froggo's head.

Sharon was surprised at this action, as she had never seen her new boyfriend angry before.

"Hey, don't do that; that hurt, okay?" El Froggo said in a gentle, soft voice whilst he rubbed the back of his head.

"Oh my Lord, he can speak," Sharon said softly. She could now understand why Brad was so angry.

Remi went quiet for a long moment, and his face became very pale.

Here it comes, Sharon thought.

"Are you fucking kidding me!" Remi then shouted.

Mercury was still watching the band, as was Mercedes now, who was still muttering the name 'Kirstin' and 'bitch' under her breath. A young effeminate-looking man now walked tentatively up to both of the sisters and asked for a donation for his charity.

"I thought you were from South America somewhere!" Remi continued shouting. *Or was it Central America?*

Frank thought Remi was going to punch the small-statured man, so he stepped in between the two.

"I never said that, okay? So just lay off, okay," Froggo said nervously from behind Frank's shoulder. "And I'm from New York, okay, and you're giving me a headache with all this shouting, okay?"

Remi now went very red in the face. "No, you never said *anything* at all, did you, *Froggo*? All you did was smash things and try to crash our plane." Then he tried to get closer to Froggo so he could thump the little bastard.

"Settle, Little Brother," Frank said in a non-committal way as he held Remi back.

"I'm sorry, okay?" Froggo was almost crying now. "It's just the stress gets to me sometimes, okay, and I need to, you know . . . relax sometimes, okay?"

"Relax!" Remi said in disbelief. "You call that relaxing!"

"Yes," Froggo whispered.

"Well, what do we do?" Sharon asked, glancing curiously as her two sisters were now talking with three odd-looking charity workers. "He can't go on like that; he would bore everybody to death. And all we were meant to do was be interviewed by Brad and sign autographs and look pretty."

That's all we ever do, Sharon thought in dismay.

Frank was looking thoughtful, but not at the dilemma about El

Froggo's lack of confidence and lack of really heavy drugs fueling his system. He was looking at his boy band performing on stage, especially Matthew, who now had confidence and really heavy drugs fueling his system.

"What!" his brother, Remi, snapped at Frank. "Why are you looking like that?"

Frank shrugged his shoulders at his brother, but now had a big smile on his face. *No such thing as bad publicity*, Frank thought, *and Matthew had to get rid of his reputation as being a wimp after that limp-wristed fight with Grantee-Grant.*

"You didn't flush Froggo's drugs, did you?" Remi said, knowing his brother all too well.

"Nope." Frank smiled.

Jerry McGuiness moved quickly through the audience and towards the side of the stage. *I'm going to save them*, he thought gleefully, but a part of his mind was distracted by the lead singer of Street United Cat Kings jumping around stage like he was a punk rock singer from the 1970s.

'Fuck you, all you teenage bitches!' he screamed to the shocked crowd. *'You're all sheep, do you know that?'*

His fellow boy band members were looking at their lead singer in horror and dancing to their choreographed routine, but Matthew was running around in no particular direction and was even spitting on the front row of the crowd.

'You suck, the whole lot of you suck,' he screamed, whilst the backing track kept playing a song about how a young boy loved his sexy baby girl with all of his sad and lonely heart.

"So rude," Jerry murmured, and then flashed his fake undercover policeman's badge to the security guards at the side of the stage.

"Police business," Jerry said in a deep and manly voice.

"Yeah, go through," one of the security guards said, all the while he never looked at Jerry and was watching the band on stage with his eyes wide and his mouth hanging open.

I'm coming to save you, Jerry thought once more.

Paulo Smythen was talking to Mercury Radonculus with a false smile on his pretty face. The plan was to wait until one of the sisters had to visit Mother Nature in the toilets at the back of the stage and then abduct them, but ever since the three of them arrived in the VIP area, Paulo wanted to get things underway immediately.

I can't wait. I can't wait any longer, Paulo thought frantically. *My fat cousin has all the fun, why can't I?*

"And what charity do you work for?" she asked in her breathless kind of voice as she twirled her shoulder-length hair.

Reginald looked at Mercury curiously for a long moment before muttering "too old" under his breath and continued calmly looking around the room as he occasionally swept his ridiculous comb-over, over his head. Colin, on the other hand, looked terrified; he was also bewildered at Paulo's sudden change of plan.

"Cancer research, of course, Miss Radonculus," Paulo replied politely in a nervous voice.

"That is a wonderful cause," Mercury replied kindly.

"Yes, yes, it is," Paulo stammered.

Why am I so nervous? he thought as his nervousness was now being replaced by his anger and hate. *I am a man now, and she is only a weak fame-whore who doesn't have any talent; just look at her face, just look at her pretty fucking face, pretty boy.*

"Cancer," a harsh voice said. "Well, I don't have cancer, so why should I care?"

That was Mercedes Radonculus, who was the prettiest and also the vainest and nastiest sister; even the reality show editing couldn't hide that fact from the observant viewer. She only cared about herself and what her so-called fans thought of her and had just gone to number one in his mind in regards to kidnapping. Judging by the way Colin was glaring at her, he was in agreement.

"We must prepare for all eventualities," Colin said angrily, then coughed a little. "Cancer affects us all."

"That's bullshit." Mercedes moaned. "Only a few people get cancer."

"A few! There's more than a few! What world or planet do you live on? It's an epidemic," Colin said in shock, then coughed all the more.

Yes, it is definitely Mercedes I want killed, Paulo thought, feeling at the knife in his jacket pocket. *I want to cut someone up this time, that fat fucking cousin of mine has had his day.*

"I would like to donate," sixteen-year-old Mercury said with a pretty smile.

"Well, thanks!" Paulo snapped with a grimace on his own pretty face, which seemed to make Mercury's smile falter a little.

Colin felt at the gun in his pocket, now thinking that Paulo's unusual aggressiveness would end in ruin.

"I didn't mean to make you angry," Mercury said uncertainly.

Well, you fucking did, you pretty little bitch, Paulo thought, now nearing a state of insanity.

Mercury now took a wary step back and away from Paulo.

"Perhaps we better move on," Colin said quietly, grabbing Paulo's arm with his free hand. "C'mon, let's not bother the young lady anymore."

"No, I won't move on," Paulo snarled, shaking off Colin's hand. "I'm sick of moving on; this is my time. Mine!"

Something had indeed just snapped in the eighteen-year-old's mind. He wanted to hurt someone; he wanted to hurt someone badly.

"Mercury, are you all right?" her eldest sister, Sharon, called out from across the room, concerned. Remi and Brad seemed to notice something was wrong as well.

"Yeah, what is wrong with you, why are you being such an arsehole, pretty boy?" Mercedes whined.

Paulo now turned his angry face towards Mercedes.

"You called me a what?" he said in a soft voice, finally bringing out his knife.

"Paulo," Colin said nervously, nearing a state of panic. He slowly took out his gun from his pocket, whilst trying not to cough his lungs up; if he was going to get caught, he was going to kill a lot of people in the process.

Reginald said nothing; he stepped away from the two men and looked around the room with those intense eyes of his.

Where are my girls? he thought. *Where are the ones just for me?*

He stopped still as he focused on the two young girls who had entered the room with what were obviously their parents.

Behind them followed a young man with short brown hair, who had a keen look on his face. The young man immediately gave a start when he saw the father of the girls, and an even bigger start when he saw the men talking to two of the famous sisters.

He's a cop, Reginald thought. *We've been caught out.*

"Halt," the young man with brown hair called out as he brought out his own pistol and aimed it in the two men's direction whilst glancing at Reginald. "You three men stay right where you are."

Yep, he's a cop. But I won't be denied today.

"It's time," Reginald said in that soft voice of his as he stepped farther away from his two cohorts. Then, to his colleagues' surprise, he pointed at Paulo and Colin and yelled at the top of his lungs: "Help us! These two men are here to kidnap the sisters!"

The young man's gun moved towards Reginald.

Victor was sitting in his grey van, looking impatiently down the road in the hope of seeing a red van coming in his direction.

Something has gone wrong, he thought, starting to feel the effects of panic building up. *This was too risky a plan; the sisters are too famous to kidnap. What was I thinking?*

He knew what he was thinking, and he knew what he used to do his thinking.

"Shut up and settle," he snapped as he felt the longing in his loins when he dwelt on the three sisters.

"Just shut up—"

Victor then almost pissed his pants in terror when his mobile phone rang.

"Jesus Christ," he growled as he answered the phone. "Yeah, what do you want? I'm busy."

"What I want is for you to get a large pizza with extra cheese and pepperoni," the caller replied. It was his brother, Bruce.

"Wh-what do you mean?" Victor said, dumfounded. He could only recall one moment when his brother said that and . . .

"You mean it, you want that pizza?" Victor replied. *He knows, somehow Bruce knows. I am in so deep a shit right now.*

His comment was code for when one of the brothers was in

trouble, big trouble. Basically, it meant you had to get the hell out of the immediate vicinity you were in or you were going to jail.

Bruce and Victor had been involved in some minor crime gangs when they were young and stupid. They never got caught, which was why Bruce had a clean record for parliament, but the gang he had been in had secret codes for various situations.

"Yes, and I want it now, right now, at your place," Bruce replied and hung up.

Pizza with extra cheese and pepperoni. It meant run, run for your life. Victor started the van, did a quick U-turn, slammed on the accelerator, and headed back to Hobart.

Sorry, boys, he thought. *Sorry, but you are on your own.*

The two policemen who had him under surveillance watched as he drove towards them.

Jeff Brady had been, to his surprise, enjoying the day, even though the singer from the boy band turned out to be the foulest-mouthed singer he had seen in a long time.

That singer is off his nut, Jeff thought, glancing back at the stage. But as he walked into the backstage area with the VIP access tickets Gena and Fiona had won on a radio show, he suddenly felt the cold stillness of tension in the air. He was a former cop after all and could see from the body language of two of the men talking to two of the Radonculus sisters that something was wrong; something was very wrong.

"Do you see that, Jeff?" Susan asked him in a quiet voice.

Jeff was astounded as he looked over at her worried face. How did Susan Milligan of all people pick up on what was going on? Fiona and Gena looked nervous as well, but only because they were within twenty feet of some of their heroes.

"Oh no, it's them," Susan continued.

"What do you mean, it's—" Jeff started to reply, then realised that the two men closely talking to the sisters were the friends of the one and only Victor Cunnington, whom he had been spying on only days earlier.

"Bloody hell," Jeff muttered. "What are they up to?"

"No good," Susan said as her face turned very cold.

"Halt," the young man suddenly called out from behind them. "You three men stay right where you are."

Three? Did I miss someone?

Jeff turned around behind him and saw that the young man had a gun pointed towards the two strange-looking men.

"Help us!" a man suddenly called out. "These two men are here to kidnap the sisters."

Who was that? Jeff thought, and he then heard someone screaming out in pain.

But Jeff had no more time to think, as he saw the young man point the gun in the direction of whoever had just called out and then immediately fall back to the ground with a bullet hole in the chest.

Paulo Smythen heard Reginald's betrayal just after he heard another man call out loudly for him and his two companions to stay right where they were. The jig was up, he thought, but he didn't care if they were caught and were headed for jail; he didn't care when he heard Colin fire his gun, he didn't care as he stepped forward and stabbed a surprised Mercedes deeply in the stomach; he even didn't care when he slashed a screaming Mercury hard across the face with the same knife. But he did care when a bullet entered his shoulder.

"Fuck . . . someone shot me," he cried out as he fell to the ground and as the pain of the bullet wound coursed through his body, a tiny bit of sanity entered his thoughts.

I killed her, he thought as he looked at one of the sisters lying still on the ground. The eldest sister, Chardonnay, was kneeling over her sister, wailing in grief.

"You're a fucking dead man," someone with dark hair and a widow's peak hairline screamed as they stood over him. Paulo then felt that man kick him hard in the ribs. Another man with a similar hairline now stood over him as well and did the exact same thing.

Grunting in pain from the two hard kicks, Paulo looked over at the massive crowd watching the gruesome event. Some were crying, some were running in no particular direction, but most were holding their mobile phones in the air and videoing the whole incident.

Vultures, he thought, but he himself was worse than a vulture, he, like his cousin, was now a murderer.

Security guards and a few policemen had now replaced the two angry men and were standing over him, looking down with cold faces, the latter with guns in their hands; none of them made any attempt to attend his wounds. Paulo laughed at their cold demeanor and winced once more at the pain in his shoulder.

They are just fame-whores, he thought in contempt. *Why be so upset about simple TV-fodder such as these?*

He looked over to his left and saw the youngest sister, Mercury, who was now sitting up and trembling as a handsome man with short blond hair and a chiseled chin was bandaging half of her face.

She's not so pretty now, he thought viciously and felt a strong wave of pleasure that came with that thought.

"Brad, I can't see out of one eye," Mercury cried out.

"It's just the blood and the swelling," Brad said softly. "Just be brave."

"Where is Mercedes?" Mercury asked.

"Just be brave," Brad said again, glancing at her dead sister. Mercury then burst into tears.

You're not so pretty anymore, are you? Paulo thought again. *You should be thanking me for the scar, not crying.*

He looked over to his right and saw Colin lying dead on the floor with a bullet hole straight in his forehead.

That was either a lucky shot or an unusually gifted one.

He then looked around for the other man in their little group and was surprised that he couldn't see him.

Where's that traitor Reginald? he thought.

Jeff felt and heard the sound of a bullet being fired so close to him, and as the young man fell to the ground, he swiveled quickly back towards the two men and brought out his own gun. He had years of training as a policeman, so he was prepared for all situations. He was prepared when he saw a frail-looking man who had obviously fired the gun fall down dead with a bullet hole in his forehead, he was prepared when he shot the effeminate-looking man who had just stabbed two of the sisters in the shoulder, but he was not prepared at all when he saw Susan standing next to him with her own gun in her hands.

"Did . . . did you just shoot the first guy?" he stammered whilst looking around the room for any other threats.

He watched as people ran, screaming madly, in all directions, but his mind was mostly focused on his secretary.

Something is wrong, he thought.

"Yes," she said softly. She seemed just as shocked as him.

Jeff noticed that Susan was holding the gun in the exact same position he held his own.

Jeff, something is wrong.

"Did your husband teach you that?" he asked, ignoring the voice in his head.

"Yes," she replied again. She looked very pale, and her hands were shaking, and her eyes had not moved from the dead body lying on the floor.

"It was a good shot," he said.

"He was a good teacher," she replied, still staring numbly at the body.

Jeff, wake up! his mind raged.

Jeff looked around him again, and like an alarm bell, the answer rang out through his mind.

"Susan," he said, "where are the girls?"

Susan's blue eyes snapped towards him, and there was a look of panic in her eyes, but there was something else, something that seemed to be very cold.

Constables Eric Woods and Razan Hussein looked on as Victor Cunnington turned his vehicle around and headed back in their direction.

"He looks in a hurry," Razan said, frowning.

"What do we do?" Eric exclaimed.

"We can't pull him over; he hasn't done anything yet," Razan replied now, through gritted teeth.

"Do we follow him?" Eric asked.

"I don't know," Razan said uncertainly.

"What!" Eric said in surprise. "Look, you make the decisions, and I just follow, all right? That's how we do things."

Eric always let Razan take the lead; they were both of equal rank, but Razan had the leadership skills out of the two.

Victor's grey van was getting closer, and it was travelling fast.

"His accomplices may still come this way," Razan said, wiping a hand over his face.

"But we don't know that," Eric replied, "and he is breaking the speed limit now, so we can pull him over."

He was really giving it to that old van, Razan thought. *Perhaps I could just pull him over and check to see what he has in the back.*

Victor's van now reached them and then quickly continued on back towards Hobart.

"We could, Eric, but I'm sure the others were up to something," Razan said, looking back as Victor's grey van drove off into the distance.

"I think you are right," Eric said, now looking straight ahead.

"Why is that?" Razan said, looking at his partner.

"Here comes that red van again," Eric said.

Razan's eyes snapped forward as he looked down the road and saw the same red van from Hobart racing towards them.

"It's moving very fast," Razan said.

"What do you expect with a van colour like that?" Eric replied.

"Do you always have to make jokes?" Razan asked.

"Not always."

"You ready then?" Razan said to his partner.

"You bet your sweet arse I am." Eric grinned.

"I could have done without that last comment." Razan sighed as he started up their vehicle.

Eric chuckled a little, but checked to see his pistol was where it should be and made sure his seat belt was on as Razan slowly moved his car into the middle of the road.

Susan was screaming her daughters' names as she raced out of the backstage area. Jeff was only half a step behind her.

Where are they? he thought worriedly. *Did they panic when they saw the killings; did they panic when they saw their own mother shoot and kill that man?*

People were still running around looking for some sort of safety, but here, at the back of the concert stage, thankfully, there weren't as many people around.

"Fiona, Gena!" Susan screamed once more.

"They may not have come this way," Jeff said to her.

They weren't in the backstage VIP area, or if they were, they were hiding from their mother, as she was screaming so loud there was no way they wouldn't have heard her. But it was possible that they had run back out to the front of the stage. If that was what they had done, they would not be able to find them quickly, for thousands of members of the audience were still listening to the band, oblivious to what had just happened backstage.

Those poor girls, Jeff thought, thinking of the famous sisters. But he had these other sisters to find.

"They had to come this way," Susan said, sounding terrified. "They saw what I did and panicked."

And why do you carry a gun? Jeff thought.

"Perhaps we should split up," Jeff said.

"Maybe. That's a good—"

"Mum!" they heard someone call out. It was one of Susan's daughters, running towards them. She had a bruise already on her face, as well as trickles of blood running down her legs.

"Gena!" Susan cried out and ran desperately towards her thirteen-year-old daughter. "Where is your sister?" she said as she wrapped Gena in her arms.

"She's in a van, a red one," Gena said as tears ran down her face. "A man grabbed us when the guns started firing. I managed to get away, but he took Fi, Mum! He took her."

"What man?" Susan asked in a hard voice, which made her daughter flinch a little.

"You three men stay right where you are."

Jeff knew who the weird-looking third man was; he had seen him before, with Victor.

"Get in the car, now!" Jeff shouted.

The red van didn't slow down as it travelled down the highway. In fact, when it saw the car in its way, it sped up and tried to go around Razan's vehicle. So the policemen quickly moved their own vehicle towards the red van and rammed it off the side of the road and into the adjoining pastures. The result was both vehicles being totaled and all occupants now being completely dazed.

"Was that the right thing to do?" Eric mumbled as he tried to undo his seat belt and get out of the car.

"I'm not sure," Razan said, then winced and felt at the back of his neck. "This could be my job if I rammed an innocent citizen off the road."

There could be anyone in that van, Razan realised. He really needed to control his temper sometimes.

The red van had spun four times in a three hundred sixty-degree circle when it was struck by Razan's vehicle, but fortunately for all involved, it had not rolled over.

"Could be mine too."

Eric now saw another vehicle drive up and skid to a halt. A woman rushed out of the car, then a young girl, and then . . .

"Is that Jeff Brady?" Eric said in shock.

"It is," Razan replied as he tried to open his car door. "Bloody thing," he muttered as he slammed his shoulder into the now-damaged door.

The woman now ripped open the back of the van, and a young girl, looking bruised and sore, jumped out and into her arms.

The other young girl joined them, and they all hugged each other in a family embrace.

"That's nice to see," Eric said groggily, "but I am still stuck."

"So am I," Razan said angrily, as he continued to ram the car door in an attempt to open it.

Jeff Brady glanced curiously at them and then took his gun out from his jacket pocket as he moved to the front out of the red vehicle.

"Bloody hell, he is doing my job," Razan growled.

He felt like an idiot now, being stuck in the car like this.

A middle-aged man with a bad comb-over climbed gingerly out of the red van. He had a bloodied face from the collision and was looking in confusion at their surroundings.

He looks as dazed as I feel, Razan thought.

Jeff Brady now trained his gun on the man. Razan could hear

Jeff tell him clearly to put his hands behind his head and to get down on his knees.

Definitely an ex-policeman, Razan thought in approval.

"Knees!" they heard the mother now scream. "I'll show him some bloody knees!" And before anybody could protest, Susan Milligan walked up to the kidnapper, brought out her own gun, and shot Reginald Yeasmith once in each kneecap.

Jeff Brady looked on in horror and then went to say something to his friend, but looking at the sight of her angry face, he wisely thought better of it.

The ex-policeman also knows the wisdom of never getting in the way of an angry mother protecting her child, Razan thought, thinking about his own dear wife who would do anything to protect their three boys.

"Well, you don't see that every day," Eric said as he watched the man writhe on the ground in agony.

"We should," Razan said softly, as he finally managed to open the car door. "With people who hurt children, we should see it all the time."

But despite what the public wanted, he was a policeman; the law was the law, and vigilantes meant chaos, so after finally getting out of his vehicle, he arrested Reginald Yeasmith, and then reluctantly arrested Susan Milligan as well.

Hobart, Tasmania

Bruce Cunnington walked as quickly as he could towards his brother's house. His mind was racing, screaming almost, with what Brook Raller had told him.

'Your brother is a serial killer,' Raller said. 'He and his associates have been involved in at least six deaths that we know of.'

'My brother wouldn't have done that,' Bruce said in anger. 'Someone must have set him up.'

'Your brother was the one who did the killing,' Raller said calmly. 'He cut those girls into pieces.'

Bruce immediately thought of Henry Abel's death on the news, and how his head seemed to be cut into pieces as well.

"This is messed up," Bruce muttered as he took one last drag on his cigarette and stubbed it out on the street path.

Victor had brought shame on his family. Their mother would die of a broken heart if she found out; their father would turn in his grave if he knew. And most important of all, Bruce's political future would be ruined.

"Victor, open up," Bruce said as he knocked on his door.

Victor, who looked very similar to Bruce in appearance, albeit even fatter, soon opened the door. He looked terrified, and his eyes darted around as if expecting policemen to arrest him at any moment.

"Can I come in?" Bruce said grumpily. "Unless, of course, you expect me to discuss your *predicament* on your front doorstep?"

"Yes," Victor said as he quivered, his extra chins wobbling with nervousness. "Come in, Brother, come in."

Bruce followed his brother into his kitchen. Victor sat down with a heavy thump on the breakfast table chair, whilst Bruce looked around for some food to eat.

"So," Bruce eventually said, his hands clenching into fists, "it appears you and your friends have an unusual hobby."

"How-how did you know?" Victor stammered.

"I have some powerful friends," Bruce replied, took a very large cold chicken out of the fridge, and placed it on an equally large plate on the table. "They have been watching you for over a year now."

"A year!" Victor said in shock.

"Yes, over a year," Bruce snapped. "They said nothing to the authorities, as they wanted to protect me."

Bruce's Holophone rang for an incoming text message.

'Check the news,' was all the message said.

Bruce switched the Holophone over to the latest news.

'Mercedes Radonculus was murdered today by a man armed with a knife. The man is believed to be Paulo Smythen, cousin of politician Bruce Cunnington. Mercury Radonculus was also attacked . . .'

"Here, eat some bloody chicken," Bruce growled and almost threw the large plate at his brother.

"What am I going to do?" Victor babbled as he started wolfing down large chunks of the chicken. "You can fix this, Brother," he now mumbled. "You can make things right with your powerful friends."

Yes, he could make things right, but did he really want to?

"Why did you do these *things*?" Bruce had to ask. Victor had shown no psychopathic tendencies when he was younger that he knew of, nor had Paulo, who had once been a nice young kid.

"I don't know," Victor mumbled, as he took another huge bite of the chicken. "It was fun, I guess."

"Fun?" Bruce said as he shook his head. "And our cousin Paulo thought it was fun too?"

"Yes." Victor smiled, with grease now running down his fat face and chicken all in his teeth. "He is just like me; he likes to have fun."

"Oh, well, we all like some fun, don't we, Brother?" Bruce said, then waited for his gluttonous brother to take another huge bite of chicken and slapped his back, hard.

Victor lurched forward from the strength of that slap, the breath leaving his mouth instantly, and then automatically being sucked back in just as quickly. He started choking on the large amount of food he still had in his mouth.

"Choking, are we?" Bruce said angrily, and then clamped one of his huge hands under Victor's chin and another on top of his head and started pushing them towards each other.

"This is fun, isn't it?" Bruce grunted as he grappled with his brother, who was struggling desperately to breathe. "Lots of fun causing pain and terror, isn't it, Victor? Those girls you cut up must have had *so* much fun."

The two huge brothers fought desperately with each other. Victor was trying to lift his brother's hands from around his head as his brother pushed downwards, but only Bruce was able to breathe, and very soon Victor's face began turning a dark shade of purple. Bruce was also using his huge body weight to crush his brother against the table, just as Victor had crushed the prostitutes he killed.

"I want to be Premier," Bruce said with gritted teeth as his brother's hands tried to pry open his fingers, "and I can't if you are around for someone to bribe me over."

Bill Cooper had planned to do just that, he was told, but his friends in The Cabal had taken care of that problem.

"I won't have you, or anybody else, stand in my way," he continued. "Not you, my cousin, or anybody."

There was a madness in Bruce. He may well believe his brother and cousin were the evil ones, but Bruce had the same genes.

"Anybody," Bruce muttered once more.

Sweat was now pouring down from Bruce's face; he had not exercised like this for—well, ever, really.

Finally, Victor's struggles began to subside, and after another minute of holding his brother's jaw shut, Bruce let him go, and Victor slumped lifelessly forward onto the kitchen table with a loud thud.

Bruce then checked to see that there weren't any scratches or bruises underneath his brother's chin and on top of his head or on his own fingers. There weren't. He would pay off any corrupt coroner or policeman anyway, if they started asking too many questions. He knew of quite a few.

"Well, here goes some more exercise," Bruce muttered and lifted his now-dead brother's body and started performing the Heimlich maneuver. "At least bruise, you bastard," he grunted, hoping that he might crack his brother's ribs. "I want the cops to see that I tried."

I couldn't save him, Bruce thought in his mind as he prepared the lies he was to tell the police. *He just choked to death right before my very eyes.* Bruce could now smell the rest of the chicken still sitting on the table. He started to salivate as he squeezed hard under his dead brother's ribcage.

Canberra, Mainland Australia

It had been a long, successful day of debate and boredom as Senators Braiths and Howles sat alone in one of the bars at Parliament House, drinking and watching the television.

'In a day of dramatic news, firstly, we reported on the gruesome death of renowned scientist Henry Abel, who was found tied up and mutilated in an underpass. This was followed later on that very afternoon by the horrific stabbing of reality star Mercedes Radonculus and the terrible facial injuries to her sister Mercury in the same attack. And it is now believed that Tasmanian politician Bruce Cunnington's own cousin Paulo

Smythen was the man who killed Mercedes, along with three other accomplices, including Bruce Cunnington's own brother, Victor. And in another twist to this story, Victor Cunnington himself was found dead this evening after choking to death on a large piece of chicken . . .'

"Chicken!" Natalie said in shock and almost spilt her drink all over her power suit. "Who would have thought Bruce, of all people, would have been so inventive," she said now in hushed tones. "I need to contact Johan Franz and Brandon Townsworth to calm these stories down a little."

Chicken! The fat man used a chicken! she thought in wonder.

"You know, Natalie, I think we could have changed the country's entire constitution today with all that has happened," Howles replied quietly with a shake of his head.

Chicken! Bruce used a chicken! he thought in amazement.

"Instead, we had to listen to the Opposition drone on about people's rights to privacy, even though they secretly agree with us," Natalie replied.

That happened so many times in parliament that she couldn't keep count. The Opposition parties always complained about a new law or economic package that they actually agreed with.

Perhaps that is why we have become a nation of complainers, she thought. *Perhaps the people picked this up from their elected leaders.*

"Well, we still have the last part of our laws to pass through the senate, and then we can finally have a look through these Holophones to see what we can find," Natalie said with a careful look around her to make sure the bartender was not within earshot.

"Yes, but after today's events, what can we come up with that will keep the public's attention away from us?" Howles said with a frown, as he watched dozens of people running quickly down the corridor. "It would have to be something earth-shattering, I think."

And why are those IT people running like that?

Aiden Wilkinson now walked into the bar with a look of puzzlement on his young face.

"Senator, I think we may have found a new distraction," he said quietly, also glancing to see if the bartender was well away from overhearing them.

"What do you mean?" Howles asked, leaning forward in his chair.

"Has someone else died?" Natalie asked keenly. "I didn't think there was anybody else left to die. Who has died now, Aiden? I need a good laugh."

"It's not that," Wilkinson said with a shrug of his shoulders. "It's just . . ."

"Just what?" Howles prompted.

"Well, the IT people are in a bit of a flap at the moment," Wilkinson replied. "I was talking to Axel Rigozzi a few days ago about how they were going to fix up the problem with the Enter key on the government's computers."

"Yeah, so?" Natalie frowned. "What does a computer problem have to do with us?" It didn't really bother her; she barely touched any computers nowadays.

"Well, they put through a 'fix' for this problem about an hour ago," Wilkinson continued.

"Look, will you get to the point, Aiden." Howles sighed. "It's been a very tiring day."

"The fix didn't work, sir," Wilkinson replied formally. "In fact, the other Enter key on the keyboard no longer works, along with the computer mouse."

Senator Howles and Braiths were very tired, but they very quickly worked out the implications of this event.

"Are you telling me that all the government computers around the country no longer work?" Howles said in disbelief.

"That all the Call Centres and processing work of twenty thousand public service employees will be put on hold?" Natalie added with a look of incredulity.

"Everything stops, Senators; the whole government service will grind to a sudden halt, and, of course, the public will get very irate," Wilkinson replied. "At least until we can fix the problem . . . again."

Howles looked at Natalie, then quickly drank the last of his drink and slammed the glass down on the bar.

"Quick, Natalie," Howles said urgently. "I'll arrange for a senate sitting tomorrow."

"I'll arrange the fifth part of our plan," Natalie said, as she followed him out of the bar.

Well, what do you know, Wilkinson thought as he watched the senators race out of the room. *The wheels of politics do move fast sometimes.*

He now needed to discuss the events of today with O'Sullivan and Raller and the other ASIO agents at one of their private meetings.

Sydney, Mainland Australia

McLaren sat at home in his expensive Sydney house, in despair at what the news reporter said was the tragic death of Henry Abel. And indeed it was a tragic death to McLaren, a tragedy for the entire human race.

"We had such good plans," he muttered as he contemplated his mentor's horrible death only a few days ago. "We were trying to save the world."

McLaren had gone to Henry Abel's laboratory in the hope of finding some answers, and he soon found them all right. He found the security guard named Richards pointing a gun at his head and telling him to hand over his security card access and to never come back again. All the while Richards told him this, he had a blank look on his face, which seemed to totally contradict the intensity of the words he was saying.

"Something was wrong with him," McLaren said to himself, but he wouldn't go back there to find out what. He had a very strong feeling that if he went back there, he would be killed instantly. He had thought about calling the cops and telling them about the laboratory, but that would lead to questions being asked, and some of those questions may have led back to McLaren himself.

"I guess I need to find a new partner," McLaren said despondently.

"Yes, you do," a clown image said, suddenly appearing on his TV screen and making McLaren almost scream in fear.

"What are you doing here?" he squeaked. "How do you know who I am?"

"Oh, McLaren, or Biggus Walker I should say,"—McShane chuckled—"I knew who you and Henry Abel truly were all this time."

"Then . . . wh-what do you want?" McLaren stammered. "And how the bloody hell did you just suddenly appear on my TV screen like that?"

"I have spying technologies that have inspired even your own government," she replied cryptically.

What? McLaren thought in confusion.

"But I just wanted you to know that I have been greatly influenced by your late friend McDermott," she continued. "And his studies on the brain and the tardigrades were *fascinating*."

"You-you know about that?" McLaren said in shock.

"Of course." McShane giggled. "And should you ever need me in the future, I will be there for you."

"That is . . . very kind of you to say," McLaren replied.

Please go away, he thought.

"Good luck with finding a new partner too," McShane said. "Hopefully you won't find someone as mean and horrible as McCredie," she finished in a disgusted tone and then disappeared from the screen.

"Who was that on the TV, Dad?" a young boy with blond hair said, coming into the room wiping at his tired eyes. "It looked like a clown."

McLaren's ex-wife had allowed his son to stay with him over the school holidays.

"Just a . . . friend of mine, Sev," McLaren said as he put an arm around his teenage son's shoulder to comfort him, and to his embarrassment, be comforted by his son as well. "Just a friend," he murmured.

McLaren moved house the next day, but he threw the TV outside that night.

When is she going to call? It's been a few days already.

"Oh, c'mon, man," the caller said angrily. "Paulo Smythen killed Mercedes Radonculus and was said to be closely involved with his cousin Victor Cunnington, who allegedly murdered all those prostitutes in Hobart, and who, by the way, is the politician Bruce Cunnington's own brother. And then Victor suddenly dies on the same day by choking to death. That's bullshit! This is all a cover-up, man, a black fucking flag for the number of privacy changes in the Senate, man!"

"Yeah, it does look suspicious and uncool, I must say, dude," Johan Franz replied. "But this is all hearsay; there is no proof that this was a black flag operation."

It did look suspicious, Franz had to agree, but one of his directives from Braiths was to keep the callers saying the term black flag. As soon as you did that, the majority would lose interest and call you a conspiracy theorist nutjob.

Bruce Cunnington himself, though, seemed to be applying the woe-is-me tactic to get the public back onside. He looked like he was about to cry every time he was interviewed. And he was being interviewed a lot. The word 'courageous' and the phrases 'he is not perfect' and 'he is one of us' seemed to be used a lot by the media now when describing him.

I wonder if that will work, Johan thought. *With the media onside, he just may survive this.*

"No proof!" the caller said in exasperation. "How more black flag could it be? Here, you mindless drones called the public, look at all of these spectacular deaths on the TV whilst I take your rights away behind your back."

"So you think it was a black flag?" Johan asked.

"Are you freaking deaf?" the caller shouted. "I just said it was. It's the blackest black flag I have ever seen."

Is there such a thing as blackest black?

"And how black is the blackest black flag?"

"What is wrong with you, man? Stop saying black flag; are you wasted or something?" the caller said, then hung up.

"Next caller," Johan said.

"Light refraction," a male caller said.

"What?" Johan replied confused.

"Light refraction," the caller said again.

"What do you mean?"

"Light refraction is the key to everything. It is the layer that protects all of the truths of our world and beyond. Scientists acknowledge it, and ignore it at the same time."

"I still don't know what you mean, dude. Is this something to do with, you know, black flags?"

"No, this is to do with the pre-programmed computers giving you the incorrect, but also, the expected and wanted answers in the search for the so-called truth."

"Computers?" Johan said even more confused.

"Just look up into the sky, everything our eyes tell our brain is a lie, just as it is with telescopes. I have to go now, they are watching me." the caller said, then hung up.

I bet they are, Johan thought tiredly.

"Next caller, please," he said trying not to sigh.

"Did you notice?" a female caller now asked.

At last she is here, Johan thought.

"Notice what?" he asked.

"The chicken."

"The what?" Johan replied, dumbfounded. Braiths was supposed to say something stupid over the radio . . . but a chicken?

"The chicken is indeed the symbol of The Cabal," the caller replied. "The chicken choking was a sign that Victor Cunnington had defied The Cabal and needed to die."

Johan was now nearly choking himself.

Chicken choking! Is she fucking serious?

"Well, umm, what did he know exactly?" Johan asked.

"He knew that his brother, Bruce Cunnington, was part of The Cabal, who had intentions of creating the greatest black flag that the world had ever seen . . ."

And so Johan had to listen tiredly to many callers over the coming weeks that were hired by Natalie Braiths to ring up and say the words 'black flag' as much as humanly possible.

The public soon lost interest in the connection between Paulo Smythen, Bruce Cunnington, and Victor Cunnington's chicken choking, not that they were that interested to begin with.

Conspiracy theories were, of course, only for nutters, after all.

The security guard known as Richards, who was once a strong man both physically and mentally, was now struggling desperately in his very own mind.

I have to get out of here, he thought as a giant battle raged across his brain. *I am a free man. I am not a slave.*

He was now walking very slowly up the stairwell to freedom. He had been instructed by those evil little children to protect and feed them, along with Lia Read, Lloyd, and Holding, and to never leave them, but days later, his own mind had finally rebelled, and he was now making a desperate grab for freedom. *Keep going, Richards*, he told himself, *one step followed by another.*

"Where is he?" he heard a little girl's voice say from below.

No, no no, Richards thought despairingly. *Leave me alone, evil child, just leave me be.*

"Who?" another child said.

"Richards," the girl replied. "He has—oh, there he is."

Richards had cut into Abel's head on the command of the children; he had betrayed his boss and acted like an animal. *That poor man*, he thought. *He conducted experiments on the others, but he didn't deserve to die in agony like that, and then they made Lloyd and Holding kill all of the other captives.*

"Richards, come back down here," the little girl said with that cute lisp in her voice. "You are a very naughty boy."

Richards kept walking slowly up the stairs.

Rainbow slapped her tiny hands together, causing Richards to automatically look over his shoulder.

"Come here," she said firmly once she had caught his eyes.

Try as he might to continue walking up the stairs to freedom, Richards could now no longer move forward, and as he slowly turned around to begin his descent back into his very own prison, he saw the complete whiteness in the girl-child's eyes.

"I hate you," he managed to say as he reached her.

One of the other children, Klusta, laughed at this comment.

"So?" The little three-year-old girl shrugged.

Sharon stood silently with her arm around her injured sister as the coffin carrying Mercedes was lowered into the ground. Brad and Remi stood at a respectable distance away from them. Both of the men seemed just as devastated as the sisters.

"I have to find a new name," Mercury said softly.

"What?" Sharon said with a concerned look at her sister.

Mercury looked up at her sister, revealing the scar that went from her chin to her hairline, and the blind eye on the right side of her face.

"I need a new name, just like yours, Sharon, for a new beginning," Mercury replied.

She was really breaking Sharon's heart; Mercury was only sixteen years of age, but had a sadness about her now that Sharon thought would take years to get over, if she ever did at all.

"Yes, a new name would be nice," Sharon said, hugging her sister tighter.

"But where will we live?" Mercury asked.

"We will live somewhere private, a huge tower maybe, somewhere where nobody can see us," Sharon said firmly. "Just you and me, no more cameras, no more fans and fakeness, just peace and quiet and anonymity."

"And Brad." Mercury smiled, making half of her face crinkle up tightly.

"And Brad, of course," Sharon said, blushing.

Brad had announced today, to the media's horror, that he would be retiring from the entertainment business. Like Sharon, he had had enough of the fame game.

'There are people who may be upset by me doing this,' he had confided in her, 'but there is always someone in the wings to take over.'

'Just like my reality show,' Sharon replied, thinking about the new Bourgeois Sisters being groomed by Remi.

'Yes, exactly,' Brad said with a sad sigh. 'We are expendable, Sharon; we are just products to make money.'

The sisters watched silently as fresh earth was now thrown over Mercedes' coffin.

I will look after you, Sharon thought protectively of her little sister, *and you and I will get through this.*

And with the money they had secured through their now-defunct reality show, the sisters did go into a semi-reclusive lifestyle, and the fickle public, after spending a brief time being fascinated about all the trauma they had been through, eventually forgot all about them and moved on to other reality stars. But the sisters did choose to live in the centre of Sydney; in fact, they lived in a well-protected tower block just across the busy street from the underground hidden laboratory of the late and renowned scientist Henry Abel.

"Well, I am glad we are all back as a family again," Martin Marsh said as he sat in front of the fire on the most comfortable lounge room chair. "Just the four of us, the way it was meant to be." His granddaughters were sitting quietly on the floor beside their grandfather with their heads resting against his knees. For the moment, they no longer looked at their mobile phones and wondered what their friends were up to every five minutes of the day; they were quiet for the most part and just wanted to stay indoors in the shelter of their own home. Their grandfather was stroking both of their hair tenderly whilst looking like he wanted to burst out crying.

"The young man who was initially shot was never mentioned on the news," Jeff said quietly to Susan.

"I know. He just disappeared," Susan replied just as quietly. Unbeknownst to them, Jerry McGuiness was now in a Canberra hospital with wounds to his chest, and more importantly, his career. He would soon be transferred to another city and work in an office from now on. He would never work as a spy again. Jeff Brady now paused for a moment to give himself time to think. He really didn't want to talk about this touchy subject, but a part of him knew he had to.

"That man won't ever be able to ever walk again properly, you know," he said quietly to Susan.

"So?" Susan replied, her expression hard, as he had sometimes seen it lately.

"The judge allowed us bail because of all that had happened," Jeff replied with a glance at Susan's daughters, "but you shot and killed a man, no matter how bad he was, and you could . . . you know."

"Go to jail like my husband," Susan said in a soft voice.

"Yes," Jeff said in frustration. "Who would look after the girls then, their grandfather?"

Susan Milligan looked at her old father and sighed. He would look after them, she had no doubt, but it was a heavy burden for an old man to look after two willful young teenagers.

"You would help him," Susan said, looking directly at him.

Jeff sighed; he knew he would help the old man look after them if it came to that.

"This whole thing stinks to high heaven, Susan," Jeff continued. "Is there anything I need to know?"

"No. No, there isn't, Jeff," Susan replied, now looking at her two daughters. "And if there was anything I was involved in . . . well, let's just say that it's all done and dusted."

"Are you sure, Susan?" Jeff asked uncertainly.

"Yes, I am sure," Susan replied firmly and smiled to make Jeff feel better.

It didn't.

He was a policeman in his heart, and he knew something was really wrong with all that had just taken place. He had talked to the two constables who were there at the kidnapping, and they agreed that this whole event was full of holes. Who had told Bill Cooper about Victor Cunnington's murders to begin with? Who killed Bill Cooper? Where did that young man who was shot disappear to? Why didn't the media mention him? Had Bruce Cunnington then killed his brother to protect his career?

It was enough to do Jeff's head in. He would never believe that Victor simply choked to death on the same day that the reality show sisters were attacked by his friends.

"You know, due to the publicity my daughter has received in shooting that bastard's kneecaps off, she is a bit of a hero with the everyday public," Martin Marsh said suddenly with a look of pride on his face. "The public, and more importantly, the media, is right behind her. She will avoid jail time, mark my words."

Damn, the old codger was listening the whole time.

"I hope so, and she *has* become a hero," Jeff agreed. "In fact, we have received quite a few new callers requesting our services."

"Is that so?" Martin said, chuckling. "Perhaps you should change your business name to 'The Kneecappers'."

"Umm, I don't think that is a good idea." Jeff grinned.

I wonder if the father has a criminal record too.

"Lots of big fat blubbery extramarital affairs, I believe," Susan said with a small grin at her father. "Jeff can't wait to watch."

"Yeah." Jeff sighed. He wasn't smiling any longer. In fact, he felt a bit ill.

The Tasmanian Midlands

Roger Tyson gave a sad sigh as he talked to the two constables who had informed him that his nephew Terry could not be found.

What would his father and mother say if they knew? Roger thought. *I promised my brother when he passed that I would look after him.*

"You say he was acting strange?" Constable Hussein asked.

"Yes, he was," Roger replied. "Well, more than usual anyway."

"Was he depressed about losing his job?" Constable Woods asked.

Roger gathered his thoughts for a moment and saw through the dark cloud of grief.

"He has not taken his own life, if that is what you are suggesting, Constable!" Roger snapped.

"We have to ask these questions," Hussein replied formally. "We do need to consider all possibilities."

"Yes, yes, I know, and I apologise," Roger muttered, feeling a little ashamed of his outburst. "Terry was lazy and self-opinionated, and also had a cocky nature, but he wouldn't have committed suicide, I assure you."

"Well, we will let you know if anything else turns up," Constable Woods replied.

Terry, Roger thought sadly.

Just as the two policemen walked back to their vehicle, another car drove up towards the house.

The two policemen froze in shock as the big figure of Bruce Cunnington got out of the vehicle.

"What the hell does *he* want?" Roger said softly.

"Gentlemen," Bruce said with a friendly wave of his hand as he walked past the two shell-shocked policemen.

"I never thought I would see you again," Roger said as Bruce walked up to his doorstep.

"Me neither," Bruce replied, glancing back at the policemen, who were still riveted to the spot. "But I have come again to offer my services," he continued.

"Your services?" Roger said in shock. "In regards to what?"

"Politics, my friend." Bruce grinned. "My State electorate is

Lyons, and you want to run as a Fed for this Electorate as well."

"As an Independent, Bruce," Roger replied. "Not for your, or any other, political party."

Bruce chuckled at this comment and shook his fat head condescendingly. "That is a hard road, Roger," he said. "As I have told you before, it may take you years to win the seat. But our party has not won this electorate in decades, and my people in Canberra would like to see this seat lost to the government, so I have been told to offer you all the assistance you need if you simply join our party."

They think I am a threat, Roger thought, astounded. *They think I might be a chance.*

"You hate Independents, don't you?" Roger asked.

"You are nothing," Bruce said contemptuously.

Liar, Roger thought.

"Anyway, I don't know whether you are a good man to seek assistance from, as people tend to die around you," he said, thinking of the arrogant Henry Abel and Bruce's psychopathic brother, Victor.

"And you," Bruce snapped back angrily. "People die around *you*; where is your nephew, hey?"

Roger felt like he had been punched in the stomach.

"I-I," he stammered.

"He's dead," Bruce said with a heartless smile.

Roger looked at the large politician for a long moment.

"You didn't . . . you didn't," Roger stumbled, knowing that Bruce had gotten his nephew fired from his old job.

"Didn't what?" Bruce snapped.

"Terry . . ." Roger couldn't think straight.

"No, I didn't murder *him*," Bruce said with the hidden meaning showing clearly in his eyes.

He did it, Roger thought. *He murdered his own brother.*

"Get off my land, murderer," he finally managed to say.

"Oh, another horrible lie about my dear deceased brother," Bruce said as his fat face crumpled into sadness and he wiped a crocodile tear from his eye. "I tried to save him; why do people persecute me so?"

Bruce Cunnington then gave him an almost friendly smile and

turned and walked back to his self-driven vehicle, waving amiably to the two policemen, who still hadn't left.

Terry, Roger thought again and wiped a real tear from his eye, *I am so sorry.*

Hobart Prison

The prison door slammed shut, and Paulo Smythen huddled nervously in the corner of the lower bunk bed, which would be his home for the next decade or so.

"My, oh my, you are such a pretty sight," a deep voice said from the above bunk bed.

Paulo flinched; he hadn't even been aware there was another person in the room.

"Who are you?" Paulo said nervously.

"I am a man who wants to know where Reginald Yeasmith is," the deep voice replied. "I have been following him very keenly in the news, shall we say."

The man with the deep voice now jumped off the top bunk with a loud thud as his big shoes hit the floor.

Paulo flinched again as he looked up and saw a huge bald-headed man with tree trunks for arms and tattoos all over his body looking down at him.

"Now where is he?" the man demanded.

"I don't know," Paulo said in a quivering voice. "He is a pedo, so perhaps he is in a different area."

"Of course." The big man grimaced. "Those cunts get protection where the children they violate don't."

"Yeah, it's a messed-up world," Paulo said, giving him a groveling smile.

"Yeah, it is, isn't it?" the big man replied with a smile that didn't reach his eyes. "A world where young famous girls get stabbed and cut up."

Shit, I am a dead man, Paulo thought.

"And what are you in here for?" Paulo risked asking.

"None of your fucking business," the big man snapped, "and I ask the fucking questions here, not you."

"Of course, of course," Paulo replied timidly, "and . . . and how long till you get out?"

"Ten years, pretty boy, ten years till the big day arrives in 2044 and I get my arse back into the real world," he replied with a thoughtful look at the young man.

Pretty boy! Normally Paulo would be upset at being called that, but not today, not with this man.

"If you really want to know, I was a standover man," the big man suddenly said. "It was good fun for a while, except my last job got a bit out of hand, and one person was accidentally killed when his head fell off."

Paulo was about to laugh, but then, looking at the huge, muscled man, he wisely decided not to.

"That's a tough job," Paulo said, trying to ingratiate himself to his new cell mate.

"It is," the big man said as he swelled his chest in pride. "I may not be as tough and resourceful as my wife, but it was a hard life out there."

His wife! What the hell did his wife do for a living?

"Do you like cutting people?" the big man asked.

Should I lie? Paulo thought. *No, he knew what I did, as it's all over the media.*

"I love it," Paulo replied honestly, thinking of the now-dead Mercedes Radonculus, who had grunted in the most satisfying way when he stabbed her in the stomach, and her sister Mercury, who screamed in agony when he slashed her face.

I do love it, he thought, almost getting aroused at the memory.

"Good," the big man replied, "for I am in need of another inmate who likes to hurt people, as one of my offsiders did something very stupid and got paroled and I need someone else to help my mate Brooks with the bashings."

"I would be honoured," Paulo replied amazed at how quickly he had just moved up the prisoner hierarchy.

"Of course you would." The big man smiled. "But betray me and . . ." He then made a cutting gesture across his throat.

"I would never do that," Paulo replied. *Not yet anyway.*

"Good," the big man said again with his harsh grin. "Stick with me, boy, and you will learn something. But you may need to do something about your pretty face, though," he continued more seriously. "It's not scary enough, and some of the men in here might find you a bit *too* attractive, if you know what I mean." Paulo knew what he meant, and he knew what to do. He had been cutting himself for over a year now; he knew that cutting into his face was only a matter of time.

"Yes, I shall do that," Paulo said, nodding his head. "Umm . . . sorry to ask, but what is your name?"

"Brent," the big man said. "Brent Milligan."

I am going to kill you one day, Brent, and have my own gang, Paulo thought whilst gazing into the future for a brief moment. *The Smythen Gang. That has a good sound to it.*

"Nice to meet you," he said instead.

(FIA) Fields Intelligence Agency Report: Year 2123

Subject: The secretive group known as The Cabal
Estimated Existence: started approximately in 1992 and ended
on the day of The Collapse, 2044

Known Members:
Natalie Braiths – Senator
(Believed to be killed in Canberra on the day of The Collapse)
Brook Raller – A high-ranking member of ASIO
(Believed to be killed in Canberra on the day of The Collapse)
Brandon Townsworth – Media Tycoon
(Believed to be killed in Sydney on the day of The Collapse)
Phil Miller – Banker (father of Professor James Miller. Killed in
Sydney on the day of The Collapse)
Gary Miller – Banker (son of Phil Miller and brother of
Professor James Miller. Killed in Sydney on the day of The
Collapse)
Mark Howles – Senator and Environment Minister
(Believed to be killed in Canberra on the day of The Collapse)
Bruce Cunnington – Tasmanian Opposition Leader
(Killed in Hobart Parliament on the day of The Collapse)
Henry Abel – Scientist (possible member of The McKay Group
as well. Murdered gruesomely by unknown assailants in the year
2034)
Aiden Wilkinson – Minister Advisor, then later Health Minister
(Killed in Hobart on the day of The Collapse)
James O'Sullivan – Minister Advisor
(Killed in Hobart on the day of The Collapse)
Florian Grainger – Water Corporation Executive
(Believed to be killed in Canberra on the day of The Collapse)
Johan Franz– Radio Conspiracy Theorist (not considered a true
member, fate unknown)
Jake Symonds – Federal Opposition Leader
(Killed in the Cykam siege of Canberra 2052)
Brad 'Sparkles' Hoffington – TV Interviewer and Celebrity
Presenter (not considered a true member, fate unknown)

Anonymous Members:
Flowers – Assassin (fate, as well as true identity, unknown)

Level of Secrecy:
Poor. Very easily monitored, excluding the person known only as Flowers.

Origins of The Cabal:
The Cabal was born out of the oppression known then as Political Correctness, a movement with initial good intentions in the early decades of its reign, which, over time, became one of fear and control.

Objectives of The Cabal:
Control the public via all media outlets.
Promote as much as you can of the Left and Right Extremism to increase the disillusionment of the powerful but silent Majority.
Promote TV shows and entertainment of low-level intelligence with the hope of making the viewers dumb and uneducated about what happens in the real world.
Lower the general population's IQ through the restrictive grip of the so-called 'Nanny State'.
Keep the public fearful so you may indeed give them an enemy to worry about—real or not—which will then help you achieve your pre-designed objectives.
Harass anybody who voices a differing opinion than The Cabal by labeling them racist or un-Australian.
Promote the cashless society with the aim of controlling any future financial crisis.
Keep the public quiet through endless promotion of political correctness and the culture of always looking to be offended.
Make sure the public are scared of having an opinion for fear that they may offend somebody.

Recorded Quotes:
Phil Miller: "Nobody can say anything about anybody at all in today's world because of PC, even though there are some things that obviously needed to be discussed, at the very least. Society

has been led into a sort of silent stalemate, where nobody is allowed, or even dares to, offend anybody for fear of being vilified by the righteous do-gooders. This has allowed us, The Cabal, to control the agenda."

Bruce Cunnington: (A loud burp) "Just the other day, I got in trouble with a bleeding heart do-gooder for saying manhole. (Takes a big swig from a can of beer.) But it wasn't as if I was saying manhole as if I was talking about a bloke's bumhole or anything. (Burps loudly again, inhales a product once known as a cigarette, burps one more time, decides to munch on a large slice of pizza.) I was talking about (pauses for a moment, followed by loud chewing on the pizza)—this is good bloody pizza, extra cheese and pepperoni always does the trick, as my brother Victor used to say (prolonged chewing and chuckling). I was talking about the bloody manhole on the street that allowed the council workers to perform maintenance underneath the street footpaths. (Takes a big swig from a can of beer, burps once more.) They said I should have called it a personhole, of all things. What the fuck is wrong with people? Has the world gone insane! Jesus Christ, don't worry about inequality or human rights or anything trivial like that; no, let's change the fucking word manhole to personhole, as that is *far* more important for our society. These people are odd, when will the public wake up to this?"

Gary Miller: "The world, collectively, is over 300 trillion dollars in debt. I hope that the public doesn't ponder too much on whom exactly that debt is owed too; I like my life as it is. We should all be safe, though. I don't think they even realise where the buck stops."

Aiden Wilkinson: "Who gave you that black eye?"
James O'Sullivan: "Nobody (sounds embarrassed). Can we . . . can we just move on, with what we were discussing earlier about last week's protests?"
Aiden Wilkinson: "Sure, James, sure." (He sounds very uncertain.)

James O'Sullivan: "All right, so the Extreme Left thinks anybody who isn't one of their own people is automatically in the right and their needs come first, whilst the Extreme Right thinks anybody is who isn't one of their own people is automatically in the wrong and their needs come last."

Aiden Wilkinson: "Yes. So we have the masochistic, self-loathing Extreme Left, or the big and tough but really scared of everybody who isn't one of them Extreme Right." (Laughs a little.)

James O'Sullivan: (a loud sigh) "Yep."

Aiden Wilkinson: "And they both step on people but think they are doing the just thing."

James O'Sullivan: "Exactly. There is no balance to their thinking whatsoever."

Aiden Wilkinson: "And the majority in the middle just wants to be left alone and hopes the whole problem will just go away somehow, which it most definitely won't."

(A long pause followed by another loud sigh could be heard.)

James O'Sullivan: "I'm starting to think Henry may be on to something. A new era, a new beginning."

Aiden Wilkinson: "Really?"

James O'Sullivan: "I think so, and so do a lot of people in high places."

Aiden Wilkinson: "The Prime Minister!"

James O'Sullivan: (laughter) "No, the real powers."

(Long pause)

Aiden Wilkinson: "Oh my God, did Natalie give you that black eye?" (sounds shocked)

James O'Sullivan: "Shut up!" (sounds angry)

Senator Natalie Braiths: "Do protests today do any good? Ha! On one hand is the sanctimonious Extreme Left who, whilst pretending to be the champions of free speech, would not only oppose but drown out completely anyone expressing any such free speech which differed from their own views. On the other hand is the Extreme Right, who say they are not racists and tried their best not to be seen as racist, but everybody and their dogs could see they were indeed dumb racists. They use their macho aggressiveness to sway the masses, which is kind of a turn-on, to be honest. (A deep sigh) So the result is, these two groups stand metres apart and hurl abuse at each other, whilst the police kept them apart and the controlled media watches on. What a horrible violent choice it was for the public majority, and what a narrow voice it was to represent the people. It. Is. Brilliant."

Jake Symonds: "All that the protesting from both the Extreme Left and Right achieved was to make the majority, who had all of the power but were, thankfully, blissfully unaware of it, sick of both sides. It has made them so disillusioned, with what they referred to as the rent-a-crowd protesters, that they have become quieter and quieter as the years went by. From the first decade of the new century to the fifth decade, gone now completely were the days of protesting and people power. The majority has become jaded and apathetic. That is the way things should be, if you want good and cohesive government."

John France, aka Johan Franz: "I chose the lamest conspiracy theory out there and promoted the absolute shit out of it, dude. Some of the public even believe me, which is great, as they keep me employed, but the rest think I am a complete tool, which is what some of my backers wanted. It's . . . it's, you know, kind of upsetting, I guess, to know the general public think I am an idiot and, and hiding my real identity can be embarrassing, and my close friends who know the truth laugh at me, and I don't get laid much and . . . and . . . why do I do this job again?"

Brad 'Sparkles' Hoffington: "I'm tired. I am so tired. How long do I have to ask these fame-whores the same soulless and stupid questions? And how long will the public keep jumping up and down and screaming at other human beings, as if they are superior somehow? They are not, believe me. I have spent a lot of time with the famous, and they are as hopeless, kind, nasty, lovely, vain, modest, intelligent, or dumb as the rest of us. People need to wake up and focus on more important things; our world is crumbling around us, and we are just staring at the television, oblivious as to what awaits us all."

Henry Abel: "The blinkers are truly on, the Politically Correct cannot think outside the square. They are as narrow-minded and as ruthless as the people they are meant to be standing against. And the idiots actually feel good about it; they feel all warm and fuzzy inside about oppressing people's rights to an opinion that disagreed with their own. They actually have the gall to believe that they alone own the moral high ground about nearly everything (breaks into laughter). Their arrogance is astounding (more chuckling). They should leave the way the world is run to people like us." (Loud applause in the background.)

Senator Mark Howles: "The public must not be allowed to think too much about the world and how it works, in order for control to prevail. They must be encouraged at all times to watch their favourite sports teams and to yell at them, not us. They must always be glued to the TV, watching the gossips shows about which star is going out with whom, or the reality shows and riveting crap like that. They must be entertained to make sure they leave the way the world is run to us. For we are trained for this; we know what we are doing: climate change, if it exists at all, environmental damage, the increasing gap between the rich and the poor, the Resource Wars, the Space Planes and the Satellite Wars, and even the population crisis are all under control. So sit back and let us do the thinking for you."

Florian Grainger: "I earn twenty times more in wages than the average worker gets in a year. Isn't that wrong? Shouldn't somebody get angry about the injustice of this? But nobody does; the public are just plain used to it and accept it as how things are. They throw their hands in the air and say 'what can I do about it?' and so they should, as they indeed cannot do anything about it at all, as our society is built on commerce. It's just the way things are—the big end of town get paid more than you, and the political parties in parliament do not represent you; they represent us, as they are, in fact, one of us. Trickle-down economics! What a bloody joke, the trickle you feel is the 'one percent' urinating on your heads. So suck it up, those people who are aware, and deal with it, or join with the others in their sleep and watch reality TV or the footy. I really don't care. My life is good."

Brandon Townsworth: "Some of the floggers out there wonder how I managed to get the top like I have. I wasn't a smart kid at school. I wasn't rich or popular; in fact, and you may well be surprised by this, mate, I had no people skills whatsoever (laughs). Yeah, I know, who out there would fucking believe that I have no fucking people skills? (laughs) Shit for brains, the lot of them (laughs some more). So do you know how I made my way to being the most powerful man in Australia? I made it because I am a bully.

"Yes, I know bullies are complete bastards, and even I don't like them, but read your history; it is the bully who *always* gets his way. Look around you; look at the people in your work place, look at the politicians in parliament, look at the people above you, take a good look at those floggers who dominated us in the past with all this political correctness crap. Was the PC movement the fucking majority back in the day? No, of course they weren't, far from it in fact; they were just a handful of self-righteous, sanctimonious gits who thought they know better than everyone else. But I tell you one thing, the PC were as well, one thing that not even they themselves were aware of. They were the biggest bullies God put on this green Earth. Yes, those few arty-farty pricks forced their beliefs and opinions down the whole bloody country's throat, and the public had to gag on it because they were brow-beaten if they objected.

"Yeah, that's right; bullying doesn't necessarily involve violence; there is emotional bullying as well, which is just as powerful. And you know what was really funny and also quite sad about all of this? The public didn't collectively tell them all to piss off like they should have. No, the average person, so it turned out, couldn't handle the constant PC righteous big-brother barrage from the TV and media personalities and soon wilted, bent over, and took it fair up the clacker. And as the decades went by, the 'children of political correctness' or the 'bunch of weak self-centred pussies', as I like to call this generation, joined with the old minority do-gooders in believing this was the normal way to behave, and now, in the year 2034, we are stuck with citizens who have no backbone, get offended by the slightest thing, and believe they are automatically entitled to everything. It was unbelievable how it happened; it was like a mass hypnosis the way they changed everybody's personalities and our whole culture.

"So, my friend, if you want to be successful and make your mark in today's world, mate, if you want to climb as far up the ladder as you can and rule people, then you need to become a bully, because we always get our way."

Last Known Activity:
Health Minister Aiden Wilkinson was involved in a plot to introduce a biological disease to the Tasmanian city of Hobart to reduce the island's population. To some degree, it was a success, but by chance, it was made irrelevant by the zombie plague introduced by The McKay Group. Whilst the biological disease did have an affect in the year 2044, and yet again in 2091, some of the unreleased disease was returned to a secretive location known as Pine Gap by an ASIO spy known as The Hipster.

The Ramifications on Today:
In the year 2102, Cykam Soldiers invaded Pine Gap, executing all of the residents and somehow accidentally reintroducing the same Hobart biological disease on a return trip back into the Victorian city of Melbourne. A Bomber Plane, which contained numerous other conventional weapons and many other top-secret bombs obtained from Pine Gap, was used in an attempt to attack Hobart by the then Governor-General Maz Wyndham and was destroyed by Professor James Miller and the Midlands Tower. The wreckage still lies approximately seventy kilometres west of that Tower, and the land—once owned by the Tyson family—is still uninhabitable to humans but is now being cleaned by mechanical robots with the hope of being habitable in just a few decades.

CPSIA information can be obtained
at www.ICGtesting.com
Printed in the USA
BVHW04s2050280418
514707BV00001B/6/P